The Half-Hearted

By

John Buchan

The Echo Library 2006

Published by

The Echo Library

Echo Library
131 High St.
Teddington
Middlesex TW11 8HH

www.echo-library.com

Please report serious faults in the text to complaints@echo-library.com

ISBN 1-84702-948-5

NOTE

For the convenience of the reader it may be stated that the period of this tale is the closing years of the 19th Century.

4

CONTENTS

PART I

I.   EVENING IN GLENAVELIN
II.   LADY MANORWATER'S GUESTS
III.   UPLAND WATER
IV.   AFTERNOON IN A GARDEN
V.   A CONFERENCE OF THE POWERS
VI.   PASTORAL
VII.   THE MAKERS OF EMPIRE
VIII.   MR. WRATISLAW'S ADVENT
IX.   THE Episodes OF A DAY
X.   HOME TRUTHS
XI.   THE PRIDE BEFORE A FALL
XII.   PASTORAL AND TRAGEDY
XIII.   THE PLEASURES OF A CONSCIENCE
XIV.   A GENTLEMAN IN STRAITS
XV.   THE NEMESIS OF A COWARD
XVI.   A MOVEMENT OF THE POWERS
XVII.   THE BRINK OF THE RUBICON
XVIII.   THE FURTHER BRINK
XIX.   THE BRIDGE OF BROKEN HEARTS

PART II

XX.   THE EASTERN ROAD
XXI.   IN THE HEART OF THE HILLS
XXII.   THE OUTPOSTS
XXIII.   THE DINNER AT GALETTI'S
XXIV.   THE TACTICS OP A CHIEF
XXV.   MRS. LOGAN'S BALL
XXVI.   FRIEND TO FRIEND
XXVII.   THE ROAD TO FORZA
XXVIII.   THE HILL-FORT
XXIX.   The WAY TO NAZRI
XXX.   EVENING IN THE HILLS
XXXI.   EVENTS SOUTH OF THE BORDER
XXXII.   THE BLESSING OF GAD

PART I

CHAPTER I

EVENING IN GLENAVELIN

From the heart of a great hill land Glenavelin stretches west and south to the wider Gled valley, where its stream joins with the greater water in its seaward course. Its head is far inland in a place of mountain solitudes, but its mouth is all but on the lip of the sea, and salt breezes fight with the flying winds of the hills. It is a land of green meadows on the brink of heather, of far-stretching fir woods that climb to the edge of the uplands and sink to the fringe of corn. Nowhere is there any march between art and nature, for the place is in the main for sheep, and the single road which threads the glen is little troubled with cart and crop-laden wagon. Midway there is a stretch of wood and garden around the House of Glenavelin, the one great dwelling-place in the vale. But it is a dwelling and a little more, for the home of the real lords of the land is many miles farther up the stream, in the moorland house of Etterick, where the Avelin is a burn, and the hills hang sharply over its source. To a stranger in an afternoon it seems a very vale of content, basking in sun and shadow, green, deep, and silent. But it is also a place of storms, for its name means the "glen of white waters," and mist and snow are commoner in its confines than summer heats.

On a very wet evening in June a young man in a high dogcart was driving up the glen. A deer-stalker's cap was tied down over his ears, and the collar of a great white waterproof defended his neck. A cheerful bronzed face was shadowed by the peak of his cap, and two very keen grey eyes peered out into the mist. He was driving with tight rein, for the mare was fresh and the road had awkward slopes and corners; but none the less he was dreaming, thinking pleasant thoughts, and now and then looking cheerily at the ribs of hill which at times were cleared of mist. His clean-shaven face was wet and shining with the drizzle, pools formed on the floor of the cart, and the mare's flanks were plastered with the weather.

Suddenly he drew up sharp at the sight of a figure by the roadside.

"Hullo, Doctor Gracey," he cried, "where on earth have you come from? Come in and I'll give you a lift."

The figure advanced and scrambled into the vacant seat. It was a little old man in a big topcoat with a quaint-fashioned wide-awake hat on his head. In ill weather all distinctions are swept away. The stranger might have been a statesman or a tramp.

"It is a pleasure to see you, Doctor," and the young man grasped a mittened hand and looked into his companion's face. There was something both kindly and mirthful in his grey eyes.

The old man arranged his seat comfortably, buttoned another button at the neck of the coat, and then scrutinised the driver. "It's four years--four years in October since I last cast eyes on you, Lewie, my boy," he said. "I heard you were coming, so I refused a lift from Haystounslacks and the minister. Haystounslacks was driving from Gledsmuir, and unless the Lord protects him he will be in Avelin water ere he gets home. Whisky and a Glenavelin road never agree, Lewie, as I who have mended the fool's head a dozen times should know. But I thought you would never come, and was prepared to ride in the next baker's van." The Doctor spoke with the pure English and high northern voice of an old school of professional men, whose tongue, save in telling a story, knew not the vernacular, and yet in its pitch and accent inevitably betrayed their birthplace. Precise in speech and dress, uncommonly skilful, a mild humorist, and old in the world's wisdom, he had gone down the evening way of life with the heart of a boy.

"I was delayed--I could not help it, though I was all afternoon at the job," said the young man. "I've seen a dozen and more tenants and I talked sheep and drains till I got out of my depth and was gravely corrected. It's the most hospitable place on earth, this, but I thought it a pity to waste a really fine hunger on the inevitable ham and eggs, so I waited for dinner. Lord, I have an appetite! Come and dine, Doctor. I am in solitary state just now, and long, wet evenings are dreary."

"I'm afraid I must excuse myself, Lewie," was the formal answer, with just a touch of reproof. Dinner to Doctor Gracey was a serious ceremony, and invitations should not be scattered rashly. "My housekeeper's wrath is not to be trifled with, as you should know."

"I do," said the young man in a tone of decent melancholy. "She once cuffed my ears the month I stayed with you for falling in the burn. Does she beat you, Doctor?"

"Indeed, no," said the little old gentleman; "not as yet. But physically she is my superior and I live in terror." Then abruptly, "For heaven's sake, Lewie, mind the mare."

"It's all right," said the driver, as the dogcart swung neatly round an ugly turn. "There's the mist going off the top of Etterick Law, and--why, that's the end of the Dreichill?"

"It's the Dreichill, and beyond it is the Little Muneraw. Are you glad to be home, Lewie?"

"Rather," said the young man gravely. "This is my own countryside, and I fancy it's the last place a man forgets."

"I fancy so--with right-thinking people. By the way, I have much to congratulate you on. We old fogies in this desert place have been often seeing your name in the newspapers lately. You are a most experienced traveller."

"Fair. But people made a great deal more of that than it deserved. It was very simple, and I had every chance. Some day I will go out and do the same thing again with no advantages, and if I come back you may praise me then."

"Right, Lewie. A bare game and no chances is the rule of war. And now, what will you do?"

"Settle down," said the young man with mock pathos, "which in my case means settling up also. I suppose it is what you would call the crucial moment in my life. I am going in for politics, as I always intended, and for the rest I shall live a quiet country life at Etterick. I've a wonderful talent for rusticity."

The Doctor shot an inquiring glance from beneath the flaps of his hat. "I never can make up my mind about you, Lewie."

"I daresay not. It is long since I gave up trying to make up my mind about myself."

"When you were a very small and very bad boy I made the usual prophecy that you would make a spoon or spoil a horn. Later I declared you would make the spoon. I still keep to that opinion, but I wish to goodness I knew what shape your spoon would take."

"Ornamental, Doctor, some odd fancy spoon, but not useful. I feel an inner lack of usefulness."

"Humph! Then things are serious, Lewie, and I, as your elder, should give advice; but confound it, my dear, I cannot think what it should be. Life has been too easy for you, a great deal too easy. You want a little of the salt and iron of the world. You are too clever ever to be conceited, and you are too good a fellow ever to be a fool, but apart from these sad alternatives there are numerous middle stages which are not very happy."

The young man's face lengthened, as it always did either in repose or reflection.

"You are old and wise, Doctor. Have you any cure for a man with sufficient money and no immediate profession to prevent stagnation?"

"None," said the Doctor; "but the man himself can find many. The chief is that he be conscious of his danger, and on the watch against it. As a last expedient I should recommend a second course of travel."

"But am I to be barred from my home because of this bogey of yours?"

"No, Lewie lad, but you must be kept, as you say, 'up to scratch,'" and the old face smiled. "You are too good to waste. You Haystouns are high-strung, finicking people, on whom idleness sits badly. Also you are the last of your race and have responsibilities. You must remember I was your father's friend, and knew you all well."

At the mention of his father the young man's interest quickened.

"I must have been only about six years old when he died. I find so few people who remember him well and can tell me about him."

"You are very like him, Lewie. He began nearly as well as you; but he settled down into a quiet life, which was the very thing for which he was least fitted. I do not know if he had altogether a happy time. He lost interest in things, and grew shy and rather irritable. He quarrelled with most of his neighbours, and got into a trick of magnifying little troubles till he shrank from the slightest discomfort."

"And my mother?"

"Ah, your mother was different--a cheery, brave woman. While she lived she kept him in some measure of self-confidence, but you know she died at your birth, Lewie, and after that he grew morose and retiring. I speak about these things from the point of view of my profession, and I fancy it is the special disease which lies in your blood. You have all been over-cultured and enervated; as I say, you want some of the salt and iron of life."

The young man's brow was furrowed in a deep frown which in no way broke the good-humour of his face. They were nearing a cluster of houses, the last clachan of sorts in the glen, where a kirk steeple in a grove of trees proclaimed civilization. A shepherd passed them with a couple of dogs, striding with masterful step towards home and comfort. The cheery glow of firelight from the windows pleased both men as they were whirled through the raw weather.

"There, you see," said the Doctor, nodding his head towards the retreating figure; "there's a man who in his own way knows the secret of life. Most of his days are spent in dreary, monotonous toil. He is for ever wrestling with the weather and getting scorched and frozen, and the result is that the sparse enjoyments of his life are relished with a rare gusto. He sucks his pipe of an evening with a zest which the man who lies on his back all day smoking knows nothing about. So, too, the labourer who hoes turnips for one and sixpence the day. They know the arduousness of life, which is a lesson we must all learn sooner or later. You people who have been coddled and petted must learn it, too; and for you it is harder to learn, but pleasanter in the learning, because you stand above the bare need of things, and have leisure for the adornments. We must all be fighters and strugglers, Lewie, and it is better to wear out than to rust out. It is bad to let choice things become easily familiar; for, you know, familiarity is apt to beget a proverbial offspring."

The young man had listened attentively, but suddenly he leaned from the seat and with a dexterous twitch of his whip curled it round the leg of a boy of sixteen who stood before a cottage.

"Hullo, Jock," he cried. "When are you coming up to see me? Bring your brother some day and we'll go and fish the Midburn." The urchin pulled off a ragged cap and grinned with pleasure.

"That's the boy you pulled out of the Avelin?" asked the Doctor. "I had heard of that performance. It was a good introduction to your home-coming."

"It was nothing," said the young man, flushing slightly. "I was crossing the ford and the stream was up a bit. The boy was fishing, wading pretty deep, and in turning round to stare at me he slipped and was carried down. I merely rode my horse out and collared him. There was no danger."

"And the Black Linn just below," said the Doctor, incredulously. "You have got the usual modesty of the brave man, Lewie."

"It was a very small thing. My horse knew its business--that was all." And he flicked nervously with the whip.

A grey house among trees rose on the left with a quaint gateway of unhewn stone. The dogcart pulled up, and the Doctor scrambled down and stood shaking the rain from his hat and collar. He watched the young man till, with a skilful turn, he had entered Etterick gates, and then with a more meditative face than is usual in a hungry man he went through the trees to his own dwelling.

CHAPTER II

LADY MANORWATER'S GUESTS

When the afternoon train from the south drew into Gledsmuir station, a girl who had been devouring the landscape for the last hour with eager eyes, rose nervously to prepare for exit. To Alice Wishart the country was a novel one, and the prospect before her an unexplored realm of guesses. The daughter of a great merchant, she had lived most of her days in the ugly environs of a city, save for such time as she had spent at the conventional schools. She had never travelled; the world of men and things was merely a name to her, and a girlhood, lonely and brightened chiefly by the companionship of books, had not given her self-confidence. She had casually met Lady Manorwater at some political meeting in her father's house, and the elder woman had taken a strong liking to the quiet, abstracted child. Then came an invitation to Glenavelin, accepted gladly yet with much fear and searching of heart. Now, as she looked out on the shining mountain land, she was full of delight that she was about to dwell in the heart of it. Something of pride, too, was present, that she was to be the guest of a great lady, and see something of a life which seemed infinitely remote to her provincial thoughts. But when her journey drew near its end she was foolishly nervous, and scanned the platform with anxious eye.

The sight of her hostess reassured her. Lady Manorwater was a small middle-aged woman, with a thin classical face, large colourless eyes, and untidy fair hair. She was very plainly dressed, and as she darted forward to greet the girl with entire frankness and kindness, Alice forgot her fears and kissed her heartily. A languid young woman was introduced as Miss Afflint, and in a few minutes the three were in the Glenavelin carriage with the wide glen opening in front.

"Oh, my dear, I hope you will enjoy your visit. We are quite a small party, for Jack says Glenavelin is far too small to entertain in. You are fond of the country, aren't you? And of course the place is very pretty. There is tennis and golf and fishing; but perhaps you don't like these things? We are not very well off for neighbours, but we are large enough in number to be sufficient to ourselves. Don't you think so, Bertha?" And Lady Manorwater smiled at the third member of the group.

Miss Afflint, a silent girl, smiled back and said nothing. She had been engaged in a secret study of Alice's face, and whenever the object of the study raised her eyes she found a pair of steady blue ones beaming on her. It was a little disconcerting, and Alice gazed out at the landscape with a fictitious curiosity.

They passed out of the Gled valley into the narrower strath of Avelin, and soon, leaving the meadows behind, went deep into the recesses of woods. At a narrow glen bridged by the road and bright with the spray of cascades and the fresh green of ferns, Alice cried out in delight, "Oh, I must come back here some day and sketch it. What a Paradise of a place!"

"Then you had better ask Lewie's permission." And Lady Manorwater laughed.

"Who is Lewie?" asked the girl, anticipating some gamekeeper or shepherd.

"Lewie is my nephew. He lives at Etterick, up at the head of the glen."

Miss Afflint spoke for the first time. "A very good man. You should know Lewie, Miss Wishart. I'm sure you would like him. He is a great traveller, you know, and has written a famous book. Lewis Haystoun is his full name."

"Why, I have read it," cried Alice. "You mean the book about Kashmir. But I thought the author was an old man."

"Lewie is not very old," said his aunt; "but I haven't seen him for years, so he may be decrepit by this time. He is coming home soon, he says, but he never writes. I know two of his friends who pay a Private Inquiry Office to send them news of him."

Alice laughed and became silent. What merry haphazard people were these she had fallen among! At home everything was docketed and ordered. Meals were immovable feasts, the hour for bed and the hour for rising were more regular than the sun's. Her father was full of proverbs on the virtue of regularity, and was wont to attribute every vice and misfortune to its absence. And yet here were men and women who got on very well without it. She did not wholly like it. The little doctrinaire in her revolted and she was pleased to be censorious.

"You are a very learned young woman, aren't you?" said Lady Manorwater, after a short silence. "I have heard wonderful stories about your learning. Then I hope you will talk to Mr. Stocks, for I am afraid he is shocked at Bertha's frivolity. He asked her if she was in favour of the Prisons Regulation Bill, and she was very rude."

"I only said," broke in Miss Afflint, "that owing to my lack of definite local knowledge I was not in a position to give an answer commensurate with the gravity of the subject." She spoke in a perfect imitation of the tone of a pompous man.

"Bertha, I do not approve of you," said Lady Manorwater. "I forbid you to mimic Mr. Stocks. He is very clever, and very much in earnest over everything. I don't wonder that a butterfly like you should laugh, but I hope Miss Wishart will be kind to him."

"I am afraid I am very ignorant," said Alice hastily, "and I am very useless. I never did any work of any sort in my life, and when I think of you I am ashamed."

"Oh, my dear child, please don't think me a paragon," cried her hostess in horror. "I am a creature of vague enthusiasms and I have the sense to know it. Sometimes I fancy I am a woman of business, and then I take up half a dozen things till Jack has to interfere to prevent financial ruin. I dabble in politics and I dabble in philanthropy; I write review articles which nobody reads, and I make speeches which are a horror to myself and a misery to my hearers. Only by the possession of a sense of humour am I saved from insignificance."

To Alice the speech was the breaking of idols. Competence, responsibility were words she had been taught to revere, and to hear them light-heartedly disavowed seemed an upturning of the foundation of things. You will perceive that her education had not included that valuable art, the appreciation of the flippant.

By this time the carriage was entering the gates of the park, and the thick wood cleared and revealed long vistas of short hill grass, rising and falling like moorland, and studded with solitary clumps of firs. Then a turn in the drive brought them once more into shadow, this time beneath a heath-clad knoll where beeches and hazels made a pleasant tangle. All this was new, not three years old; but soon they were in the ancient part of the policy which had surrounded the old house of Glenavelin. Here the grass was lusher, the trees antique oaks and beeches, and grey walls showed the boundary of an old pleasure-ground. Here in the soft sunlit afternoon sleep hung like a cloud, and the peace of centuries dwelt in the long avenues and golden pastures. Another turning and the house came in sight, at first glance a jumble of grey towers and ivied walls. Wings had been built to the original square keep, and even now it was not large, a mere moorland dwelling. But the whitewashed walls, the crow-step gables, and the quaint Scots baronial turrets gave it a perfection to the eye like a house in a dream. To Alice, accustomed to the vulgarity of suburban villas with Italian campaniles, a florid lodge a stone's throw from the house, darkened too with smoke and tawdry with paint, this old-world dwelling was a patch of wonderland. Her eyes drank in the beauty of the place--the great blue backs of hill beyond, the acres of sweet pasture, the primeval woods.

"Is this Glenavelin?" she cried. "Oh, what a place to live in!"

"Yes, it's very pretty, dear." And Lady Manorwater, who possessed half a dozen houses up and down the land, patted her guest's arm and looked with pleasure on the flushed girlish face.

Two hours later, Alice, having completed dressing, leaned out of her bedroom window to drink in the soft air of evening. She had not brought a maid, and had refused her hostess's offer to lend her her own on the ground that maids were a superfluity. It was her desire to be a very practical young person, a scorner of modes and trivialities, and yet she had taken unusual care with her toilet this evening, and had spent many minutes before the glass. Looking at herself carefully, a growing conviction began to be confirmed--that she was really rather pretty. She had reddish-brown hair and--a rare conjunction--dark eyes and eyebrows and a delicate colour. As a small girl she had lamented bitterly the fate that had not given her the orthodox beauty of the dark or fair maiden, and in her school days she had passed for plain. Now it began to dawn on her that she had beauty of a kind--the charm of strangeness; and her slim strong figure had the grace which a wholesome life alone can give. She was in high spirits, curious, interested, and generous. The people amused her, the place was a fairyland and outside the golden weather lay still and fragrant among the hills.

When she came down to the drawing-room she found the whole party assembled. A tall man with a brown beard and a slight stoop ceased to assault the handle of a firescreen and came over to greet her. He had only come back half an hour ago, he explained, and so had missed her arrival. The face attracted and soothed her. Abundant kindness lurked in the humorous brown eyes, and a queer pucker on the brow gave him the air of a benevolent despot. If this was Lord Manorwater, she had no further dread of the great ones of the earth. There were four other men, two of them mild, spectacled people, who had the air of students and a precise affected mode of talk, and one a boy cousin of whom no one took the slightest notice. The fourth was a striking figure, a man of about forty in appearance, tall and a little stout, with a rugged face which in some way suggested a picture of a prehistoric animal in an old natural history she had owned. The high cheek-bones, large nose, and slightly protruding eyes had an unfinished air about them, as if their owner had escaped prematurely from a mould. A quantity of bushy black hair--which he wore longer than most men-enhanced the dramatic air of his appearance. It was a face full of vigour and a kind of strength, shrewd, a little coarse, and solemn almost to the farcical. He was introduced in a rush of words by the hostess, but beyond the fact that it was a monosyllable, Alice did not catch his name.

Lord Manorwater took in Miss Afflint, and Alice fell to the dark man with the monosyllabic name. He had a way of bowing over his hand which slightly repelled the girl, who had no taste for elaborate manners. His first question, too, displeased her. He asked her if she was one of the Wisharts of some unpronounceable place.

She replied briefly that she did not know. Her grandfathers on both sides had been farmers.

The gentleman bowed with the smiling unconcern of one to whom pedigree is a matter of course.

"I have heard often of your father," he said. "He is one of the local supports of the party to which I have the honour to belong. He represents one great section of our retainers, our host another. I am glad to see such friendship between the two." And he smiled elaborately from Alice to Lord Manorwater.

Alice was uncomfortable. She felt she must be sitting beside some very great man, and she was tortured by vain efforts to remember the monosyllable which had stood for his name. She did not like his voice, and, great man or not, she resented the obvious patronage. He spoke with a touch of the drawl which is currently supposed to belong only to the half-educated classes of England.

She turned to the boy who sat on the other side of her. The young gentleman--his name was Arthur and, apparently, nothing else--was only too ready to talk. He proceeded to explain, compendiously, his doings of the past week, to which the girl listened politely. Then anxiety got the upper hand, and she asked in a whisper, *a propos* of nothing in particular, the name of her left-hand neighbour.

"They call him Stocks," said the boy, delighted at the tone of confidence, and was going on to sketch the character of the gentleman in question when Alice cut him short.

"Will you take me to fish some day?" she asked.

"Any day," gasped the hilarious Arthur. "I'm ready, and I'll tell you what, I know the very burn--" and he babbled on happily till he saw that Miss Wishart had ceased to listen. It was the first time a pretty girl had shown herself desirous of his company, and he was intoxicated with the thought.

But Alice felt that she was in some way bound to make the most of Mr. Stocks, and she set herself heroically to the task. She had never heard of him, but then she was not well versed in the minutiae of things political, and he clearly was a politician. Doubtless to her father his name was a household word. So she spoke to him of Glenavelin and its beauties.

He asked her if she had seen Royston Castle, the residence of his friend the Duke of Sanctamund. When he had stayed there he had been much impressed--

Then she spoke wildly of anything, of books and pictures and people and politics. She found him well-informed, clever, and dogmatic. The culminating point was reached when she embarked on a stray remark concerning certain events then happening in India.

He contradicted her with a lofty politeness.

She quoted a book on Kashmir.

He laughed the authority to scorn. "Lewis Haystoun?" he asked. "What can he know about such things? A wandering dilettante, the worst type of the pseudo-culture of our universities. He must see all things through the spectacles of his upbringing."

Fortunately he spoke in a low voice, but Lord Manorwater caught the name.

"You are talking about Lewie," he said; and then to the table at large, "do you know that Lewie is home? I saw him to-day."

Bertha Afflint clapped her hands. "Oh, splendid! When is he coming over? I shall drive to Etterick to-morrow. No--bother! I can't go to-morrow, I shall go on Wednesday."

Lady Manorwater opened mild eyes of surprise. "Why didn't the boy write?" And the young Arthur indulged in sundry exclamations, "Oh, ripping, I say! What? A clinking good chap, my cousin Lewie!"

"Who is this Lewis the well-beloved?" said Mr. Stocks. "I was talking about a very different person--Lewis Haystoun, the author of a foolish book on Kashmir."

"Don't you like it?" said Lord Manorwater, pleasantly. "Well, it's the same man. He is my nephew, Lewie Haystoun. He lives at Etterick, four miles up the glen. You will see him over here to-morrow or the day after."

Mr. Stocks coughed loudly to cover his discomfiture. Alice could not repress a little smile of triumph, but she was forbearing and for the rest of dinner exerted herself to appease her adversary, listening to his talk with an air of deference which he found entrancing.

Meanwhile it was plain that Lord Manorwater was not quite at ease with his company. Usually a man of brusque and hearty address, he showed his discomfort by an air of laborious politeness. He was patronized for a brief minute by Mr. Stocks, who set him right on some matter of agricultural reform. Happening to be a specialist on the subject and an enthusiastic farmer from his earliest days, he took the rebuke with proper meekness. The spectacled people were talking earnestly with his wife. Arthur was absorbed in his dinner and furtive glances at his left-hand neighbour. There remained Bertha Afflint, whom he had hitherto admired with fear. To talk with her was exhausting to frail mortality, and he had avoided the pleasure except in moments of boisterous bodily and mental health. Now she was his one resource, and the unfortunate man, rashly entering into a contest of wit, found himself badly worsted by her ready tongue. He declared that she was worse than her mother, at which the unabashed young woman replied that the superiority of parents was the last retort of the vanquished. He registered an inward vow that Miss Afflint should be used on the morrow as a weapon to quell Mr. Stocks.

When Alice escaped to the drawing-room she found Bertha and her sister--a younger and ruddier copy--busy with the letters which had arrived by the evening post. Lady Manorwater, who reserved her correspondence for the late hours, seized upon the girl and carried her off to sit by the great French windows from which lawn and park sloped down to the moorland loch. She chattered pleasantly about many things, and then innocently and abruptly asked her if she had not found her companion at table amusing.

Alice, unaccustomed to fiction, gave a hesitating "Yes," at which her hostess looked pleased. "He is very clever, you know," she said, "and has been very useful to me on many occasions."

Alice asked his occupation.

"Oh, he has done many things. He has been very brave and quite the maker of his own fortunes. He educated himself, and then I think he edited some Nonconformist paper. Then he went into politics, and became a Churchman. Some old man took a liking to him and left him his money, and that was the condition. So I believe he is pretty well off now and is waiting for a seat. He has been nursing this constituency, and since the election comes off in a month or two, we asked him down here to stay. He has also written a lot of things and he is somebody's private secretary." And Lady Manorwater relapsed into vagueness.

The girl listened without special interest, save that she modified her verdict on Mr. Stocks, and allowed, some degree of respect for him to find place in her heart. The fighter in life always appealed to her, whatever the result of his struggle.

Then Lady Manorwater proceeded to hymn his excellences in an indeterminate, artificial manner, till the men came into the room, and conversation became general. Lord Manorwater made his way to Alice, thereby defeating Mr. Stocks, who tended in the same direction. "Come outside and see things, Miss Wishart," he said. "It's a shame to miss a Glenavelin evening if it's fine. We must appreciate our rarities."

And Alice gladly followed him into the still air of dusk which made hill and tree seem incredibly distant and the far waters of the lake merge with the moorland in one shimmering golden haze. In the rhododendron thickets sparse blooms still remained, and all along by the stream-side stood stately lines of yellow iris above the white water-ranunculus. The girl was sensitive to moods of season and weather, and she had almost laughed at the incongruity of the two of them in modern clothes in this fit setting for an old tale. Dickon of Glenavelin, the sworn foe of the Lord of Etterick, on such nights as this had ridden up the water with his bands to affront the quiet moonlight. And now his descendant was pointing out dim shapes in the park which he said were prize cattle.

"Whew! what a weariness is civilization!" said the man, with comical eyes. "We have been making talk with difficulty all the evening which serves no purpose in the world. Upon my word, my kyloes have the best of the bargain. And in a month or so there will be the election and I shall have to go and rave-- there is no other word for it, Miss Wishart--rave on behalf of some fool or other, and talk Radicalism which would make your friend Dickon turn in his grave, and be in earnest for weeks when I know in the bottom of my heart that I am a humbug and care for none of these things. How lightly politics and such matters sit on us all!"

"But you know you are talking nonsense," said the serious Alice. "After all, these things are the most important, for they mean duty and courage and--and-- all that sort of thing."

"Right, little woman," said he, smiling; "that is what Stocks tells me twice a day, but, somehow, reproof comes better from you. Dear me! it's a sad thing that a middle-aged legislator should be reproved by a very little girl. Come and see the herons. The young birds will be everywhere just now."

For an hour in the moonlight they went a-sightseeing, and came back very cool and fresh to the open drawing-room window. As they approached they caught an echo of a loud, bland voice saying, "We must remember our moral responsibilities, my dear Lady Manorwater. Now, for instance--"

And a strange thing happened. For the first time in her life Miss Alice Wishart felt that the use of loud and solemn words could jar upon her feelings. She set it down resignedly to the evil influence of her companion.

In the calm of her bedroom Alice reviewed her recent hours. She admitted to herself that she would enjoy her visit. A healthy and active young woman, the mere prospect of an open-air life gave her pleasure. Also she liked the people. Mentally she epitomized each of the inmates of the house. Lady Manorwater was all she had pictured her--a dear, whimsical, untidy creature, with odd shreds of cleverness and a heart of gold. She liked the boy Arthur, and the spectacled people seemed harmless. Bertha she was prepared to adore, for behind the languor and wit she saw a very kindly and capable young woman fashioned after her own heart. But of all she liked Lord Manorwater best. She knew that he had a great reputation, that he was said to be incessantly laborious, and she had expected some one of her father's type, prim, angular, and elderly. Instead she found a boyish person whom she could scold, and with women reproof is the first stone in the foundation of friendship. On Mr. Stocks she generously reserved her judgment, fearing the fate of the hasty.

CHAPTER III

UPLAND WATERS

When Alice woke next morning the cool upland air was flooding through the window, and a great dazzle of sunlight made the world glorious. She dressed and ran out to the lawn, then past the loch right to the very edge of the waste country. A high fragrance of heath and bog-myrtle was in the wind, and the mouth grew cool as after long draughts of spring water. Mists were crowding in the valleys, each bald mountain top shone like a jewel, and far aloft in the heavens were the white streamers of morn. Moorhens were plashing at the loch's edge, and one tall heron rose from his early meal. The world was astir with life: sounds of the *plonk-plonk* of rising trout and the endless twitter of woodland birds mingled with the far-away barking of dogs and the lowing of the full-uddered cows in the distant meadows. Abashed and enchanted, the girl listened. It was an elfin land where the old witch voices of hill and river were not silenced. With the wind in her hair she climbed the slope again to the garden ground, where she found a solemn-eyed collie sniffing the fragrant wind in his morning stroll.

Breakfast over, the forenoon hung heavy on her hands. It was Lady Manorwater's custom to let her guests sit idle in the morning and follow their own desire, but in the afternoon she would plan subtle and far-reaching schemes of enjoyment. It was a common saying that in her large good-nature she amused people regardless of their own expense. She would light-heartedly make town-bred folk walk twenty miles or bear the toil of infinite drives. But this was after lunch; before, her guests might do as they pleased. Lord Manorwater went off to see some tenant; Arthur, after vain efforts to decoy Alice into a fishing expedition, went down the stream in a canoe, because to his fool's head it seemed the riskiest means of passing the time at his disposal; Bertha and her sister were writing letters; the spectacled people had settled themselves below shady trees with voluminous papers and a pile of books. Alice alone was idle. She made futile expeditions to the library, and returned with an armful of volumes which she knew in her heart she would never open. She found the deepest and most comfortable chair and placed it in a shady place among beeches. But she could not stay there, and must needs wander restlessly about the gardens, plucking flowers and listlessly watching the gardeners at their work.

Lunch-time found this young woman in a slightly irritable frame of mind. The cause direct and indirect was Mr. Stocks, who had found her alone, and had saddled her with his company for the space of an hour and a half. His vein had been *badinage* of the serious and reproving kind, and the girl had been bored to distraction. But a misspent hour is soon forgotten, and the sight of her hostess's cheery face would have restored her to good humour had it not been for a thought which could not be exorcised. She knew of Lady Manorwater's reputation as an inveterate matchmaker, and in some subtle way the suspicion came to her that that goddess had marked herself as a quarry. She found herself next Mr. Stocks at meals, she had already listened to his eulogy from her hostess's own lips, and to her unquiet fancy it seemed as if the others stood back that they two might be together. Brought up in an atmosphere of commerce, she was perfectly aware that she was a desirable match for an embryo politician, and that sooner or later she would be mistress of many thousands. The thought was a barbed vexation. To Mr. Stocks she had been prepared to extend the tolerance of a happy aloofness; now she found that she was driven to dislike him with all the bitterness of unwelcome proximity.

The result of such thoughts was that after lunch she disregarded her hostess's preparations and set out for a long hill walk. Like all perfectly healthy people, much exercise was as welcome to her as food and sleep; ten miles were refreshing; fifteen miles in an afternoon an exaltation. She reached the moor beyond the policies, and, once past this rushy wilderness, came to the Avelinside and a single plank bridge which she crossed lightly without a tremor. Then came the highway, and then a long planting of firs, and last of all the dip of a rushing stream pouring down from the hills in a lonely wooded hollow. The girl loved to explore, and here was a field ripe for adventure.

Soon she grew flushed with the toil and the excitement; climbing the bed of the stream was no child's play, for ugly corners had to be passed, slippery rocks to be skirted, and many breakneck leaps to be effected. Her spirits rose as the spray from little falls brushed her face and the thick screen of the birches caught in her hair. When she reached a vantage-rock and looked down on the chain of pools and rapids by which she had come, a cry of delight broke from her lips. This was living, this was the zest of life! The upland wind cooled her brow; she washed her hands in a rocky pool and arranged her tangled tresses. What did she care for Mr. Stocks or any man? He was far down on the lowlands talking his pompous nonsense; she was on the hills with the sky above her and the breeze of heaven around her, free, sovereign, the queen of an airy land.

With fresh wonder she scrambled on till the trees began to grow sparser and an upland valley opened in view. Now the burn was quiet, running in long shining shallows and falling over little rocks into deep brown pools where the trout darted. On either side rose the gates of the valley--two craggy knolls each with a few trees on its face. Beyond was a green lawnlike place with a great confusion of blue mountains hemmed around its head. Here, if anywhere, primeval peace had found its dwelling, and Alice, her eyes bright with pleasure, sat on a green knoll, too rapt with the sight for word or movement.

Then very slowly, like an epicure lingering at a feast, she walked up the banks of the burn, now high above a trough of rock, now down in a green winding hollow. Suddenly she came on the spirits of the place in the shape of two boys down on their faces groping among the stones of a pool.

One was very small and tattered, one about sixteen; both were barefoot and both were wet and excited. "Tam, ye stot, ye've let the muckle yin aff again," groaned the smaller. "Oh, be canny, man! If we grip him it'll be the biggest trout that the laird will have in his basket," The elder boy, who was bearing the heat and burden of the work, could only groan "Heather!" at intervals. It seemed to be his one exclamation.

Now it happened that the two ragamuffins lifted their eyes and saw to their amazement a girl walking on the bank above them, a girl who smiled comrade-like on them and seemed in no way surprised. They propped themselves on their elbows and stared. "Heather!" they ejaculated in one breath. Then they, too, grinned broadly, for it was impossible to resist so good-humoured an intruder. She held her head high and walked like a queen, till a turn of the water hid her. "It's a wumman," gasped the smaller boy. "And she's terrible bonny," commented the more critical brother. Then the two fell again to the quest of the great trout.

Meanwhile the girl pursued her way till she came to a fall where the bank needed warier climbing. As she reached the top a little flushed and panting, she became conscious that the upland valley was not without inhabitants. For, not six paces off, stood a man's figure, his back turned towards her, and his mind apparently set on mending a piece of tackle.

She stood for a moment hesitating. How could she pass without being seen? The man was blissfully unconscious of her presence, and as he worked he whistled Schubert's "Wohin," and whistled it very badly. Then he fell to apostrophizing his tackle, and then he grew irritable. "Somebody come and keep this thing taut," he cried. "Tam, Jock! where on earth are you?"

The thing in question was lying at Alice's feet in wavy coils.

"Jock, you fool, where are you?" cried the man, but he never looked round and went on biting and tying. Then an impulse took the girl and she picked up the line. "That's right," cried the man, "pull it as tight as you can," and Alice tugged heroically at the waterproof silk. She felt horribly nervous, and was conscious that she must look a very flushed and untidy young barbarian. Many times she wanted to drop it and run away, but the thought of the menaces against the absent Jock and of her swift discovery deterred her. When he was done with her help he might go on working and never look round. Then she would escape unnoticed down the burn.

But no such luck befell her. With a satisfied tug he pronounced the thing finished and wheeled round to regard his associates. "Now, you young wretches--" and the words froze on his lips, for in the place of two tatterdemalion boys he saw a young girl holding his line limply and smiling with much nervousness.

"Oh," he cried, and then became dumb and confused. He was shy and unhappy with women, save the few whom he had known from childhood. The girl was no better. She had blushed deeply, and was now minutely scanning the stones in the burn. Then she raised her eyes, met his, and the difficulty was solved by both falling into fits of deep laughter. She was the first to speak.

"I am so sorry I surprised you. I did not see you till I was close to you, and then you were abusing somebody so terribly that to stop such language I had to stop and help you. I saw Tam and Jock at a pool a long way down, so they couldn't hear you, you know."

"And I'm very much obliged to you. You held it far better than Tam or Jock would have done. But how did you get up here?"

"I climbed up the burn," said Alice simply, putting up a hand to confine a wandering tress. The young man saw a small, very simply dressed girl, with a flushed face and bright, deep eyes. The small white hat crowned a great tangle of wonderful reddish gold hair. She held herself with the grace which is born of natural health and no modish training; the strong hazel stick, the scratched shoes, and the wet fringes of her gown showed how she had spent the afternoon. The young man, having received an excellent education, thought of Dryads and Oreads.

Alice for her part saw a strong, well-knit being, with a brown, clean-shaven face, a straight nose, and a delicate, humorous mouth. He had large grey eyes, very keen, quizzical, and kindly. His raiment was disgraceful--an old knickerbocker suit with a ruinous Norfolk jacket, patched at the elbows and with leather at wrist and shoulder. Apparently he scorned the June sun, for he had no cap. His pockets seemed bursting with tackle, and a discarded basket lay on the ground. The whole figure pleased her, its rude health, simplicity, and disorder. The atrocious men who sometimes came to her father's house had been miracles of neatness, and Mr. Stocks was wont to robe his person in the most faultless of shooting suits.

A fugitive memory began to haunt the girl. She had met or heard of this man before. The valley was divided between Glenavelin and Etterick. He was not the Doctor, and he was not the minister. Might not he be that Lewie, the well-beloved, whose praises she had heard consistently sung since her arrival? It pleased her to think that she had been the first to meet the redoubtable young man.

To them there entered the two boys, the younger dangling a fish. "It is the big trout ye lost," he cried. "We guddled 'um. We wad has gotten 'um afore, but a wumman frichted 'um." Then turning unabashed to Alice, he said in accusing tones, "That's the wumman!"

The elder boy gently but firmly performed on his brother the operation known as "scragging." It was a subdued spirit which emerged from the fraternal embrace.

"Pit the fush in the basket, Tam," said he, "and syne gang away wide up the hill till I cry ye back." The tones implied that his younger brother was no fit company for two gentlemen and a lady.

"I won't spoil your fishing," said Alice, fearing fratricidal strife. "You are fishing up, so I had better go down the burn again." And with a dignified nod to the others she turned to go.

Jock sprang forward with a bound and proceeded to stone the small Tarn up the hill. He coursed that young gentleman like a dog, bidding him "come near," or "gang wide," or "lie down there," to all of which the culprit, taking the sport in proper spirit, gaily responded.

"I think you had better not go down the burn," said the man reflectively. "You should keep the dry hillside. It is safer."

"Oh, I am not afraid," said the girl, laughing.

"But then I might want to fish down, and the trout are very shy there," said he, lying generously.

"Well, I won't then, but please tell me where Glenavelin is, for the stream-side is my only direction."

"You are staying there?" he asked with a pleased face. "We shall meet again, for I shall be over to-morrow. That fence on the hillside is their march, and if you follow it you will come to the footbridge on the Avelin. Many thanks for taking Jock's place and helping me."

He watched her for a second as she lightly jumped the burn and climbed the peaty slope. Then he turned to his fishing, and when Alice looked back from the vantage-ground of the hill shoulder she saw a figure bending intently below a great pool. She was no coquette, but she could not repress a tinge of irritation at so callous and self-absorbed a young man. Another would have been profuse in thanks and would have accompanied her to point out the road, or in some way or other would have declared his appreciation of her presence. He might have told, her his name, and then there would have been a pleasant informal introduction, and they could have talked freely. If he came to Glenavelin to-morrow, she would have liked to appear as already an acquaintance of so popular a guest.

But such thoughts did not long hold their place. She was an honest young woman, and she readily confessed that fluent manners and the air of the *cavaliere servente* were things she did not love. Carelessness suited well with a frayed jacket and the companionship of a hill burn and two ragged boys. So, comforting her pride with proverbs, she returned to Glenavelin to find the place deserted save for dogs, and in their cheering presence read idly till dinner.

CHAPTER IV
AFTERNOON IN A GARDEN

The gardens of Glenavelin have an air of antiquity beyond the dwelling, for there the modish fashions of another century have been followed with enthusiasm. There are clipped yews and long arched avenues, bowers and summer-houses of rustic make, and a terraced lawn fringed with a Georgian parapet. A former lord had kept peacocks innumerable, and something of the tradition still survived. Set in the heart of hilly moorlands, it was like a cameo gem in a tartan plaid, a piece of old Vauxhall or Ranelagh in an upland vale. Of an afternoon sleep reigned supreme. The shapely immobile trees, the grey and crumbling stone, the lone green walks vanishing into a bosky darkness were instinct with the quiet of ages. It needed but Lady Prue with her flounces and furbelows and Sir Pertinax with his cane and buckled shoon to re-create the ancient world before good Queen Anne had gone to her rest.

In one of the shadiest corners of a great lawn Lady Manorwater sat making tea. Bertha, with a broad hat shading her eyes, dozed over a magazine in a deck-chair. That morning she and Alice had broken the convention of the house and gone riding in the haughlands till lunch. Now she suffered the penalty and dozed, but her companion was very wide awake, being a tireless creature who knew not lethargy. Besides, there was sufficient in prospect to stir her curiosity. Lady Manorwater had announced some twenty times that day that her nephew Lewis would come to tea, and Alice, knowing the truth of the prophecy, was prepared to receive him.

The image of the forsaken angler remained clear in her memory, and she confessed to herself that he interested her. The girl had no connoisseur's eye for character; her interest was the frank and unabashed interest in a somewhat mysterious figure who was credited by all his friends with great gifts and a surprising amiability. After breakfast she had captured one of the spectacled people, whose name was Hoddam. He was a little shy man, one of the unassuming tribe of students by whom all the minor intellectual work of the world is done, and done well. It is a great class, living in the main in red-brick villas on the outskirts of academic towns, marrying mild blue-stockings, working incessantly, and finally attaining to the fame of mention in prefaces and foot-notes, and a short paragraph in the *Times* at the last. . . . Mr. Hoddam did not seek the company of one who was young, pretty, an heiress, and presumably flippant, but he was flattered when she plainly sought him.

"Mr. Lewis Haystoun is coming here this afternoon," she had announced. "Do you know him?"

"I have read his book," said her victim.

"Yes, but did you not know him at Oxford? You were there with him, were you not?"

"Yes, we were there together. I knew him by sight, of course, for he was a very well-known person. But, you see, we belonged to very different sets."

"How do you mean?" asked the blunt Alice.

"Well, you see," began Mr. Hoddam awkwardly--absolute honesty was one of his characteristics--"he was very well off, and he lived with a sporting set, and he was very exclusive."

"But I thought he was clever--I thought he was rather brilliant?"

"Oh, he was! Indubitably! He got everything he wanted, but then he got them easily and had a lot of time for other things, whereas most of us had not a moment to spare. He got the best First of his year and the St. Chad's Fellowship, but I think he cared far more about winning the 'Varsity Grind. Men who knew him said he was an extremely good fellow, but he had scores of rich sporting friends, and nobody else ever got to know him. I have heard him speak often, and his manner gave one the impression that he was a tremendous swell, you know, and rather conceited. People used to think him a sort of universal genius who could do everything. I suppose he was quite the ablest man that had been there for years, but I should think he would succeed ultimately as the man of action and not as the scholar."

"You give him a most unlovely character," said the girl.

"I don't mean to. I own to being entirely fascinated by him. But he was never, I think, really popular. He was supposed to be intolerant of mediocrity; and also he used to offend quite honest, simple-minded people by treating their beliefs very cavalierly. I used to compare him with Raleigh or Henri IV.--the proud, confident man of action."

Alice had pondered over Mr. Hoddam's confessions and was prepared to receive the visitor with coldness. The vigorous little democrat in her hated arrogance. Before, if she had asked herself what type on earth she hated most, she would have decided for the unscrupulous, proud man. And yet this Lewis must be lovable. That brown face had infinite attractiveness, and she trusted Lady Manorwater's acuteness and goodness of heart.

Lord Manorwater had gone off on some matter of business and taken the younger Miss Afflint with him. As Alice looked round the little assembly on the lawn, she felt for the first time the insignificance of the men. The large Mr. Stocks was not at his best in such surroundings. He was the typical townsman, and bore with him wherever he went an atmosphere of urban dust and worry. He hungered for ostentation, he could only talk well when he felt that he impressed his hearers; Bertha, who was not easily impressed, he shunned like a plague. The man, reflected the censorious Alice, had no shades or half-tones in his character; he was all bald, strong, and crude. Now he was talking to his hostess with the grace of the wise man unbending.

"I shall be pleased indeed to meet your nephew," he said. "I feel sure that we have many interests in common. Do you say he lives near?"

Lady Manorwater, ever garrulous on family matters, readily enlightened him. "Etterick is his, and really all the land round here. We simply live on a patch in the middle of it. The shooting is splendid, and Lewie is a very keen sportsman. His mother was my husband's sister, and died when he was born. He is wonderfully unspoiled to have had such a lonely boyhood."

"How did the family get the land?" he asked. It was a matter which interested him, for democratic politician though he was, he looked always forward to the day when he should own a pleasant country property, and forget the troubles of life in the Nirvana of the respectable.

"Oh, they've had it for ages. They are a very old family, you know, and look down upon us as parvenus. They have been everything in their day--soldiers, statesmen, lawyers; and when we were decent merchants in Abbeykirk three centuries ago, they were busy making history. When you go to Etterick you must see the pictures. There is a fine one by Jameson of the Haystoun who fought with Montrose, and Raeburn painted most of the Haystouns of his time. They were a very handsome race, at least the men; the women were too florid and buxom for my taste."

"And this Lewis--is he the only one of the family?"

"The very last, and of course he does his best to make away with himself by risking his precious life in Hindu Kush or Tibet or somewhere." Her ladyship was geographically vague.

"What a pity he does not realize his responsibilities!" said the politician. "He might do so much."

But at the moment it dawned upon the speaker that the skirker of responsibilities was appearing in person. There strode towards them, across the lawn, a young man and two dogs.

"How do you do, Aunt Egeria?" he cried, and he caught her small woman's hand in a hard brown one and smiled on the little lady.

Bertha Afflint had flung her magazine to the winds and caught his available left hand. "Oh, Lewie, you wretch! how glad we are to see you again." Meantime the dogs performed a solemn minuet around her ladyship's knees.

The young man, when he had escaped from the embraces of his friends, turned to the others. He seemed to recognize two of them, for he shook hands cordially with the two spectacled people. "Hullo, Hoddam, how are you? And Imrie! Who would have thought of finding you here?" And he poured forth a string of kind questions till the two beamed with pleasure.

Then Alice heard dimly words of introduction: "Miss Wishart, Mr. Haystoun," and felt herself bowing automatically. She actually felt nervous. The disreputable fisher of the day before was in ordinary riding garments of fair respectability. He recognized her at once, but he, too, seemed to lose for a moment his flow of greetings. His tone insensibly changed to a conventional politeness, and he asked her some of the stereotyped questions with which one greets a stranger. She felt sharply that she was a stranger to whom the courteous young man assumed more elaborate manners. The freedom of the day before seemed gone. She consoled herself with the thought that whereas then she had been warm, flushed, and untidy, she was now very cool and elegant in her prettiest frock.

Then Mr. Stocks arose and explained that he was delighted to meet Mr. Lewis Haystoun, that he knew of his reputation, and hoped to have some pleasant talk on matters dear to the heart of both. At which Lewis shunned the vacant seat between Bertha and that gentleman, and stretched himself on the lawn beside Alice's chair. A thrill of pleasure entered the girl's heart, to her own genuine surprise.

"Are Tam and Jock at peace now?" she asked. "Tam and Jock are never at peace. Jock is sedate and grave and old for his years, while Tam is simply a human collie. He has the same endearing manners and irresponsible mind. I had to fish him out of several rock-pools after you left."

Alice laughed, and Lady Manorwater said in wonder, "I didn't know you had met Lewie before, Alice."

"Miss Wishart and I forgathered accidentally at the Midburn yesterday," said the man.

"Oh, you went there," cried the aggrieved Arthur, "and you never told me! Why, it is the best water about here, and yesterday was a first-rate day. What did you catch, Lewie?"

"Twelve pounds-about four dozen trout."

"Listen to that! And to think that that great hulking chap got all the sport!" And the boy intercepted his cousin's tea by way of retaliation.

Then Mr. Stocks had his innings, with Lady Manorwater for company, and Lewis was put through a strict examination on his doings for the past years.

"What made you choose that outlandish place, my dear?" asked his aunt.

"Oh, partly the chance of a shot at big game, partly a restless interest in frontier politics which now and then seizes me. But really it was Wratislaw's choice."

"Do you know Wratislaw?" asked Mr. Stocks abruptly.

"Tommy?--why, surely! My best of friends. He had got his fellowship some years before I went up, but I often saw him at Oxford, and he has helped me innumerable times." The young man spoke eagerly, prepared to extend warm friendship to any acquaintance of his friend's.

"He and I have sometimes crossed swords," said Mr. Stocks pompously.

Lewis nodded, and forbore to ask which had come off the better.

"He is, of course, very able," said Mr. Stocks, making a generous admission.

His hearer wondered why he should be told of a man's ability when he had spoken of him as his friend.

"Have you heard much of him lately?" he asked. "We corresponded regularly when I was abroad, but of course he never would speak about himself, and I only saw him for a short time last week in London."

The gentleman addressed waved a deprecating hand.

"He has had no popular recognition. Such merits as he has are too aloof to touch the great popular heart. But we who believe in the people and work for them have found him a bitter enemy. The idle, academic, superior person, whatever his gifts, is a serious hindrance to honest work," said the popular idol.

"I shouldn't call him idle or superior," said Lewis quietly. "I have seen hard workers, but I have never seen anything like Tommy. He is a perfect mill-horse, wasting his fine talent on a dreary routine, merely because he is conscientious and nobody can do it so well."

He always respected honesty, so he forbore to be irritated with this assured speaker.

But Alice interfered to prevent jarring.

"I read your book, Mr. Haystoun. What a time you must have had! You say that north of Bardur or some place like that there are two hundred miles of utterly unknown land till you come to Russian territory. I should have thought that land important. Why doesn't some one penetrate it?

"Well, for various causes. It is very high land and the climate is not mild. Also, there are abundant savage tribes with a particularly effective crooked kind of knife. And, finally, our Government discourages British enterprise there, and Russia would do the same as soon as she found out."

"But what a chance for an adventurer!" said Alice, with a face aglow.

Lewis looked up at the slim figure in the chair above him, and caught the gleam of dark eyes.

"Well, some day, Miss Wishart--who knows?" he said slowly and carelessly.

But three people looked at him, Bertha, his aunt, and Mr. Stocks, and three people saw the same thing. His face had closed up like a steel trap. It was no longer the kindly, humorous face of the sportsman and good fellow, but the keen, resolute face of the fighter, the schemer, the man of daring. The lines about his chin and brow seemed to tighten and strengthen and steel, while the grey eyes had for a moment a glint of fire.

Three people never forgot that face. It was a pity that the lady at his side was prevented from seeing it by her position, for otherwise life might have gone differently with both. But the things which we call chance are in the power of the Fateful Goddesses who reserve their right to juggle with poor humanity.

Alice only heard the words, but they pleased her. Mr. Stocks fell farther into the background of disfavour. She had imagination and fire as well as common sense. It was the purple and fine gold which first caught her fancy, though on reflection she might decide for the hodden-grey. So she was very gracious to the young adventurer. And Arthur's brows grew dark as Erebus.

Lewis rode home in the late afternoon to Etterick in a haze of golden weather with an abstracted air and a slack bridle. A small, dainty figure tripped through the mazes of his thoughts. This man, usually oblivious of woman's presence, now mooned like any schoolboy. Those fresh young eyes and the glory of that hair! And to think that once he had sworn by black!

CHAPTER V

A CONFERENCE OP THE POWERS

It was the sultriest of weather in London--days when the city lay in a fog of heat, when the paving cracked, and the brow was damp from the slightest movement and the mind of the stranger was tortured by the thought of airy downs and running rivers. The leaves in the Green Park were withered and dusty, the window-boxes in Mayfair had a tarnished look, and horse and man moved with unwilling languor. A tall young man in a grey frockcoat searched the street for shadow, and finding none entered the doorway of a club which promised coolness.

Mr. George Winterham removed his top-hat, had a good wash, and then sought the smoking room. Seen to better advantage, he was sufficiently good-looking, with an elegant if somewhat lanky frame, a cheerful countenance, and a great brown moustache which gave him the air military. But he was no soldier, being indeed that anomalous creature, the titular barrister, who shows his profession by rarely entering the chambers and by an ignorance of law more profound than Necessity's.

He found the shadiest corner of the smoking room and ordered the coolest drink he could think of. Then he smiled, for he saw advancing to him across the room another victim of the weather. This was a small, thin man, with a finely-shaped dark head and the most perfectly-fitting clothes. He had been deep in a review, but at the sight of the wearied giant in the corner he had forgotten his interest in the "Entomology of the Riviera." He looked something of the artist or the man of letters, but in truth he had no taint of Bohemianism about him, being a very respectable person and a rising politician. His name was Arthur Mordaunt, but because it was the fashion at the time for a certain class of people to address each other in monosyllables, his friends invariably knew him as "John."

He dropped into a chair and regarded his companion with half-closed eyes.

"Well, John. Dished, eh? Most infernal heat I ever endured! I can't stand it, you know. I'll have to go away."

"Think," said the other, "think that at this moment somewhere in the country there are great, cool, deep woods and lakes and waterfalls, and we might be sitting in flannels instead of being clothed in these garments of sin."

"Think," said George, "of nothing of the kind. Think of high upland glens and full brown rivers, and hillsides where there is always wind. Why do I tantalize myself and talk to a vexatious idiot like you?"

This young man had a deep voice, a most emphatic manner of speech, and a trick of cheerfully abusing his friends which they rather liked than otherwise.

"And why should I sit opposite six feet of foolishness which can give me no comfort? Whew! But I think I am getting cool at last. I have sworn to make use of my first half-hour of reasonable temperature and consequent clearness of mind to plan flight from this place."

"May I come with you, my pretty maid? I am hideously sick of July in town. I know Mabel will never forgive me, but I must risk it."

Mabel was the young man's sister, and the friendship between the two was a perpetual joke. As a small girl she had been wont to con eagerly her brother's cricketing achievements, for George had been a famous cricketer, and annually went crazy with excitement at the Eton and Harrow match. She exercised a maternal care over him, and he stood in wholesome fear of her and ordered his doings more or less at her judgment. Now she was married, but she still supervised her tall brother, and the victim made no secret of the yoke.

Suddenly Arthur jumped to his feet. "I say, what about Lewis Haystoun? He is home now, somewhere in Scotland. Have you heard a word about him?"

"He has never written," groaned George, but he took out a pocket-book and shook therefrom certain newspaper cuttings. "The people I employ sent me these about him to-day." And he laid them out on his knee.

The first of them was long, and consisted of a belated review of Mr. Haystoun's book. George, who never read such things, handed it to Arthur, who glanced over the lines and returned it. The second explained in correct journalese that the Manorwater family had returned to Glenavelin for the summer and autumn, and that Mr. Lewis Haystoun was expected at Etterick shortly. The third recorded the opening of a bazaar in the town of Gledsmuir which Mr. Haystoun had patronised, "looking," said the fatuous cutting, "very brown and distinguished after his experiences in the East."--"Whew!" said George. "Poor beggar, to have such stuff written about him!"--The fourth discussed the possible retirement of Sir Robert Merkland, the member for Gledsmuir, and his possible successor. Mr. Haystoun's name was mentioned, "though indeed," said the wiseacre, "that gentleman has never shown any decided leanings to practical politics. We understand that the seat will be contested in the Radical interest by Mr. Albert Stocks, the well-known writer and lecturer."

"You know everybody, John. Who's the fellow?" George asked.

"Oh, a very able man indeed, one of the best speakers we have. I should like to see a fight between him and Lewie: they would not get on with each other. This Stocks is a sort of living embodiment of the irritable Radical conscience, a very good thing in its way, but not quite in Lewie's style."

The fifth cutting mentioned the presence of Mr. Haystoun at three garden-parties, and hinted the possibility of a mistress soon to be at Etterick.

George lay back in his chair gasping. "I never thought it would come to this. I always thought Lewie the least impressionable of men. I wonder what sort of woman he has fallen in love with. But it may not be true."

"We'll pray that it isn't true. But I was never quite sure of him. You know there was always an odd romantic strain in the man. The ordinary smart, pretty girl, who adorns the end of a dinner-table and makes an admirable mistress of a house, he would never think twice about. But for all his sanity Lewie has many cranks, and a woman might get him on that side."

"Don't talk of it. I can picture the horrid reality. He will marry some thin-lipped creature who will back him in all his madness, and his friends will have to bid him a reluctant farewell. Or, worse still, there are scores of gushing, sentimental girls who might capture him. I wish old Wratislaw were here to ask him what he thinks, for he knows Lewie better than any of us. Is he a member here?"

"Oh yes, he is a member, but I don't think he comes much. You people are too frivolous for him."

"Well, that is all the good done by subscribing to a news-cutting agency for news of one's friends. I feel as low as ditch water. There is that idiot who goes off to the ends of the earth for three years, and when he comes back his friends get no good of him for the confounded women." George echoed the ancient complaint which is doubtless old as David and Jonathan.

Then these two desolated young men, in view of their friend's defection, were full of sad memories, much as relations after a funeral hymn the acts of the deceased.

George lit a cigar and smoked it savagely. "So that is the end of Lewis! And to think I knew the fool at school and college and couldn't make a better job of him than this! Do you remember, John, how we used to call him 'Vaulting Ambition,' because he won the high jump and was a cocky beggar in general?"

"And do you remember when he got his First, and they wanted him to stand for a fellowship, but he was keen to get out of England and travel? Do you remember that last night at Heston, when he told us all he was going to do, and took a bet with Wratislaw about it?"

It is probable that this sad elegy would have continued for hours, had not a servant approached with letters, which he distributed, two to Arthur Mordaunt and one to Mr. Winterham. A close observer might have seen that two of the envelopes were identical. Arthur slipped one into his pocket, but tore open the other and read.

"It's from Lewie," he cried. "He wants me down there next week at Etterick. He says he is all alone and crazy to see old friends again."

"Mine's the same!" said George, after puzzling out Mr. Haystoun's by no means legible writing. "I say, John, of course we'll go. It's the very chance we were wishing for."

Then he added with a cheerful face, "I begin to think better of human nature. Here were we abusing the poor man as a defaulter, and ten minutes after he heaps coals of fire on our heads. There can't be much truth in what that newspaper says, or he wouldn't want his friends down to spoil sport."

"I wonder what he'll be like? Wratislaw saw him in town, but only for a little, and he notices nothing. He's rather famous now, you know, and we may expect to find him very dignified and wise. He'll be able to teach us most things, and we'll have to listen with proper humility."

"I'll give you fifty to one he's nothing of the kind," said George. "He has his faults like us all, but they don't run in that line. No, no, Lewie will be modest enough. He may have the pride of Lucifer at heart, but he would never show it.

His fault is just this infernal modesty, which makes him shirk fighting some blatant ass or publishing his merits to the world."

Arthur looked curiously at his companion. Mr. Winterham was loved of his friends as the best of good fellows, but to the staid and rising politician he was not a person for serious talk. Hence, when he found him saying very plainly what had for long been a suspicion of his own, he was willing to credit him with a new acuteness.

"You know I've always backed Lewie to romp home some day," went on the young man. "He has got it in him to do most things, if he doesn't jib and bolt altogether."

"I don't see why you should talk of your friends as if they were racehorses or prize dogs."

"Well, there's a lot of truth in the metaphor. You know yourself what a mess of it he might make. Say some good woman got hold of him--some good woman, for we will put aside the horrible suggestion of the adventuress. I suppose he'd be what you call a 'good husband.' He would become a magistrate and a patron of local agricultural societies and flower shows. And eveybody would talk about him as a great success in life; but we--you and I and Tommy-- who know him better, would feel that it was all a ghastly failure."

Mr. Lewis Haystoun's character erred in its simplicity, for it was at the mercy of every friend for comment.

"What makes you dread the women so?" asked Arthur with a smile.

"I don't dread 'em. They are all that's good, and a great deal better than most men. But then, you know, if you get a man really first-class he's so much better than all but the very best women that you've got to look after him. To ordinary beggars like myself it doesn't matter a straw, but I won't have Lewie throwing himself away."

"Then is the ancient race of the Haystouns to disappear from the earth?"

"Oh, there are women fit for him, sure enough, but you won't find them at every garden party. Why, to find the proper woman would be the making of the man, and I should never have another doubt about him. But I am afraid. He's a deal too kindly and good-natured, and he'd marry a girl to-morrow merely to please her. And then some day quite casually he would come across the woman who was meant by Providence for him, and there would be the devil to pay and the ruin of one good man. I don't mean that he'd make a fool of himself or anything of that sort, for he's not a cad; but in the middle of his pleasant domesticity he would get a glimpse of what he might have been, and those glimpses are not forgotten."

"Why, George, you are getting dithyrambic," said Arthur, still smiling, but with a new vague respect in his heart.

"For you cannot harness the wind or tie--tie the bonds of the wild ass," said George, with an air of quotation. "At any rate, we're going to look after him. He is a good chap and I've got to see him through."

For Mr. Winterham, who was very much like other men, whose language was free, and who respected few things indeed in the world, had unfailing tenderness for two beings-his sister and his friend.

The two young men rose, yawned, and strolled out into the hall. They scanned carelessly the telegram boards. Arthur pointed a finger to a message typed in a corner.

"That will make a good deal of difference to Wratislaw."

George read: "The death is announced, at his residence in Hampshire, of Earl Beauregard. His lordship had reached the age of eighty-five, and had been long in weak health. He is succeeded by his son the Right Hon. Lord Malham, the present Secretary of State for Foreign Affairs."

"It means that if Wratislaw's party get back with a majority after August, and if Wratislaw gets the under-secretaryship as most people expect, then, with his chief in the Lords, he will be rather an important figure in the Commons."

"And I suppose his work will be pretty lively," said George. He had been reading some of the other telegrams, which were, as a rule, hysterical messages by way of foreign capitals, telling of Russian preparations in the East.

"Oh, lively, yes. But I've confidence in Tommy. I wish the Fate which decides men's politics had sent him to our side. He knows more about the thing than any one else, and he knows his own mind, which is rare enough. But it's too hot for serious talk. I suppose my seat is safe enough in August, but I don't relish the prospect of a three weeks' fight. Wratislaw, lucky man, will not be opposed. I suppose he'll come up and help Lewis to make hay of Stock's chances. It's a confounded shame. I shall go and talk for him."

On the steps of the club both men halted, and looked up and down the sultry white street. The bills of the evening papers were plastered in a row on the pavement, and the glaring pink and green still further increased the dazzle. After the cool darkness within each shaded his eyes and blinked.

"This settles it," said George. "I shall wire to Lewie to-night."

"And I," said the other; "and to-morrow evening we'll be in that cool green Paradise of a glen. Think of it! Meantime I shall grill through another evening in the House, and pair."

CHAPTER VI

PASTORAL

I

A July morning had dawned over the Dreichill, and the glen was filled with sunlight, though as yet there seemed no sun. Behind a peak of hill it displayed its chastened morning splendours, but a stray affluence of brightness had sought the nooks of valley in all the wide uplands, courier of the great lord of heat and light and the brown summer. The house of Etterick stands high in a crinkle of hill, with a background of dark pines, and in front a lake, set in shores of rock and heather. When the world grew bright Lewis awoke, for that strange young man had a trick of rising early, and as he rubbed sleep from his eyes at the window he saw the exceeding goodliness of the morning. He roused his companions with awful threats, and then wandered along a corridor till he came to a low verandah, whence a little pier ran into a sheltered bay of the loch. This was his morning bathing-place, and as he ran down the surface of rough moorland stone he heard steps behind him, and George plunged into the cold blue waters scarcely a second after his host.

It was as chill as winter save for the brightness of the morning, which made the loch in open spaces a shining gold. As they raced each other to the far end, now in the dark blue of shade, now in the gold of the open, the hill breeze fanned their hair, and the great woody smell of pines was sweet around them. The house stood dark and silent, for the side before them was the men's quarters, and at that season given up to themselves; but away beyond, the smoke of chimneys curled into the still air. A man was mowing in some field on the hillside, and the cry of sheep came from the valley. By and by they reached the shelving coast of fine hill gravel, and as they turned to swim easily back a sleepy figure staggered down the pier and stumbled rather than plunged into the water.

"Hullo!" gasped George, "there's old John. He'll drown, for I bet you anything he isn't awake. Look!"

But in a second a dark head appeared which shook itself vigorously, and a figure made for the other two with great strokes. He was by so much the best swimmer of the three that he had soon reached them, and though in all honesty he first swam to the farther shore, yet he touched the pier very little behind them. Then came a rush for the house, and in half an hour three fresh-coloured young men came downstairs, whistling for breakfast.

The breakfast-room was a place to refresh a townsman's senses. Long and cool and dark, it was simply Lewis's room, and he preferred to entertain his friends there instead of wandering among unused dining-rooms. It had windows at each end with old-fashioned folding sashes; and the view on one side was to a great hill shoulder, fir-clad and deep in heather, and on the other to the glen below and the shining links of the Avelin. It was panelled in dark oak, and the furniture was a strange medley. The deep arm-chairs by the fire and the many pipes savoured of the smoking-room; the guns, rods, polo sticks, whips, which were stacked or hung everywhere, and the heads of deer on the walls, gave it an atmosphere of sport. The pictures were few but good--two water-colours, a small Raeburn above the fireplace, and half a dozen fine etchings. In a corner were many old school and college groups--the Eton Ramblers, the O.U.A.C., some dining clubs, and one of Lewis on horseback in racing costume, looking deeply miserable. Low bookcases of black oak ran round the walls, and the shelves were crammed with books piled on one another, many in white vellum bindings, which showed pleasantly against the dark wood. Flowers were everywhere-common garden flowers of old-fashioned kinds, for the owner hated exotics, and in a shallow silver bowl in the midst of the snowy table-cloth was a great mass of purple heather-bells.

Three very hungry young men sat down to their morning meal with a hearty goodwill. The host began to rummage among his correspondence, and finally extracted an unstamped note, which he opened. His face brightened as he read, and he laid it down with a broad smile and helped himself to fish.

"Are you people very particular what you do to-day?" he asked.

Arthur said, No. George explained that he was in the hands of his beneficent friend.

"Because my Aunt Egeria down at Glenavelin has got up some sort of a picnic on the moors, and she wants us to meet her at the sheepfolds about twelve."

"Oh," said George meditatively. "Excellent! I shall be charmed." But he looked significantly at Arthur, who returned the glance.

"Who are at Glenavelin?" asked that simple young man with an air of innocence.

"There's a man called Stocks, whom you probably know."

Arthur nodded.

"And there's Bertha Afflint and her sister."

It was George's turn to nod approvingly. The sharp-witted Miss Afflint was a great ally of his.

"And there's a Miss Wishart--Alice Wishart," said Lewis, without a word of comment. "And with my Aunt Egeria that will be all."

The pair got the cue, and resolved to subject the Miss Wishart whose name came last on their host's tongue to a friendly criticism. Meanwhile they held their peace on the matter like wise men.

"What a strange name Egeria is!" said Arthur. "Very," said Lewis; "but you know the story. My respectable aunt's father had a large family of girls, and being of a classical turn of mind he called them after the Muses. The Muses held out for nine, but for the tenth and youngest he found himself in a difficulty. So he tried another tack and called the child after the nymph Egeria. It sounds outlandish, but I prefer it to Terpsichore."

Thereafter they lit pipes, and, with the gravity which is due to a great subject, inspected their friend's rods and guns.

"I see no memorials of your travels, Lewie," said Arthur. "You must have brought back no end of things, and most people like to stick them round as a remembrance."

"I have got a roomful if you want to see them," said The traveller; "but I don't see the point of spoiling a moorland place with foreign odds and ends. I like homely and native things about me when I am in Scotland."

"You're a sentimentalist, old man," said his friend; and George, who heard only the last word, assumed that Arthur had then and there divulged his suspicions, and favoured that gentleman with a wild frown of disapproval.

As Lewis sat on the edge of the Etterick burn and looked over the shining spaces of morning, forgetful of his friends, forgetful of his past, his mind was full of a new turmoil of feeling. Alice Wishart had begun to claim a surprising portion of his thoughts. He told himself a thousand times that he was not in love--that he should never be in love, being destined for other things; that he liked the girl as he liked any fresh young creature in the morning of life, with youth's beauty and the grace of innocence. But insensibly his everyday reflections began to be coloured by her presence. "What would she think of this?" "How that would please her!" were sentences spoken often by the tongue of his fancy. He found charm in her presence after his bachelor solitude; her demure gravity pleased him; but that he should be led bond-slave by love--that was a matter he valiantly denied.

II

The sheepfolds of Etterick lie in a little fold of glen some two miles from the dwelling, where the heathy tableland, known all over the glen as "The Muirs," relieves the monotony of precipitous hills. On this day it was alert with life. The little paddock was crammed with sheep, and more stood huddling in the pens. Within was the liveliest scene, for there a dozen herds sat on clipping-stools each with a struggling ewe between his knees, and the ground beneath him strewn with creamy folds of fleece. From a thing like a gallows in a corner huge bags were suspended which were slowly filling. A cauldron of pitch bubbled over a fire, and the smoke rose blue in the hot hill air. Every minute a bashful animal was led to be branded with a great E on the left shoulder and then with awkward stumbling let loose to join her naked fellow-sufferers. Dogs slept in the sun and wagged their tails in the rear of the paddock. Small children sat on gates and lent willing feet to drive the flocks. In a corner below a little shed was the clippers' meal of ale and pies, with two glasses of whisky each, laid by under a white cloth. Meantime from all sides rose the continual crying of sheep, the intermittent bark of dogs, and the loud broad converse of the men.

Lewis and his friends jumped a fence, and were greeted heartily in the enclosure. He seemed to know each herd by name or rather nickname, for he had a word for all, and they with all freedom grinned *badinage* back.

"Where's my stool, Yed?" he cried. "Am I not to have a hand in clipping my own sheep?"

An obedient shepherd rose and fetched one of the triangular seats, while Lewis with great ease caught the ewe, pulled her on her back, and proceeded to call for shears. An old pair was found for him, and with much dexterity he performed the clipping, taking little longer to the business than the expert herd, and giving the shears a professional wipe on the sacking with which he had prudently defended his clothes.

From somewhere in the back two boys came forward--the Tam and Jock of a former day--eager to claim acquaintance. Jock was clearly busy, for his jacket was off and a very ragged shirt was rolled about two stout brown arms. The "human collie" seemed to be a gentleman of some leisure, for he was arrayed in what was for him the pink of fashion in dress. The two immediately lay down on the ground beside Lewis exactly in the manner of faithful dogs.

The men talked cheerfully, mainly on sheep and prices. Now talk would touch on neighbours, and there would be the repetition of some tale or saying. "There was a man in the glen called Rorison. D'ye mind Jock Rorison, Sandy?" And Sandy would reply, "Fine I mind Jock," and then both would proceed to confidences.

"Hullo, Tam," said Lewis at last, realizing his henchman's grandeur. "Why this magnificence of dress?

"I'm gaun to the Sabbath-school treat this afternoon," said that worthy.

"And you, Jock-are you going too?"

"No me! I'm ower auld, and besides, I've cast out wi' the minister."

"How was that?"

"Oh, I had been fechtin'," said Jock airily. "It was Andra Laidlaw. He called me ill names, so I yokit on him and bate him too, but I got my face gey sair bashed. The minister met me next day when I was a' blue and yellow, and, says he, 'John Laverlaw, what have ye been daein'? Ye're a bonny sicht for Christian een. How do ye think a face like yours will look between a pair o' wings in the next warld?' I ken I'm no bonny," added the explanatory Jock; "but ye canna expect a man to thole siccan language as that."

Lewis laughed and, being engaged in clipping his third sheep, forgot the delicacy of his task and let the shears slip. A very ugly little cut on the animal's neck was the result.

"Oh, confound it!" cried the penitent amateur. "Look what I've done, Yed. I'll have to rub in some of that stuff of yours and sew on a bandage. The files will kill the poor thing if we leave the cut bare in this infernal heat."

The old shepherd nodded, and pointed to where the remedies were kept. Jock went for the box, which contained, besides the ointment, some rolls of stout linen and a huge needle and twine. Lewis doctored the wound as best he could, and then proceeded to lay on the cloth and sew it to the fleece. The ewe grew restless with the heat and the pinching of the cut, and Jock was given the task of holding her head.

Clearly Lewis was not meant by Providence for a tailor. He made lamentable work with the needle. It slipped and pricked his fingers, while his unfeeling friends jeered and Tam turned great eyes of sympathy upwards from his Sunday garments.

"Patience, patience, man!" said the old herd. "Ca' cannier and be a wee thing quieter in your langwidge. There's a wheen leddies comin' up the burn."

It was too late. Before Lewis understood the purport of the speech Lady Manorwater and her party were at the folds, and as he made one final effort with the refractory needle a voice in his ear said:

"Please let me do that, Mr. Haystoun. I've often done it before."

He looked up and met Alice Wishart's laughing eyes. She stood beside him and deftly finished the bandage till the ewe was turned off the stool. Then, very warm and red, he turned to find a cool figure laughing at his condition.

"I'll have to go and wash my hands, Miss Wishart," he said gravely. "You had better come too." And the pair ran down to a deep brown pool in the burn and cleansed from their fingers the subtle aroma of fleeces.

"Ugh! my clothes smell like a drover's. That's the worst of being a dabbler in most trades. You can never resist the temptation to try your hand."

"But, really, your whole manner was most professional, Mr. Haystoun. Your language--"

"Please, don't," said the penitent; and they returned to the others to find that once cheerful assembly under a cloud. Every several man there was nervously afraid of women and worked feverishly as if under some great Taskmistress's eye. The result was a superfluity of shear-marks and deep, muffled profanity. Lady Manorwater ran here and there asking questions and confusing the workers; while Mr. Stocks, in pursuance of his democratic sentiments, talked in a stilted fashion to the nearest clipper, who called him "Sir" and seemed vastly ill at ease.

Lewis restored some cordiality. Under her nephew's influence Lady Manorwater became natural and pleasing. Jock was ferreted out of some corner and, together with the reluctant Tam, brought up for presentation.

"Tam," said his patron, "I'll give you your choice. Whether will you go to the Sabbath-school treat, or come with us to a real picnic? Jock is coming, and I promise you better fun and better things to eat."

It was no case for hesitation. Tam executed a doglike gambol on the turf, and proceeded to course up the burn ahead of the party, a vision of twinkling bare legs and ill-fitting Sunday clothes. The sedate Jock rolled down his sleeves, rescued a ragged jacket, and stalked in the rear.

III

Once on the heathy plateau the party scattered. Mr. Stocks caught the unwilling Arthur and treated him to a disquisition on the characteristics of the people whose votes he was soon to solicit. As his acquaintance with the subject was not phenomenal, the profit to the aggrieved listener was small. George, Lady Manorwater, and the two Miss Afflints sought diligently for a camping-ground, which they finally found by a clear spring of water on the skirts of a great grey rock. Meanwhile, Alice Wishart and Lewis, having an inordinate love of high places, set out for the ridge summit, and reached it to find a wind blowing from the far Gled valley and cooling the hot air.

Alice found a scrap of rock and climbed to the summit, where she sat like a small pixie, surveying a wide landscape and her warm and prostrate companion. Her bright hair and eyes and her entrancing grace of form made the callous Lewis steal many glances upwards from his lowly seat. The two had become excellent friends, for the man had that honest simplicity towards women which is the worst basis for love and the best for friendship. She felt that at any moment he might call her by some one or other of the endearing expressions used between men. He, for his part, was fast drifting from friendship to another feeling, but as yet he gave no sign of it, and kept up the brusque, kindly manners of his common life.

As she looked east and north to the heart of the hill-land, her eyes brightened, and she rose up and strained on tiptoe to scan the farthest horizon. Eagerly she asked the name of this giant and that, of this glint of water--was it loch or burn? Lewis answered without hesitation, as one to whom the country was as well known as his own name.

By and by her curiosity was satisfied and she slipped back into her old posture, and with chin on hand gazed into the remote distances. "And most of that is yours? Do you know, if I had a land like this I should never leave it again. You, in your ingratitude, will go wandering away in a year or two, as if any place on earth could be better than this. You are simply 'sinning away your mercies,' as my grandfather used to say."

"But what would become of the heroic virtues that you adore?" asked the cynical Lewis. "If men were all home-keepers it would be a prosaic world."

"Can you talk of the prosaic and Etterick in the same breath? Besides, it is the old fallacy of man that the domestic excludes the heroic," said Alice, fighting for the privileges of her sex.

"But then, you know, there comes a thing they call the go-fever, which is not amenable to reason. People who have it badly do not care a straw for a place in itself; all they want is to be eternally moving from one spot to another."

"And you?"

"Oh, I am not a sufferer yet, but I walk in fear, for at any moment it may beset me." And, laughing, he climbed up beside her.

It may be true that the last subject of which a man tires is himself, but Lewis Haystoun in this matter must have been distinct from the common run of men. Alice had given him excellent opportunities for egotism, but the blind young man had not taken them. The girl, having been brought up to a very simple and natural conception of talk, thought no more about it, except that she would have liked so great a traveller to speak more generously. No doubt, after all, this reticence was preferable to self-revelation. Mr. Stocks had been her companion that morning in the drive to Etterick, and he had entertained her with a sketch of his future. He had declined, somewhat nervously, to talk of his early life, though the girl, with her innate love of a fighter, would have listened with pleasure. But he had sketched his political creed, hinted at the puissance of his friends, claimed a monopoly of the purer sentiments of life, and rosily augured the future. The girl had been silent--the man had thought her deeply impressed; but now the morning's talk seemed to point a contrast, and Mr. Lewis Haystoun climbed to a higher niche in the temple of her esteem.

Afar off the others were signaling that lunch was ready, but the two on the rock were blind.

"I think you are right to go away," said Alice. "You would be too well off here. One would become a very idle sort of being almost at once."

"And I am glad you agree with me, Miss Wishart. 'Here is the shore, and the far wide world's before me,' as the song says. There is little doing in these uplands, but there's a vast deal astir up and down the earth, and it would be a pity not to have a hand in it."

Then he stopped suddenly, for at that moment the light and colour went out of his picture of the wanderer's life, and he saw instead a homelier scene-a dainty figure moving about the house, sitting at his table's head, growing old with him in the fellowship of years. For a moment he felt the charm of the red hearth and the quiet life. Some such sketch must the Goddess of Home have drawn for Ulysses or the wandering Olaf, and if Swanhild or the true Penelope were as pretty as this lady of the rock there was credit in the renunciation. The man forgot the wide world and thought only of the pin-point of Glenavelin.

Some such fancy too may have crossed the girl's mind. At any rate she cast one glance at the abstracted Lewis and welcomed a courier from the rest of the party. This was no other than the dandified Tam, who had been sent post-haste by George-that true friend having suffered the agonies of starvation and a terrible suspicion as to what rash step his host might be taking. Plainly the young man had not yet made Miss Wishart's acquaintance.

IV

The sun set in the thick of the dark hills, and a tired and merry party scrambled down the burnside to the highway. They had long outstayed their intention, but care sat lightly there, and Lady Manorwater alone was vexed by thoughts of a dinner untouched and a respectable household in confusion. The sweet-scented dusk was soothing to the senses, and there in the narrow glen, with the wide blue strath and the gleam of the river below, it was hard to find the link of reality and easy to credit fairyland. Arthur and Miss Wishart had gone on in front and were now strayed among boulders. She liked this trim and precise young man, whose courtesy was so grave and elaborate, while he, being a recluse by nature but a humanitarian by profession, was half nervous and half entranced in her cheerful society. They talked of nothing, their hearts being set on the scramble, and when at last they reached the highway and the farm where the Glenavelin traps had been put up, they found themselves a clear ten minutes in advance of the others.

As they sat on the dyke in the soft cool air Alice spoke casually of the place. "Where is Etterick?" she asked; and a light on a hillside farther up the glen was pointed out to her.

"It's a very fresh and pleasant place to stay at," said Arthur. "We're much higher than you are at Glenavelin, and the house is bigger and older. But we simply camp in a corner of it. You can never get Lewie to live like other people. He is the best of men, but his tastes are primeval. He makes us plunge off a verandah into a loch first thing in the morning, you know, and I shall certainly drown some day, for I am never more than half awake, and I always seem to go straight to the bottom. Then he is crazy about long expeditions, and when the Twelfth comes we shall never be off the hill. He is a long way too active for these slack modern days."

Lewie, Lewie! It was Lewie everywhere! thought the girl. What could become of a man who was so hedged about by admirers? He had seemed to court her presence, and her heart had begun to beat faster of late when she saw his face. She dared not confess to herself that she was in love--that she wanted this Lewis to herself, and bated the pretensions of his friends. Instead she flattered herself with a fiction. Her ground was the high one of an interest in character. She liked the young man and was sorry to see him in a way to be spoiled by too much admiration. And the angel who records our innermost thoughts smiled to himself, if such grave beings can smile.

Meantime Lewis was delivered bound and captive to the enemy. All down the burn his companion had been Mr. Stocks, and they had lagged behind the others. That gentleman had not enjoyed the day; he had been bored by the landscape and scorched by the sun; also, as the time of contest approached, he was full of political talk, and he had found no ears to appreciate it. Now he had seized on Lewis, and the younger man had lent him polite attention though inwardly full of ravening and bitterness.

"Your friend Mr. Mordaunt has promised to support my candidature. You, of course, will be in the opposite camp."

Lewis said he did not think so-that he had lost interest in party politics, and would lie low.

Mr. Stocks bowed in acquiescence.

"And what do you think of my chances?"

Lewis replied that he should think about equal betting. "You see the place is Radical in the main, with the mills at Gledfoot and the weavers at Gledsmuir. Up in Glenavelin they are more or less Conservative. Merkland gets in usually by a small majority because he is a local man and has a good deal of property down the Gled. If two strangers fought it the Radical would win; as it is it is pretty much of a toss-up either way."

"But if Sir Robert resigns?"

"Oh, that scare has been raised every time by the other party. I should say that there's no doubt that the old man will keep on for years."

Mr. Stocks looked relieved. "I heard of his resignation as a certainty, and I was afraid that a stronger man might take his place."

So it fell out that the day which began with pastoral closed, like many another day, with politics. Since Lewis refrained from controversy, Mr. Stocks seemed to look upon him as a Gallio from whom no danger need be feared, nay, even as a convert to be fostered. He became confident and talked jocularly of the tricks of his trade. Lewis's boredom was complete by the time they reached the farmhouse and found the Glenavelin party ready to start.

"We want to see Etterick, so we shall come to lunch to-morrow, Lewie," said his aunt. "So be prepared, my dear, and be on your best behaviour."

Then, with his two friends, he turned towards the lights of his home.

CHAPTER VII

THE MAKERS OF EMPIRE

The day before the events just recorded two men had entered the door of a certain London club and made their way to a remote little smoking-room on the first floor. It was not a handsome building, nor had it any particular outlook or position. It was a small, old-fashioned place in a side street, in style obviously of last century, and the fittings within were far from magnificent. Yet no club carried more distinction in its membership. Its hundred possible inmates were the cream of the higher professions, the chef and the cellar were things to wonder at, and the man who could write himself a member of the Rota Club had obtained one of the rare social honours which men confer on one another. Thither came all manner of people--the distinguished foreigner travelling incognito, and eager to talk with some Minister unofficially on matters of import, the diplomat on a secret errand, the traveller home for a brief season, the soldier, the thinker, the lawyer. It was a catholic assembly, but exclusive--very. Each man bore the stamp of competence on his face, and there was no cheap talk of the "well-informed" variety. When the members spoke seriously they spoke like experts; otherwise they were apt to joke very much like schoolboys let loose. The Right Hon. Mr. M---- was not above twitting Lord S---- with gunroom stories, and suffering in turn good-natured libel.

Of the two men lighting their pipes in the little room one was to the first glance a remarkable figure. About the middle height, with a square head and magnificent shoulders, he looked from the back not unlike some professional strong man. But his face betrayed him, for it was clearly the face of the intellectual worker, the man of character and mind. His jaw was massive and broad, saved from hardness only by a quaintly humorous mouth; he had, too, a pair of very sharp blue eyes looking from under shaggy eyebrows. His age was scarcely beyond thirty, but one would have put it ten years later, for there were lines on his brow and threads of grey in his hair. His companion was slim and, to a hasty glance, insignificant. He wore a peaked grey beard which lengthened his long, thin face, and he had a nervous trick of drumming always with his fingers on whatever piece of furniture was near. But if you looked closer and marked the high brow, the keen eyes, and the very resolute mouth, the thought of insignificance disappeared. He looked not unlike a fighting Yankee colonel who had had a Puritan upbringing, and the impression was aided by his simplicity in dress. He was, in fact, a very great man, the Foreign Secretary of the time, formerly known to fame as Lord Malham, and at the moment, by his father's death, Lord Beauregard, and, for his sins, an exile to the Upper House. His companion, whose name was Wratislaw, was a younger Member of Parliament who was credited with peculiar knowledge and insight on the matters which formed his lordship's province. They were close friends and allies of some years' standing, and colloquies between the two in this very place were not unknown to the club annals.

Lord Beauregard looked at his companion's anxious face. "Do you know the news?" he said.

"What news?" asked Wratislaw. "That your family position is changed, or that the dissolution will be a week earlier, or that Marka is busy again?"

"I mean the last. How did you know? Did you see the telegrams?"

"No, I saw it in the papers."

"Good Heavens!" said the great man. "Let me see the thing," and he snatched a newspaper cutting from Wratislaw's hand, returning it the next moment with a laugh. It ran thus: "Telegrams from the Punjab declare that an expedition, the personnel of which is not yet revealed, is about to start for the town of Bardur in N. Kashmir, to penetrate the wastes beyond the frontier. It is rumoured that the expedition has a semi-official character."

"That's our friend," said Wratislaw, putting the paper into his pocket.

Lord Beauregard wrinkled his brow and stared at the bowl of his pipe. "I see the motive clearly, but I am hanged if I understand why an evening paper should print it. Who in this country knows of the existence of Bardur?"

"Many people since Haystoun's book," said the other.

"I have just glanced at it. Is there anything important in it?"

"Nothing that we did not know before. But things are put in a fresh light. He covered ground himself of which we had only a second-hand account."

"And he talks of this Bardur?"

"A good deal. He is an expert in his way on the matter and uncommonly clever. He kept the best things out of the book, and it would be worth your while meeting him. Do you happen to know him?"

"No--o," said the great man doubtfully. "Oh, stop a moment. I have heard my young brother talk of somebody of the same name. Rather a figure at Oxford, wasn't he?"

Wratislaw nodded. "But to talk of Marka," he add.

"His mission is, of course, official, and he has abundant resources."

"So much I gathered," said Wratislaw. "But his designs?

"He knows the tribes in the North better than any living man, but without a base at hand he is comparatively harmless. The devil in the thing is that we do not know how close that base may be. Fifty thousand men may be massed within fifty miles, and we are in ignorance."

"It is the lack of a secret service," said the other. "Had we that, there are a hundred young men who would have risked their necks there and kept us abreast of our enemies. As it is, we have to wait till news comes by some roundabout channel, while that cheerful being, Marka, keeps the public easy by news of hypothetical private expeditious."

"And meantime there is that thousand-mile piece of desert of which we know nothing, and where our friends may be playing pranks as they please. Well, well, we must wait on developments. It is the last refuge of the ill-informed. What about the dissolution? You are safe, I suppose?"

Wratislaw nodded.

"I have been asked my forecast fifty times to-day, and I steadily refuse to speak. But I may as well give it to you. We shall come back with a majority of from fifty to eighty, and you, my dear fellow, will not be forgotten."

"You mean the Under-Secretaryship," said the other. "Well, I don't mind it."

"I should think not. Why, you will get that chance your friends have hoped so long for, and then it is only a matter of time till you climb the last steps. You are a youngish man for a Minister, for all your elderly manners."

Wratislaw smiled the pleased smile of the man who hears kind words from one whom he admires. "It won't be a bed of roses, you know. I am very unpopular, and I have the grace to know it."

The elder man looked on the younger with an air of kindly wisdom. "Your pride may have a fall, my dear fellow. You are young and confident, I am old and humble. Some day you will be glad to hope that you are not without this despised popularity."

Wratislaw looked grave. "God forbid that I should despise it. When it comes my way I shall think that my work is done, and rest in peace. But you and I are not the sort of people who can court it with comfort. We are old sticks and very full of angles, but it would be a pity to rub them off if the shape were to be spoiled."

Lord Beauregard nodded. "Tell me more about your friend Haystoun."

Wratislaw's face relaxed, and he became communicative.

"He is a Scots laird, rather well off, and, as I have said, uncommonly clever. He lives at a place called Etterick in the Gled valley."

"I saw Merkland to-day, and he spoke his farewell to politics. The Whips told me about it yesterday."

"Merkland! But he always raised that scare!"

"He is serious this time. He has sold his town house."

"Then that settles it. Lewis shall stand in his place."

"Good," said the great man. "We want experts. He would strengthen your feeble hands and confirm your tottering knees, Tommy."

"If he gets in; but he will have a fight for it. Our dear friend Albert Stocks has been nursing the seat, and the Manorwaters and scores of Lewie's friends will help him. That young man has a knack of confining his affections to members of the opposite party."

"What was Merkland's majority? Two-fifty or something like that?"

"There or about. But he was an old and well-liked country laird, whereas Lewie is a very young gentleman with nothing to his credit except an Oxford reputation and a book of travels, neither of which will appeal to the Gledsmuir weavers."

"But he is popular?"

"Where he is known--adored. But his name does not carry confidence to those who do not know the man, for his family were weak-kneed gentry."

"Yes, I knew his father. Able, but crotchety and impossible! Tommy, this young man must get the seat, for we cannot afford to throw away a single chance. You say he knows the place," and he jerked his head to indicate that

East to which his thoughts were ever turning. "Some time in the next two years there will be the devil's own mess in that happy land. Then your troubles will begin, my friend, and I can wish nothing better for you than the support of some man in the Commons who knows that Bardur is not quite so pastoral as Hampshire. He may relieve you of some of the popular odium you are courting, and at the worst he can be sent out."

Wratislaw whistled long and low. "I think not," he said. "He is too good to throw away. But he must get in, and as there is nothing in the world for me to do I shall go up to Ettorick tomorrow and talk to him. He will do as I tell him, and we can put our back into the fight. Besides, I want to see Stocks again. That man is the joy of my heart!"

"Lucky beggar!" said the Minister. "Oh, go by all means and enjoy yourself, while I swelter here for another three weeks over meaningless telegrams enlivened by the idiot diplomatist. Good-bye and good luck, and bring the young man to a sense of his own value."

CHAPTER VIII

MR. WRATISLAW'S ADVENT

As the three men went home in the dusk they talked of the day. Lewis had been in a bad humour, but the company of his friends exorcised the imp of irritation, and he felt only the mellow gloom of the evening and the sweet scents of the moor. In such weather he had a trick of walking with his head high and his nostrils wide, sniffing the air like the wild ass of the desert with which the metaphorical George had erstwhile compared him. That young man meanwhile was occupied with his own reflections. His good nature had been victimized, he had been made to fetch and carry continually, and the result was that he had scarcely spoken a word to Miss Wishart. His plans thus early foiled, nothing remained but to draw the more fortunate Arthur, so in a conspirator's aside he asked him his verdict. But Arthur refused to speak. "She is pretty and clever," he said, "and excellent company." And with this his lips were sealed, and his thoughts went off on his own concerns.

Lewis heard and smiled. The sun and wind of the hills beat in his pulses like wine. To have breathed all day the fragrance of heather and pines, to have gladdened the eye with an infinite distance and blue lines of mountain, was with this man to have drunk the cup of intoxicating youth. The cool gloaming did not chill; rather it was the high and solemn aftermath of the day's harvesting. The faces of gracious women seemed blent with the pageant of summer weather; kindly voices, simple joys--for a moment they seemed to him the major matters in life. So far it was pleasing fancy, but Alice soon entered to disturb with the disquieting glory of her hair. The family of the Haystouns had ever a knack of fine sentiment. Fantastic, unpractical, they were gluttons for the romantic, the recondite, and the dainty. But now had come a breath of strong wind which rent the meshes of a philandering fancy. A very new and strange feeling was beginning to make itself known. He had come to think of Alice with the hot pained affection which makes the high mountains of the world sink for the time to a species of mole-hillock. She danced through his dreams and usurped all the paths of his ambition. Formerly he had thought of himself--for the man was given to self-portraiture--as the adventurer, the scorner of the domestic; now he struggled to regain the old attitude, but he struggled in vain. The ways were blocked, a slim figure was ever in view, and lo! when he blotted it from his sight the world was dark and the roads blind. For a moment he had lost his bearings on the sea of life. As yet the discomfiture was sweet, his confusion was a joy; and it is the first trace of weakness which we have seen in the man that he accepted the unsatisfactory with composure.

At the door of Etterick it became apparent that something was astir. Wheel-marks were clear in the gravel, and the ancient butler had an air of ceremony. "Mr. Wratislaw has arrived, sir," he whispered to Lewis, whereat that young man's face shone.

"When? How? Where is he now?" he cried, and with a word to his companions he had crossed the hall, raced down a lengthy passage, and flung open the door of his sanctum. There, sure enough, were the broad shoulders of Wratislaw bending among the books.

"Lord bless me, Tommy, what extraordinary surprise visit is this? I thought you would be over your ears in work. We are tremendously pleased to see you."

The sharp blue eyes had been scanning the other's frank sunburnt face with an air of affectionate consideration. "I got off somehow or other, as I had to see you, old man, so I thought I would try this place first. What a fortressed wilderness you live in! I got out at Gledsmuir after travelling some dreary miles in a train which stopped at every farm, and then I had to wait an hour till the solitary dogcart of the inn returned. Hullo! you've got other visitors" And he stretched out a massive hand to Arthur and George.

The sight of him had lifted a load from these gentlemen's hearts. The old watchdog had come; the little terriers might now take holiday. The task of being Lewis's keeper did not by right belong to them; they were only amateurs acting in the absence of the properly qualified Wratislaw. Besides, it had been anxious work, for while each had sworn to himself aforetime to protect his friend from the wiles of Miss Wishart, both were now devoted slaves drawn at that young woman's chariot wheel. You will perceive that it is a delicate matter to wage war with a goddess, and a task unblest of Heaven.

Supper was brought, and the lamps lit in the cool old room, where, through the open window, they could still catch the glint of foam on the stream and the dark gloom of pines on the hill. They fell ravenously on the meal, for one man had eaten nothing since midday and the others were fresh from moorland air. Thereafter they pulled armchairs to a window, and lit the pipes of contentment. Wratislaw stretched his arms on the sill and looked out into the fragrant darkness.

"Any news, Tommy?" asked his host. "Things seem lively in the East."

"Very, but I am ill-informed. Did you lay no private lines of communication in your travels?"

"They were too short. I picked up a lot of out-of-the-way hints, but as I am not a diplomatist I cannot use them. I think I have already made you a present of most. By the by, I see from the papers that an official expedition is going north from Bardur. What idiot invented that?"

Wratislaw pulled his head in and sat back in his chair. "You are sure you don't happen to know?"

"Sure. But it is just the sort of canard which the gentry on the other side of the frontier would invent to keep things quiet. Who are the Englishmen at Bardur now?"

The elder man looked shrewdly at the younger, who was carelessly pulling a flower to pieces. "There's Logan, whom you know, and Thwaite and Gribton."

"Good men all, but slow in the uptake. Logan is a jewel. He gave me the best three days' shooting I ever dreamed of, and he has more stories in his head than George. But if matters got into a tangle I would rather not be in his company. Thwaite is a gentlemanlike sort of fellow, but dull-very, while Gribton is the ordinary shrewd commercial man, very cautious and rather timid."

"Did you ever happen to hear of a man called Marka? He might call himself Constantine Marka, or Arthur Marker, or the Baron Mark--whatever happened to suit him."

Lewis puzzled for a little. "Yes, of course I did. By George! I should think so. It was a chap of that name who had gone north the week before I arrived. They said he would never be heard of again. He seemed a reckless sort of fool."

"You didn't see him?"

"No. But why?"

"Simply that you came within a week of meeting one of the cleverest men living, a cheerful being whom the Foreign Office is more interested in than any one else in the world. If you should hear again of Constantine Marka, Marker, or Mark, please note it down."

"You mean that he is the author of the *canard*," said Lewis, with sharp eyes, taking up a newspaper.

"Yes, and many more. This graceful person will complicate things for me, for I am to represent the Office in the Commons if we get back with a decent majority."

Lewis held out a cordial hand. "I congratulate you, Tommy. Now beginneth the end, and may I be spared to see!"

"I hope you may, and it's on this I want to talk to you. Merkland has resigned; it will be in the papers to-morrow. I got it kept out till I could see you!"

"Yes?" said Lewis, with quickening interest.

"And we want you to take his place. I spoke to him, and he is enthusiastic on the matter. I wired to the Conservative Club at Gledsmuir, and it seems you are their most cherished possibility. The leaders of the party are more than willing, so it only remains for you to consent, my dear boy."

"I--don't--think--I--can," said the possibility slowly. "You see, only to-day I told that man Stocks that Merkland would not resign, and that I was sick of party politics and would not interfere with his chances. The poor beggar is desperately keen, and if I stood now he would think me disingenuous."

"But there is no reason why he should not know the truth. You can tell him that you only heard about Merkland to-night, and that you act only in deference to strong external pressure."

"In that case he would think me a fool. I have a bad enough reputation for lack of seriousness in these matters already. The man is not very particular, and there is nothing to hinder him from blazoning it up and down the place that I changed my mind in ten minutes on a friend's recommendation. I should get a very complete licking."

"Do you mind, Lewie, if I advise you to take it seriously? It is really not a case for little scruples about reputation. There are rocks ahead of me, and I want a man like you in the House more than I could make you understand. You say you hate party politics, and I am with you, but there is no reason why you should not use them as a crutch to better work. You are in your way an expert, and that is what we will need above all things in the next few years. Of course, if you feel yourself bound by a promise not to oppose Stocks, then I have nothing more to say; but, unless the man is a lunatic, he will admit the justice of your case."

"You mean that you really want me, Tommy?" said the young man, in great doubt. "I hate the idea of fighting Stocks, and I shall most certainly be beaten."

"That is on the knees of the gods, and as for the rest I take the responsibility. I shall speak to Stocks myself. It will be a sharp fight, but I see no reason why you should not win. After all, it is your own countryside, and you are a better man than your opponent."

"You are the serpent who has broken up this peaceful home. I shall be miserable for a month, and the house will be divided against itself. Arthur has promised to help Stocks, while the Manorwaters, root and branch, are pledged to support him."

"I'll do my best, Lewie, for old acquaintance' sake. It had to come sooner or later, you know, and it is as well that you should seize the favourable moment. Now let us drop the subject for to-night. I want to enjoy myself."

And he rose, stretched his great arms, and wandered about the room.

To all appearance he had forgotten the very existence of things political. Arthur, who had a contest to face shortly, was eager for advice and the odds and ends of information which defend the joints in a candidate's harness, but the well-informed man disdained to help. He tested the guns, gave his verdict on rods, and ranged through a cabinet of sporting requisites. Then he fell on his host's books, and for an hour the three were content to listen to him. It was rarely that Wratislaw fell into such moods, but when the chance came it was not to be lightly disregarded. A laborious youth had given him great stores of scholarship, and Lewis's books were a curious if chaotic collection. On the fly-leaf of a little duodecimo was an inscription from the author of Waverley, who had often made Etterick his hunting-ground. A Dunbar had Hawthornden's autograph, and a set of tall classic folios bore the handwriting of George Buchanan. Lord Kames, Hume, and a score of others had dedicated works to lairds of Etterick, and the Haystouns themselves had deigned at times to court the Muse. Lewis's own special books-college prizes, a few modern authors, some well-thumbed poets, and a row in half a dozen languages on some matters of diplomatic interest-were crowded into a little oak bookcase which had once graced his college rooms. Thither Wratislaw ultimately turned, dipping, browsing, reading a score of lines.

"What a nice taste you have in arrangement!" he cried. "Scott, Tolstoi, Meredith, an odd volume of a Saga library, an odd volume of the *Corpus Boreale*, some Irish reprints, Stevenson's poems, Virgil and the *Pilgrim's Progress*, and a French Gazetteer of Mountains wedged above them. And then an odd Badminton volume, French *Memoires*, a Dante, a Homer, and a badly printed German text of Schopenhauer! Three different copies of Rabelais, a De Thou, a Horace, and-bless my soul!--about twenty books of fairy tales! Lewie, you must have a mind like a lumber-room."

"I pillaged books from the big library as I wanted them," said the young man humbly. "Do you know, Tommy, to talk quite seriously, I get more erratic every day? Knocking about the world and living alone make me a queer slave of whims. I am straying too far from the normal. I wish to goodness you would take me and drive me back to the ways of common sense."

"Meaning--?

"That I am getting cranky and diffident. I am beginning to get nervous about people's opinion and sensitive to my own eccentricity. It is a sad case for a man who never used to care a straw for a soul on earth."

"Lewie, attend to me," said Wratislaw, with mock gravity. "You have not by any chance been falling in love?"

The accused blushed like a girl, and lied withal like a trooper, to the delight of the un-Christian George.

"Well, then, my dear fellow, there is hope for you yet. If a man once gets sentimental, he desires to be normal above all things, for he has a crazy intuition that it is the normal which women really like, being themselves but a hair's-breadth from the commonplace. I suppose it is only another of the immortal errors with which mankind hedges itself about."

"You think it an error?" said Lewis, with such an air of relief that George began to laugh and Wratislaw looked comically suspicious.

"Why the tone of joy, Lewie?"

"I wanted your opinion," said the perjured young man. "I thought of writing a book. But that is not the thing I was talking about. I want to be normal, aggressively normal, to court the suffrages of Gledsmuir. Do you know Stocks?"

"Surely."

"An excellent person, but I never heard him utter a word above a child's capacity. He can talk the most shrieking platitudes as if he had found at last the one and only truth. And people are impressed."

Wratislaw pulled down his eyebrows and proceeded to defend a Scottish constituency against the libel of gullibility. But Lewis was not listening. He did not think of the impression made on the voting powers, but on one small girl who clamorously impeded all his thoughts. She was, he knew, an enthusiast for the finer sentiments of life, and of these Mr. Stocks had long ago claimed a monopoly. He felt bitterly jealous-the jealousy of the innocent man to whom woman is an unaccountable creature, whose habits and likings must be curiously studied. He was dimly conscious of lacking the stage attributes of a lover. He could not pose as a mirror of all virtues, a fanatic for the True and the Good. Somehow or other he had acquired an air of self-seeking egotism, unscrupulousness, which he felt miserably must make him unlovely in certain eyes. Nor would the contest he was entering upon improve this fancied reputation of his. He would have to say hard, unfeeling things against what all the world would applaud as generous sentiment.

When the others had gone yawning to bed, he returned and sat at the window for a little, smoking hard and puzzling out the knots which confronted him. He had a dismal anticipation of failure. Not defeat--that was a little matter;

but an abject show of incompetence. His feelings pulled him hither and thither. He could not utter moral platitudes to checkmate his opponent's rhetoric, for, after all, he was honest; nor could he fill the part of the cold critic of hazy sentiment; gladly though he would have done it, he feared the reproach in girlish eyes. This good man was on the horns of a dilemma. Love and habit, a generous passion and a keen intellect dragged him alternately to their side, and as a second sign of weakness the unwilling scribe has to record that his conclusion as he went to bed was to let things drift--to take his chance.

CHAPTER IX

THE EPISODES OF A DAY

It is painful to record it, but when the Glenavelin party arrived at noon of the next day it was only to find the house deserted. Lady Manorwater, accustomed to the vagaries of her nephew, led the guests over the place and found to her horror that it seemed undwelt in. The hall was in order, and the tart and rosy lairds of Etterick looked down from their Raeburn canvases on certain signs of habitation; but the drawing-rooms were dingy with coverings and all the large rooms were in the same tidy disarray. Then, wise from experience, she led the way to Lewis's sanctum, and found there a pretty luncheon-table and every token of men's presence. Soon the four tenants arrived, hot and breathless, from the hill, to find Bertha Afflint deep in rods and guns, Miss Wishart and Lady Manorwater ensconced in the great armchairs, and Mr. Stocks casting a critic's eye over the unruly bookshelves.

Wratislaw's presence at first cast a certain awe on the assembly. His name was so painfully familiar, so consistently abused, that it was hard to refrain from curiosity. Lady Manorwater, an ancient ally, greeted him effusively, and Alice cast shy glances at this strong man with the kind smile and awkward manners. The truth is that Wratislaw was acutely nervous. With Mr. Stocks alone was he at his ease. He shook his hand heartily, declared himself delighted to meet him again, and looked with such manifest favour on this opponent that the gentleman was cast into confusion.

"I must talk shop," cried Lady Manorwater when they were seated at table. "Lewie, have you heard the news that poor Sir Robert has retired? What a treasure of a cook you have, sir! The poor man is going to travel, as his health is bad; he wrote me this morning. Now who is to take his place? And I wish you'd get me the recipe for this tomato soup."

Lewis unravelled the tangled skein of his aunt's questions.

"I heard about Merkland last night from Wratislaw. I think, perhaps, I had better make a confession to everybody. I never intended to bother with party politics, at least not for a good many years, but some people want me to stand, so I have agreed. You will have a very weak opponent, Stocks, so I hope you will pardon my impertinence in trying the thing."

The candidate turned a little pale, but he smiled gallantly.

"I shall be glad to have so distinguished an opponent. But I thought that yesterday you would never have dreamed of the thing."

"No more I should; but Wratislaw talked to me seriously and I was persuaded."

Wratislaw tried to look guileless, failed signally, and detected a sudden unfavourable glance from Mr. Stocks in his direction.

"We must manage everything as pleasantly as possible. You have my aunt and my uncle and Arthur on your side, while I have George, who doesn't count in this show, and I hope Wratislaw. I'll give you a three days' start if you like in lieu of notice." And the young man laughed as if the matter were the simplest of jokes.

The laugh jarred very seriously on one listener. To Alice the morning had been full of vexations, for Mr. Stocks had again sought her company, and wearied her with a new manner of would-be gallantry which sat ill upon him. She had come to Etterick with a tenderness towards Lewis which was somewhat dispelled by his newly-disclosed political aims. It meant that the Glenavelin household, including herself, would be in a different camp for three dreary weeks, and that Mr. Stocks would claim more of her society than ever. With feminine inconsistency she visited her repugnance towards that gentleman on his innocent rival. But Mr. Lewis Haystoun's light-hearted manner of regarding the business struck the little Puritan deeper. Politics had always been a thing of the gravest import in her eyes, bound up with a man's duty and honour and religion, and lo! here was this Gallio who not only adorned a party she had been led to regard as reprobate, but treated the whole affair as a half-jocular business, on which one should not be serious. It was sheer weakness, her heart cried out, the weakness of the philanderer, the half-hearted. In her vexation her interest flew in sympathy to Mr. Stocks, and she viewed him for the occasion with favour.

"You are far too frivolous about it," she cried. "How can you fight if you are not in earnest, and how can you speak things you only half believe? I hate to think of men playing at politics." And she had set her little white teeth, and sat flushed and diffident, a Muse of Protest.

Lewis flushed in turn. He recognized with pain the fulfilment of his fears. He saw dismally how during the coming fight he would sink daily in the estimation of this small critic, while his opponent would as conspicuously rise. The prospect did not soothe him, and he turned to Bertha Afflint, who was watching the scene with curious eyes.

"It's very sad, Lewie," she said, "but you'll get no canvassers from Glenavelin. We have all been pledged to Mr. Stocks for the last week. Alice is a keen politician, and, I believe, has permanently unsettled Lord Manorwater's easy-going Liberalism. She believes in action; whereas, you know, he does not."

"We all believe in action nowadays," said Wratislaw. "I could wish at times for the revival of 'leisureliness' as a party catch-word."

And then there ensued a passage of light arms between the great man and Bertha which did not soothe Alice's vexation. She ignored the amiable George, seeing in him another of the half-hearted, and in a fine heat of virtue devoted herself to Mr. Stocks. That gentleman had been melancholy, but the favour of Miss Wishart made him relax his heavy brows and become communicative. He was flattered by her interest. She heard his reminiscences with a smile and his judgments with attention. Soon the whole table talked merrily, and two people alone were aware that breaches yawned under the unanimity.

Archness was not in Alice's nature, and still less was coquetry. When Lewis after lunch begged to be allowed to show her his dwelling she did not blush and simper, she showed no pretty reluctance, no graceful displeasure. She thanked him, but coldly, and the two climbed the ridge above the lake, whence the whole glen may be seen winding beneath. It was still, hot July weather, and the far hills seemed to blink and shimmer in the haze; but at their feet was always coolness in the blue depth of the loch, the heath-fringed shores, the dark pines, and the cold whinstone crags.

"You don't relish the prospect of the next month?" she asked.

He shrugged his shoulders. "After all, it is only a month, and it will all be over before the shooting begins."

"I cannot understand you," she cried suddenly and impatiently. "People call you ambitious, and yet you have to be driven by force to the simplest move in the game, and all the while you are thinking and talking as if a day's sport were of far greater importance."

"And it really vexes you--Alice?" he said, with penitent eyes.

She drew swiftly away and turned her face, so that the man might not see the vexation and joy struggling for mastery.

"Of course it is none of my business, but surely it is a pity." And the little doctrinaire walked with head erect to the edge of the slope and studied intently the distant hills.

The man was half amused, half pained, but his evil star was in the ascendant. Had he known it, he would have been plain and natural, for at no time had the girl ever been so near to him. Instead, he made some laughing remark, which sounded harshly flippant in her ears. She looked at him reproachfully; it was cruel to treat her seriousness with scorn; and then, seeing Lady Manorwater and the others on the lawn below, she asked him with studied carelessness to take her back. Lewis obeyed meekly, cursing in his heart his unhappy trick of an easy humour. If his virtues were to go far to rob him of what he most cared for, it looked black indeed for the unfortunate young man.

Meantime Wratislaw and Mr. Stocks had drawn together by the attraction of opposites. A change had come over the latter, and momentarily eclipsed his dignity. For the man was not without tact, and he felt that the attitude of high-priest of all the virtues would not suit in the presence of one whose favourite task it was to laugh his so-called virtues to scorn. Such, at least to begin with, was his honourable intention. But the subtle Wratislaw drew him from his retirement and skilfully elicited his coy principles. It was a cruel performance--a shameless one, had there been any spectator. The one would lay down a fine generous line of policy; the other would beg for a fact in confirmation. The one would haltingly detail some facts; the other would promptly convince him of their falsity. Eventually the victim grew angry and a little frightened. The real Mr. Stocks was a man of business, not above making a deal with an opponent; and for a little the real Mr. Stocks emerged from his shell.

"You won't speak much in the coming fight, will you? You see, you are rather heavy metal for a beginner like myself," he said, with commercial frankness.

"No, my dear Stocks, to set your mind at rest, I won't. Lewis wants to be knocked about a little, and he wants the fight to brace him. I'll leave him to fight his own battles, and wish good luck to the better man. Also, I won't come to your meetings and ask awkward questions."

Mr. Stocks bore malice only to his inferiors, and respected his betters when he was not on a platform. He thanked Wratislaw with great heartiness, and when Lady Manorwater found the two they were beaming on each other like the most ancient friends.

"Has anybody seen Lewie?" she was asking. "He is the most scandalous host in the world. We can't find boats or canoes and we can't find him. Oh, here is the truant!" And the renegade host was seen in the wake of Alice descending from the ridge.

Something in the attitude of the two struck the lady with suspicion. Was it possible that she had been blind, and that her nephew was about to confuse her cherished schemes? This innocent woman, who went through the world as not being of it, had fancied that already Alice had fallen in with her plans. She had seemed to court Mr. Stocks's company, while he most certainly sought eagerly for hers. But Lewis, if he entered the lists, would be a perplexing combatant, and Lady Manorwater called her gods to witness that it should not be. Many motives decided her against it. She hated that a scheme of her own once made should be checkmated, though it were by her dearest friend. More than all, her pride was in arms. Lewis was a dazzling figure; he should make a great match; money and pretty looks and parvenu blood were not enough for his high mightiness.

So it came about that, when they had explored the house, circumnavigated the loch, and had tea on a lawn of heather, she informed her party that she must get out at Haystounslacks, for she wished to see the farmer, and asked Bertha to keep her company. The young woman agreed readily, with the result that Alice and Mr. Stocks were left sole occupants of the carriage for the better half of the way. The man was only too willing to seize the chance thus divinely given him. His irritation at Lewis's projects had been tempered by Alice's kindness at lunch and Wratislaw's unlooked-for complaisance. Things looked rosy for him; far off, as on the horizon of his hopes, he saw a seat in Parliament and a fair and amply dowered wife.

But Miss Wishart was scarcely in so pleasant a humour. With Lewis she was undeniably cross, but of Mr. Stocks she was radically intolerant. A moment of pique might send her to his side, but the position was unnatural and could not be maintained. Even now Lewis was in her thoughts. Fragments of his odd romantic speech clove to her memory. His figure--for he showed to perfection in his own surroundings--was so comely and gallant, so bright with the glamour of adventurous youth, that for a moment this prosaic young woman was a convert to the coloured side of life and had forgotten her austere creed.

Mr. Stocks went about his duty with praise-worthy thoroughness. For the fiftieth time in a week he detailed to her his prospects. When he had raised a cloud-built castle of fine hopes, when he had with manly simplicity repeated his confession of faith, he felt that the crucial moment had arrived. Now, when she looked down the same avenue of prospect as himself, he could gracefully ask her to adorn the fair scene with her presence.

"Alice," he said, and at the sound of her name the girl started from a reverie in which Lewis was not absent, and looked vacantly in his face.

He took it for maidenly modesty.

"I have wanted to speak to you for long, Alice. We have seen a good deal of each other lately, and I have come to be very fond of you. I trust you may have some liking for me, for I want you to promise to be my wife."

He told his love in regular sentences. Unconsciously he had fallen into the soft patronizing tone in which aforetime he had shepherded a Sunday school.

The girl looked at the large sentimental face and laughed. She felt ashamed of her rudeness even in the act.

He caught her hands, and before she knew his face was close to hers. "Promise me, dear," he said. "We have everything in common. Your father will be delighted, and we will work together for the good of the people. You are not meant to be a casual idler like the people at Etterick. You and I are working man and woman."

It was her turn to flush in downright earnest. The man's hot face sickened her. What were these wild words he was speaking? She dimly caught their purport, heard the mention of Etterick, saw once again Lewis with his quick, kindly eyes, and turned coldly to the lover.

"It is quite out of the question, Mr. Stocks," she said calmly. "Of course I am obliged to you for the honour you have done me, but the thing is impossible."

"Who is it?" he cried, with angry eyes. "Is it Lewis Haystoun?"

The girl looked quickly at him, and he was silent, abashed. Strangely enough, at that moment she liked him better than ever before. She forgave him his rudeness and folly, his tactless speech and his comical face. He was in love with her, he offered her what he most valued, his political chances and his code of fine sentiments; it was not his blame if she found both little better than husks.

Her attention flew for a moment to the place she had left, only to return to a dismal reflection. Was she not, after all, in the same galley as her rejected suitor? What place had she in the frank good-fellowship of Etterick, or what part had they in the inheritance of herself and her kind? Had not Mr. Stocks--now sitting glumly by her side--spoken the truth? We are only what we are made, and generations of thrift and seriousness had given her a love for the strenuous and the unadorned which could never be cast out. Here was a quandary--for at the same instant there came the voice of the heart defiantly calling her to the breaking of idols.

CHAPTER X

HOME TRUTHS

I

It is told by a great writer in his generous English that when the followers of Diabolus were arraigned before the Recorder and Mayor of regenerate Mansoul, a certain Mr. Haughty carried himself well to the last. "He declared," says Bunyan, "that he had carried himself bravely, not considering who was his foe or what was the cause in which he was engaged. It was enough for him if he fought like a man and came off victorious." Nevertheless, we are told, he suffered the common doom, being crucified next day at the place of execution. It is the old fate of the freelance, the Hal o' the Wynd who fights for his own hand; for in life's contest the taking of sides is assumed to be a necessity.

Such was Lewis's reflections when he found Wratislaw waiting for him in the Etterick dogcart when he emerged from a meeting in Gledsmuir. He had now enjoyed ten days of it, and he was heartily tired. His throat was sore with much speaking, his mind was barren with thinking on the unthinkable, and his spirits were dashed with a bitter sense of futility. He had honestly done his best. So far his conscience was clear; but as he reviewed the past in detail, his best seemed a very shoddy compromise. It was comfort to see the rugged face of Wratislaw again, though his greeting was tempered by mistrust. The great man had refused to speak for him and left him to fight his own battles; moreover, he feared the judgment of the old warrior on his conduct of the fight. He was acutely conscious of the joints in his armour, but he had hoped to have decently cloaked them from others. When he heard the first words, "Well, Lewie, my son, you have been making a mess of it," his heart sank.

"I am sorry," he said. "But how?"

"How? Why, my dear chap, you have no grip. You have let the thing get out of hand. I heard your speech to-night. It was excellent, very clever, a beautiful piece of work, but worse than useless for your purpose. You forget the sort of man you are fighting. Oh, I have been following the business carefully, and I felt bound to come down to keep you in order. To begin with, you have left your own supporters in the place in a nice state of doubt."

"How?"

"Why, because you have given them nothing to catch hold of. They expected the ordinary Conservative confession of faith--a rosy sketch of foreign affairs, and a little gentle Socialism, and the old rhetoric about Church and State. Instead, they are put off with epigrams and excellent stories, and a few speculations as to the metaphysical basis of politics. Believe me, Lewie, it is only the very general liking for your unworthy self which keeps them from going over in a body to Stocks." And Wratislaw lit a cigar and puffed furiously.

"Then you would have me deliver the usual insincere platitudes?" said Lewis dismally.

"I would have you do nothing of the kind. I thought you understood my point of view. A man like Stocks speaks his platitudes with vehemence because he believes in them whole-heartedly. You have also your platitudes to get through with, not because you would stake your soul on your belief in them, but because they are as near as possible the inaccurate popular statement of your views, which is all that your constituents would understand, and you pander to the popular craving because it is honest enough in itself and is for you the stepping-stone to worthier work."

Lewis shook his head dismally.

"I haven't the knack of it. I seem to stand beside myself and jeer all the while. Besides, it would be opposing complete sincerity with a very shady substitute. That man Stocks is at least an honest fool. I met him the other day after he had been talking some atrocious nonsense. I asked him as a joke how he could be such a humbug, and he told me quite honestly that he believed every word; so, of course, I apologized. He was attacking you people on your foreign policy, and he pulled out a New Testament and said, 'What do I read here?' It went down with many people, but the thing took away my breath."

His companion looked perplexedly at the speaker. "You have had the wrong kind of education, Lewie. You have always been the spoiled child, and easily and half-unconsciously you have mastered things which the self-made man has to struggle towards with a painful conscious effort. The result is that you are a highly cultured man without any crudeness or hysteria, while the other people see things in the wrong perspective and run their heads against walls and make themselves miserable. You gain a lot, but you miss one thing. You know nothing of the heart of the crowd. Oh, I don't mean the people about Etterick. They are your own folk, and the whole air of the place is semi-feudal. But the weavers and artisans of the towns and the ordinary farm workers--what do you know of them? Your precious theories are so much wind in their ears. They want the practical, the blatantly obvious, spiced with a little emotion. Stocks knows their demands. He began among them, and at present he is but one remove from them. A garbled quotation from the Scriptures or an appeal to their domestic affections is the very thing required. Moreover, the man understands an audience. He can bully it, you know; put on airs of sham independence to cover his real obeisance; while you are polite and deferent to hide your very obvious scorn."

"Do you know, Tommy, I'm a coward," Lewis broke in. "I can't face the people. When I see a crowd of upturned faces, crass, ignorant, unwholesome many of them, I begin to despair. I cannot begin to explain things from the beginning; besides, they would not understand me if I did. I feel I have nothing in common with them. They lead, most of them, unhealthy indoor lives, their minds are half-baked, and their bodies half-developed. I feel a terrible pity, but all the same I cannot touch them. And then I become a coward and dare not face them and talk straight as man to man. I repeat my platitudes to the ceiling, and they go away thinking, and thinking rightly, that I am a fool."

Wratislaw looked worried. "That is one of my complaints. The other is that on certain occasions you cannot hold yourself in check. Do you know you have been blackguarded in the papers lately, and that there is a violent article against you in the Critic, and all on account of some unwise utterances?"

Lewis flushed deeply. "That is the worst thing I have done, and I feel horribly penitent. It was the act of a cad and a silly schoolboy. But I had some provocation, Tommy. I had spoken at length amid many interruptions, and I was getting cross. It was at Gledfoot, and the meeting was entirely against me. Then a man got up to tackle me, not a native, but some wretched London agitator. As I looked at him--a little chap With fiery eyes and receding brow--and heard his cockney patter, my temper went utterly. I made a fool of him, and I abused the whole assembly, and, funnily enough, I carried them with me. People say I helped my cause immensely."

"It is possible," said Wratislaw dryly. "The Scot has a sense of humour and has no objection to seeing his prophets put to shame. But you are getting a nice reputation elsewhere. When I read some of your sayings, I laughed of course, but I thought ruefully of your chances."

It was a penitent and desponding man who followed Wratislaw into the snuggery at Etterick. But light and food, the gleam of silver and vellum and the sweet fragrance of tobacco consoled him; for in most matters he was half-hearted, and politics sat lightly on his affections.

II

To Alice the weeks of the contest were filled with dire unpleasantness. Lewis, naturally, kept far from Glenavelin, while of Mr. Stocks she was never free. She followed Lady Manorwater's lead and canvassed vigorously, hoping to find distraction in the excitement of the fight. But her efforts did not prosper. On one occasion she found herself in a cottage on the Gledsmuir road, her hands filled with election literature. A hale old man was sitting at his meal, who greeted her cordially, and made her sit down while she stumbled through the usual questions and exhortations. "Are ye no' bidin' at Glenavelin?" he asked. "And have I no seen ye walking on the hill wi' Maister Lewie?" When the girl assented, he asked, with the indignation of the privileged, "Then what for are ye sac keen this body Stocks should win in? If Maister Lewie's fond o' ye, wad it no be wiser--like to wark for him? Poalitics! What should a woman's poalitics be but just the same as her lad's? I hae nae opeenion o' this clash about weemen's eddication." And with flaming cheeks the poor girl had risen and fled from the old reactionary.

The incident burned into her mind, and she was wretched with the anomaly of her position. A dawning respect for her rejected lover began to rise in her heart. The first of his meetings which she attended had impressed her with his skill in his own vocation. He had held those people interested. He had spoken bluntly, strongly, honestly. To few women is it given to distinguish the subtle shades of sincerity in speech, and to the rule Alice was no exception. The rhetoric and the cheers which followed had roused the speaker to a new life. His face became keen, almost attractive, without question full of power. He was an orator beyond doubt, and when he concluded in a riot of applause, Alice sat with small hands clenched and eyes shining with delight. He had spoken the main articles of her creed, but with what force and freshness! She was convinced, satisfied, delighted; though somewhere in her thought lurked her old dislike of the man and the memory of another.

As ill-luck would have it, the next night she went to hear Lewis in Gledsmuir, when that young gentleman was at his worst. She went unattended, being a fearless young woman, and consequently found herself in the very back of the hall crowded among some vehement politicians. The audience, to begin with, was not unkind. Lewis was greeted with applause, and at the first heard with patience. But his speech was vague, incoherent, and tactless. To her unquiet eyes he seemed to be afraid of the men before him. Every phrase was guarded with a proviso, and "possiblys" bristled in every sentence. The politicians at the back grew restless, and Alice was compelled to listen to their short, scathing criticisms. Soon the meeting was hopelessly out of hand. Men rose and rudely marched to the door. Catcalls were frequent from the corners, and the back of the hall became aggressive. The girl had sat with white, pained face, understanding little save that Lewis was talking nonsense and losing all grip on his hearers. In spite of herself she was contrasting this fiasco with the pithy words of Mr. Stocks. When the meeting became unruly she looked for some display of character, some proof of power. Mr. Stocks would have fiercely cowed the opposition, or at least have spoken the last word in any quarrel. Lewis's conduct was different. He shrugged his shoulders, made some laughing remark to a friend on the platform, and with all the nonchalance in the world asked the meeting if they wished to hear any more. A claque of his supporters replied with feigned enthusiasm, but a malcontent at Alice's side rose and stamped to the door. "I came to hear sense," he cried, "and no this bairn's-blethers!"

The poor girl was in despair. She had fancied him a man of power and ambition, a doer, a man of action. But he was no more than a creature of words and sentiment, graceful manners, and an engaging appearance. The despised Mr. Stocks was the real worker. She had laughed at his incessant solemnity as the badge of a fool, and adored Lewis's light-heartedness as the true air of the great. But she had been mistaken. Things were what they seemed. The light-hearted was the half-hearted, "the wandering dilettante," Mr. Stocks had called him, "the worst type of the pseudo-culture of our universities." She told herself she hated the whole affectation of breeding and chivalry. Those men--Lewis and his friends--were always kind and soft-spoken to her and her sex. Her soul hated it; she cried aloud for equal treatment, for a share of the iron and rigour of life. Their manners were a mere cloak for contempt. If they could only be rude to a woman, it would be a welcome relief from this facile condescension. What had she or any woman with brains to do in that galley? They despised her kind, with the scorn of sultans who chose their women-folk for looks and graces. The thought was degrading, and a bitterness filled her heart against the whole clique of easy aristocrats. Mr. Stocks was her true ally. To him she was a woman, an equal; to them she was an engaging child, a delicate toy.

So far she went in her heresy, but no farther. It is a true saying that you will find twenty heroic women before you may meet one generous one; but Alice was not wholly without this rarest of qualities. The memory of a frank voice, very honest grey eyes, and a robust cheerfulness brought back some affection for the erring Lewis. The problem was beyond her reconciling efforts, so the poor girl, torn between common sense and feeling, and recognizing with painful clearness the complexity of life, found refuge in secret tears.

III

The honours of the contest, so far as Lewis's party was concerned, fell to George Winterham, and this was the fashion of the event. He had been dragged reluctantly into the thing, foreseeing dire disaster for himself, for he knew little and cared less about matters political, though he was ready enough at a pinch to place his ignorance at his friend's disposal. So he had been set to the dreary work of committee-rooms; and then, since his manners were not unpleasing, dispatched as aide-de-camp to any chance orator who enlivened the county. But at last a crisis arrived in which other use was made of him. A speaker of some pretensions had been announced for a certain night at the considerable village of Allerfoot. The great man failed, and as it was the very eve of the election none could be found for his place. Lewis was in despair, till he thought of George. It was a desperate chance, but the necessity was urgent, so, shutting himself up for an hour, he wrote the better part of a speech which he entrusted to his friend to prepare. George, having a good memory, laboriously learned it by heart, and clutching the friendly paper and whole-heartedly abusing his chief, he set out grimly to his fate.

Promptly at the hour of eight he was deposited at the door of the Masonic Hall in Allerfoot. The place seemed full, and a nervous chairman was hovering around the gate. News of the great man's defection had already been received, and he was in the extremes of nervousness. He greeted George as a saviour, and led him inside, where some three hundred people crowded a small whitewashed building. The village of Allerfoot itself is a little place, but it is the centre of a wide pastoral district, and the folk assembled were brown-faced herds and keepers from the hills, plough-men from the flats of Glen Aller, a few fishermen from the near sea-coast, as well as the normal inhabitants of the village.

George was wretchedly nervous and sat in a cold sweat while the chairman explained that the great Mr. S---- deeply regretted that at the last moment he was unfortunately compelled to break so important an engagement, but that he had sent in his stead Mr. George Winterham, whose name was well known as a distinguished Oxford scholar and a rising barrister. George, who had been ploughed twice for Smalls and had eventually taken a pass degree, and to whom the law courts were nearly as unknown as the Pyramids, groaned inwardly at the astounding news. The audience might have been a turnip field for all the personality it possessed for him. He heard their applause as the chairman sat down mopping his brow, and he rose to his feet conscious that he was smiling like an idiot. He made some introductory remarks of his own--that "he was sorry the other chap hadn't turned up, that he was happy to have the privilege of expounding to them his views on this great subject "--and then with an ominous sinking of heart plucked forth his papers and launched into the unknown.

The better part of the speech was wiped clean from his memory at the start, so he had to lean heavily on the written word. He read rapidly but without intelligence. Now and again a faint cheer would break the even flow, and he would look up for a moment with startled eyes, only to go off again with quickened speed. He found himself talking neat paradoxes which he did not understand, and speaking glibly of names which to him were no more than echoes. Eventually he came to an end at least twenty minutes before a normal political speech should close, and sat down, hot and perplexed, with a horrible sense of having made a fool of himself.

The chairman, no less perplexed, made the usual remarks and then called for questions, for the time had to be filled in somehow. The words left George aghast. The wretched man looked forward to raw public shame. His ignorance would be exposed, his presumption laid bare, his pride thrown in the dust. He nerved himself for a despairing effort. He would brazen things out as far as possible; afterwards, let the heavens fall.

An old minister rose and asked in a thin ancient voice what the Government had done for the protection of missionaries in Khass-Kotannun. Was he, Mr. Winterham, aware that our missionaries in that distant land had been compelled to wear native dress by the arrogant chiefs, and so fallen victims to numerous chills and epidemics?

George replied that he considered the treatment abominable, believed that the matter occupied the mind of the Foreign Office night and day, and would be glad personally to subscribe to any relief fund. The good man declared himself satisfied, and St. Sebastian breathed freely again.

A sturdy man in homespun rose to discover the Government's intention on Church matters. Did the speaker ken that on his small holding he paid ten pound sterling in tithes, though he himself did not hold with the Establishment, being a Reformed Presbyterian? The Laodicean George said he did not understand the differences, but that it seemed to him a confounded shame, and he would undertake that Mr. Haystoun, if returned, would take immediate steps in the matter.

So far he had done well, but with the next question he betrayed his ignorance. A good man arose, also hot on Church affairs, to discourse on some disabilities, and casually described himself as a U.P. George's wits busied themselves in guessing at the mystic sign. At last to his delight he seemed to achieve it, and, in replying, electrified his audience by assuming that the two letters stood for Unreformed Presbyterian.

But the meeting was in good humour in spite of his incomprehensible address and unsatisfying answers, till a small section of the young bloods of the opposite party, who had come to disturb, felt that this peace must be put an end to. Mr. Samuel M'Turk, lawyer's clerk, who hailed from the west country and betrayed his origin in his speech, rose amid some applause from his admirers to discomfit George. He was a young man with a long, sallow face, carefully oiled and parted hair, and a resonant taste in dress. A bundle of papers graced his hand, and his air was parliamentary.

"Wis Mister Winterham aware that Mister Haystoun had contradicted himself on two occasions lately, as he would proceed to show?"

George heard him patiently, said that now he was aware of the fact, but couldn't for the life of him see what the deuce it mattered.

"After Mister Winterham's ignoring of my pint," went on the young man, "I proceed to show . . ." and with all the calmness in the world he displayed to his own satisfaction how Mr. Lewis Haystoun was no fit person to represent the constituency. He profaned the Sabbath, which this gentleman professed to hold dear, he was notorious for drunkenness, and his conduct abroad had not been above suspicion.

George was on his feet in a moment, his confusion gone, his face very red, and his shoulders squared for a fight. The man saw the effect of his words, and promptly sat down.

"Get up," said George abruptly.

The man's face whitened and he shrank back among his friends.

"Get up; up higher--on the top of the seat, that everybody may see and hear you! Now repeat very carefully all that over again."

The man's confidence had deserted him. He stammered something about meaning no harm.

"You called my friend a drunken blackguard. I am going to hear the accusation in detail." George stood up to his full height, a terrible figure to the shrinking clerk, who repeated his former words with a faltering tongue.

He heard him out quietly, and then stared coolly down on the people. He felt himself master of the situation. The enemy had played into his hands, and in the shape of a sweating clerk sat waiting on his action.

"You have heard what this man has to tell you. I ask you as men, as folk of this countryside, if it is true?"

It was the real speech of the evening, which was all along waiting to be delivered instead of the frigid pedantries on the paper. A man was speaking simply, valiantly, on behalf of his friend. It was cunningly done, with the natural tact which rarely deserts the truly honest man in his hour of extremity. He spoke of Lewis as he had known him, at school and college and in many wild sporting expeditions in desert places, and slowly the people kindled and listened. Then, so to speak, he kicked away the scaffolding of his erection. He ceased to be the apologist, and became the frank eulogist. He stood squarely on the edge of the platform, gathering the eyes of his hearers, smiling pleasantly, arms akimbo, a man at his ease and possibly at his pleasure.

"Some of you are herds," he cried, "and some are fishers, and some are farmers, and some are labourers. Also some of you call yourselves Radicals or Tories or Socialists. But you are all of you far more than these things. You are men--men of this great countryside, with blood in your veins and vigour in that blood. If you were a set of pale-faced mechanics, I should not be speaking to you, for I should not understand you. But I know you all, and I like you, and I am going to prevent you from making godless fools of yourselves. There are two men before you. One is a very clever man, whom I don't know anything about, nor you either. The other is my best friend, and known to all of you. Many of you have shot or sailed with him, many of you were born on his and his fathers' lands. I have told you of his abilities and quoted better judges than myself. I don't need to tell you that he is the best of men, a sportsman, a kind master, a very good fellow indeed. You can make up your mind between the two. Opinions matter very little, but good men are too scarce to be neglected. Why, you fools," he cried with boisterous good humour, "I should back Lewis if he were a Mohammedan or an Anarchist. The man is sound metal, I tell you, and that's all I ask."

It was a very young man's confession of faith, but it was enough. The meeting went with him almost to a man. A roar of applause greeted the smiling orator, and when he sat down with flushed face, bright eyes, and a consciousness of having done his duty, John Sanderson, herd in Nether Callowa, rose to move a vote of confidence:

"That this assembly is of opinion that Maister Lewis Haystoun is a guid man, and sae is our friend Maister Winterham, and we'll send Lewie back to Parliament or be--"

It was duly seconded and carried with acclamation.

CHAPTER XI

THE PRIDE BEFORE A FALL

The result of the election was announced in Gledsmuir on the next Wednesday evening, and carried surprise to all save Lewis's nearer friends. For Mr. Albert Stocks was duly returned member for the constituency by a majority of seventy votes. The defeated candidate received the news with great composure, addressed some good-humoured words to the people, had a generous greeting for his opponent, and met his committee with a smiling face. But his heart was sick within him, and as soon as he decently might be escaped from the turmoil, found his horse, and set off up Glenavelin for his own dwelling.

He had been defeated, and the fact, however confidently looked for, comes with a bitter freshness to every man. He had lost a seat for his party-that in itself was bad. But he had proved himself incompetent, unadaptable, a stick, a pedantic incapable. A dozen stings rankled in his soul. Alice would be justified of her suspicions. Where would his place be now in that small imperious heart? His own people had forsaken him for a gross and unlikely substitute, and he had been wrong in his estimate alike of ally and enemy. Above all came that cruelest stab--what would Wratislaw think of it? He had disgraced himself in the eyes of his friend. He who had made a fetish of competence had manifestly proved wanting; he who had loved to think of himself as the bold, opportune man, had shown himself formal and hidebound.

As he passed Glenavelin among the trees the thought of Alice was a sharp pang of regret. He could never more lift his eyes in that young and radiant presence. He pictured the successful Stocks welcomed by her, and words of praise for which he would have given his immortal soul, meted out lavishly to that owl-like being. It was a dismal business, and ruefully, but half-humorously, he caught at the paradox of his fate.

Through the swiftly failing darkness the inn of Etterick rose before him, a place a little apart from the village street. A noise of talk floated from the kitchen and made him halt at the door and dismount. The place would be full of folk discussing the election, and he would go in among them and learn the worst opinion which men might have of him. After all, they were his own people, who had known him in his power as they now saw him in his weakness. If he had failed he was not wholly foolish; they knew his few redeeming virtues, and they would be generous.

The talk stopped short as he entered, and he saw through the tobacco reek half a dozen lengthy faces wearing the air of solemnity which the hillman adopts in his pleasures. They were all his own herds and keepers, save two whom he knew for foresters from Glenavelin. He was recognized at once, and with a general nervous shuffling they began to make room for the laird at the table. He cried a hasty greeting to all, and sat down between a black-bearded giant, whose clothes smelt of sheep, and a red-haired man from one of the remoter glens. The notion of the thing pleased him, and he ordered drinks for each with a lavish carelessness. He asked for a match for his pipe, and the man who gave it wore a decent melancholy on his face and shook his head with unction.

"This is a bad job, Lewie," he said, using the privileged name of the ancient servant. "Whae would have ettled sic a calaamity to happen in your ain countryside? We a' thocht it would be a grand pioy for ye, for ye would settle down here and hae nae mair foreign stravaigins. And then this tailor body steps in and spoils a'. It's maist vexaatious."

"It was a good fight, and he beat me fairly; but we'll drop the matter. I'm sick--tired of politics, Adam. If I had been a better man they might have made a herd of me, and I should have been happy."

"Wheesht, Lewie," said the man, grinning. "A herd's job is no for the likes o' you. But there's better wark waiting for ye than poalitics. It's a beggar's trade after a', and far better left to bagman bodies like yon Stocks. It's a puir thing for sac proper a man as you."

"But what can I do?" cried Lewis in despair. "I have no profession. I am useless."

"Useless! Ye are a grand judge o' sheep and nowt, and ye ken a horse better than ony couper. Ye can ride like a jockey and drive like a Jehu, and there's no your equal in these parts with a gun or a fishing-rod. Forbye, I would rather walk ae mile on the hill wi' ye than twae, for ye gang up a brae-face like a mawkin! God! There's no a single man's trade that ye're no brawly fitted for. And then ye've a heap o' book-lear that folk learned ye away about England, though I cannot speak muckle on that, no being a jidge."

Lewis grinned at the portraiture. "You do me proud. But let's talk about serious things. You were on sheep when I came in. Get back to them and give me your mind on Cheviots. The lamb sales promise well."

For twenty minutes the room hummed with technicalities. One man might support the conversation on alien matters, but on sheep the humblest found a voice: Lewis watched the ring of faces with a sharp delight. The election had made him sick of his fellows--fellows who chattered and wrangled and wallowed in the sentimental. But now every line of these brown faces, the keen blue eyes, the tawny, tangled beards, and the inimitable soft-sounding southern speech, seemed earnest of a real and strenuous life. He began to find a new savour in existence. The sense of his flat incompetence left him, and he found himself speaking heartily and laughing with zest.

"It's as I say," said the herd of the Redswirebead. "I'm getting an auld man and a verra wise ane, and the graund owercome for the world is just 'Pay no attention.' Ye'll has heard how the word cam' to be. It was Jock Linklater o' the Caulds wha was glen notice to quit by the laird, and a' the countryside was vexed to pairt wi' Jock, for he was a popular character. But about a year after a friend meets him at Gledsmuir merkit as crouse as ever. 'Lodsake, Jock, man, I thocht ye were awa',' says he. 'No,' says Jock, 'no. I'm here as ye see.' 'But how did ye manage it?' he asked. 'Fine,' says Jock. 'They sent me a letter tellin' me I must gang; but I just payed no attention. Syne they sent me a blue letter frae the lawyer's, but I payed no attention. Syne the factor cam' to see me.' 'Ay, and what did ye do then, Jock?' says he. 'Oh, I payed no attention. Syne the laird cam' himsel.' 'Ay, that would fricht ye,' he says. 'No, no a grain,' said Jock, verra calm. 'I just payed no attention, and here I am.'"

Lewis laughed, but the rest of the audience suffered no change of feature. The gloaming bad darkened, and the little small-paned window was a fretted sheet of dark and lucent blue. Grateful odours of food and drink and tobacco hung in the air, though tar and homespun and the far-carried fragrance of peat fought stoutly for the mastery.

One man fell to telling of a fox-hunt, when he lay on the hill for the night and shot five of the destroyers of his flock before the morning, it was the sign-- and the hour--for stories of many kinds--tales of weather and adventure, humorous lowland escapades and dismal mountain realities. Or stranger still, there would come the odd, half-believed legends of the glen, told shamefully yet with the realism of men for whom each word had a power and meaning far above fiction. Lewis listened entranced, marking his interest now by an exclamation, and again by a question.

The herd of Farawa told of the salmon, the king of the Aller salmon, who swam to the head of Aller and then crossed the spit of land to the head of Callowa to meet the king of the Callowa fish. It was a humorous story, and was capped there and then by his cousin of the Dreichill, who told a ghastly tale of a murder in the wilds. Then a lonely man, Simon o' the Heid o' the Hope, glorified his powers on a January night when he swung himself on a flood-gate over the Aller while the thing quivered beneath him, and the water roared redly above his thighs.

"And that yett broke when I was three pairts ower, and I went down the river with my feet tangled in the bars and nae room for sweemin'. But I gripped an oak-ritt and stelled mysel' for an hour till the water knockit the yett to sawdust. It broke baith my ankles, and though I'm a mortal strong man in my arms, thae twisted kitts keepit me helpless. When a man's feet are broke he has nae strength in his wrist."

"I know," said Lewis, with excitement. "I have found the same myself."

"Where?" asked the man, without rudeness.

"Once on the Skifso when I was after salmon, and once in the Doorab hills above Abjela."

"Were ye sick when they rescued ye? I was. I had twae muscles sprung on my arm, but that was naething to the retching and dizziness when they laid me on the heather. Jock Jeffrey was bending ower me, and though he wasna touching me I began to suffocate, and yet I was ower weak to cry out and had to thole it."

"I know. If you hang up in the void for a little and get the feeling of great space burned on your mind, you nearly die of choking when you are pulled up. Fancy you knowing about that."

"Have you suffered it, Maister Lewie?" said the man.

"Once. There was a gully in the Doorabs just like the Scarts o' the Muneraw, only twenty times deeper, and there was a bridge of tree-trunks bound with ropes across it. We all got over except one mule and a couple of men. They were just getting off when a trunk slipped and dangled down into the abyss with one end held up by the ropes. The poor animal went plumb to the bottom; we heard it first thud on a jag of rock and then, an age after, splash in the water. One of the men went with it, but the other got his legs caught between the ropes and the tree and managed to hang on. The poor beggar was helpless with fright; and he squealed--great heavens! how he did squeal!"

"And what did ye dae?" asked a breathless audience.

"I went down after him. I had to, for I was his master, and besides, I was a bit of an athlete then. I cried to him to hang on and not look down. I clambered down the swaying trunk while my people held the ropes at the top, and when I got near the man I saw what bad happened.

"He had twisted his ankles in the fall, and though he had got them out of the ropes, yet they hung loose and quite obviously broken. I got as near him as I could, and leaned over, and I remember seeing through below his armpits the blue of the stream six hundred feet down. It made me rather sick with my job, and when I called him to pull himself up a bit till I could grip him I thought he was helpless with the same fright. But it turned out that I had misjudged him. He bad no power in his arms, simply the dead strength to hang on. I was in a nice fix, for I could lower myself no farther without slipping into space. Then I thought of a dodge. I got a good grip of the rope and let my legs dangle down till they were level with his hands. I told him to try and change his grip and catch my ankles. He did it, somehow or other, and by George! the first shock of his weight nearly ended me, for he was a heavy man. However, I managed to pull myself up a yard or two and then I could reach down and catch his arms. We both got up somehow or other, but it took a devilish time, and when they laid us both on the ground and came round like fools with brandy I thought I should choke and had scarcely strength to swear at them to get out."

The assembly had listened intently, catching its breath with a sharp *risp* as all outdoor folks will do when they hear of an escapade which strikes their fancy. One man--a stranger--hammered his empty pipe-bowl on the table in applause.

"Whae was the man, d'ye say?" he asked. "A neeger?"

Lewis laughed. "Not a nigger most certainly, though he had a brown face."

"And ye risked your life for a black o' some kind? Man, ye must be awfu' fond o' your fellow men. Wad ye dae the same for the likes o' us?

"Surely. For one of my own folk! But it was really a very small thing."

"Then I have just ae thing to say," said the brown-bearded man. "I am what ye cal a Raadical, and yestreen I recorded my vote for yon man Stocks. He crackit a lot about the rights o' man--as man, and I was wi' him. But I tell ye that you yoursel' have a better notion o' human kindness than ony Stocks, and though ye're no o' my party, yet I herewith propose a vote o' confidence in Maister Lewis Haystoun."

The health was drunk solemnly yet with gusto, and under cover of it Lewis fled out of doors. His despondency had passed, and a fit of fierce exhilaration had seized him. Men still swore by his name; he was still loved by his own folk; small matter to him if a townsman had defeated him. He was no vain talker, but a doer, a sportsman, an adventurer. This was his true career. Let others have the applause of excited indoor folk or dull visionaries; for him a man's path, a man's work, and a man's commendation.

The moon was up, riding high in a shoreless sea of blue, and in the still weather the streams called to each other from the mountain sides, as in some fantastic cosmic harmony. High on the ridge shoulder the lights of Etterick twinkled starlike amid the fretted veil of trees. A sense of extraordinary and crazy exhilaration, the recoil from the constraint of weeks, laid hold on his spirit. He hummed a dozen fragments of song, and at times would laugh with the pure pleasure of life. The quixotic, the generous, the hopeless, the successful; laughter and tears; death and birth; the warm hearth and the open road--all seemed blent for the moment into one great zest for living. "I'll to Lochiel and Appin and kneel to them," he was humming aloud, when suddenly his bridle was caught and a man's hand was at his knee.

"Lewie," cried Wratislaw, "gracious, man! have you been drinking?" And then seeing the truth, he let go the bridle, put an arm through the stirrup leathers, and walked by the horse's side. "So that's the way you take it, old chap? Do you know that you are a discredited and defeated man? and yet I find you whistling like a boy. I have hopes for you, Lewie. You have the Buoyant Heart, and with that nothing can much matter. But, confound it! you are hours late for dinner."

CHAPTER XII

PASTORAL AND TRAGEDY

The news of the election, brought to Glenavelin by a couple of ragged runners, had a different result from that forecast by Lewis. Alice heard it with a heart unquickened; and when, an hour after, the flushed, triumphant Mr. Stocks arrived in person to claim the meed of success, he was greeted with a painful carelessness. Lady Manorwater had been loud in her laments for her nephew, but to Mr. Stocks she gave the honest praise which a warm-hearted woman cannot withhold from the fighter.

"Our principles have won," she cried. "Now who will call the place a Tory stronghold? Oh, Mr. Stocks, you have done wonderfully, and I am very glad. I'm not a bit sorry for Lewis, for he well deserved his beating."

But with Alice there could be neither pleasure nor its simulation. Her terrible honesty forbade her the easy path of false congratulations. She bit her lip till tears filled her eyes. What was this wretched position into which she had strayed? Lewis was all she had feared, but he was Lewis, and far more than any bundle of perfections. A hot, passionate craving for his presence was blinding her to reason. And this man who had won--this, the fortunate politician--she cared for him not a straw. A strong dislike began to grow in her heart to the blameless Mr. Stocks.

Dinner that night was a weary meal to the girl. Lady Manorwater prattled about the day's events, and Lord Manorwater, hopelessly bored, ate his food in silence. The lively Bertha had gone to bed with a headache, and the younger Miss Afflint was the receptacle for the moment of her hostess's confidences. Alice sat between Mr. Stocks and Arthur, facing a tall man with a small head and immaculate hair who had ridden over to dine and sleep. One of the two had the wisdom to see her humour and keep silent, though the thought plunged him into a sea of ugly reflections. It would be hard if, now that things were going well with him, the lady alone should prove obdurate. For in all this politician's daydreams a dainty figure walked by his side, sat at his table's head, received his friends, fascinated austere ministers, and filled his pipe of an evening at home.

Arthur was silent, and to him the lady turned in vain. He treated her with an elaborate politeness which sat ill on his brusque manners, and for the most part showed no desire to enliven the prevailing dulness. But after dinner he carried her off to the gardens on the plea of fresh air and a fine sunset, and the girl, who liked the boy, went gladly. Then the reason of his silence was made plain. He dismayed her by becoming lovesick.

"Tell me your age, Alice," he implored.

"I am twenty at Christmas time," said the girl, amazed at the question.

"And I am seventeen or very nearly that. Men sometimes marry women older than themselves, and I don't see why I shouldn't. Oh, Alice, promise that you will marry me. I never met a girl I liked so much, and I am sure we should be happy."

"I am sure we should," said the girl, laughing. "You silly boy! what put such nonsense in your head? I am far too old for you, and though I like you very much, I don't in the least want to marry you." She seemed to herself to have got out of a sober world into a sort of Mad Tea-party, where people behaved like pantaloons and spoke in conundrums.

The boy flushed and his eyes grew cross. "Is it somebody else?" he asked; at which the girl, with a memory of Mr. Stocks, reflected on the dreadful monotony of men's ways.

A solution flashed upon his brain. "Are you going to marry Lewie Haystoun?" he cried in a more cheerful voice. After all, Lewis was his cousin, and a worthy rival.

Alice grew hotly uncomfortable. "I am not going to marry Mr. Lewis Haystoun, and I am not going to talk to you any more." And she turned round with a flaming face to the cool depths of the wood.

"Then it is that fellow Stocks. Oh, Lord!" groaned Arthur, irritated into bad manners. "You can't mean it, Alice. He's not fit to black your boots."

Some foolish impulse roused the girl to reply. She defended the very man against whom all the evening she had been unreasonably bitter. "You have no right to abuse him. He is your people's guest and a very distinguished man, and you are only a foolish boy."

He paled below his sunburn. Now he believed the truth of the horrid suspicion which had been fastening on his mind. "But--but," he stammered, "the chap isn't a gentleman, you know."

The words quickened her vexation. A gentleman! The cant word, the fetish of this ring of idle aristocrats--she knew the hollowness of the whole farce. The democrat in her made her walk off with erect head and bright eyes, leaving a penitent boy behind; while all the time a sick, longing heart drove her to the edge of tears.

The days dragged slowly for the girl. The brightness had gone out of the wide, airy landscape, and the warm August days seemed chill. She hated herself for the wrong impression she had left on the boy Arthur's mind, but she was too proud to seek to erase it; she could but trust to his honour for silence. If Lewis heard--the thought was too terrible to face! He would resign himself to the inevitable; she knew the temper of the man. Good form was his divinity, and never by word or look would he attempt to win another man's betrothed. She must see him and learn the truth: but he came no more to Glenavelin, and Etterick was a far cry for a girl's fancy. Besides, the Twelfth had come and the noise of guns on every hill spoke of other interests for the party at Etterick. Lewis had forgotten his misfortunes, she told herself, and in the easy way of the half-hearted found in bodily fatigue a drug for a mind but little in need of it.

One afternoon Lady Manorwater came over the lawn waving a letter. "Do you want to go and picnic to-morrow, Alice?" she cried. "Lewis is to be shooting on the moors at the head of the Avelin, and he wants us to come and lunch at the Pool of Ness. He wants the whole party to come, particularly Mr. Stocks, and he wants to know if you have forgiven him. What can the boy mean?"

As the cheerful little lady paused, Alice's heart beat till she feared betrayal. A sudden fierce pleasure burned in her veins. Did he still seek her good opinion? Was he, as well as herself, miserable alone? And then came like a stab the thought that he had joined her with Stocks. Did he class her with that alien world of prigs and dullards? She ceased to think, and avoiding her hostess and tea, ran over the wooden bridge to the slope of hill and climbed up among the red heather.

A month ago she had been heart-whole and young, a simple child. The same prejudices and generous beliefs had been hers, but held loosely with a child's comprehension. But now this old world had been awakened to arms against a dazzling new world of love and pleasure. She was led captive by emotion, but the cold rook of scruple remained. She had read of women surrendering all for love, but she felt dismally that this happy gift had been denied her. Criticism, a fierce, vulgar antagonism, impervious to sentiment, not to be exorcised by generous impulse--such was her unlovely inheritance.

As she leaned over a pool of clear brown water in a little burn, where scented ferns dipped and great rocks of brake and heather shadowed, she saw her face and figure mirrored in every colour and line. Her extraordinary prettiness delighted her, and then she laughed at her own vanity. A lady of the pools, with the dark eyes and red-gold hair of the north, surely a creature of dawn and the blue sky, and born for no dreary self-communings. She returned, with her eyes clear and something like laughter in her heart. To-morrow she should see him, to-morrow!

It was the utter burning silence of midday, when the man who toils loses the skin of his face, and the man who rests tastes the joys of deep leisure. The blue, airless sky, the level hilltops, the straight lines of glen, the treeless horizon of the moors--no sharp ridge or cliff caught the tired eye, only an even, sleep-lulled harmony. Five very hungry, thirsty, and wearied men lay in the shadow above the Pool of Ness, and prayed heaven for luncheon.

Lewis and George, Wratislaw and Arthur Mordaunt were there, and Doctor Gracey, who loved a day on the hills. The keepers sat farther up the slope smoking their master's tobacco--sure sign of a well-spent morning. For the party had been on the moors by eight, and for five burning hours had tramped the heather. All wore light and airy shooting-clothes save the doctor, who had merely buckled gaiters over his professional black trousers. All were burned to a tawny brown, and all lay in different attitudes of gasping ease. Few things so clearly proclaim a man's past as his posture when lounging. Arthur and Wratislaw lay, like townsmen, prone on their faces with limbs rigidly straight. Lewis and George--old campaigners both--lay a little on the side, arms lying loosely, and knees a little bent. But one and all gasped, and swore softly at the weather.

"Turn round, Tommy," said George, glancing up, "or you'll get sunstroke at the back of the neck. I've had it twice, so I ought to know. You want to wet your handkerchief and put it below your cap. Why don't you wear a deer-stalker instead of that hideous jockey thing? Feugh, I am warm and cross and thirsty.

Lewis, I'll give your aunt five minutes, and then I shall go down and drink that pool dry."

Lewis sat up and watched the narrow ribbon of road which coiled up the glen to the pool's edge. He only saw some hundreds of yards down it, but the prospect served to convince him that his erratic aunt was late.

"If my wishes had any effect," said George, "at this moment I should be having iced champagne." And he cast a longing eye to the hampers.

"You won't get any," said Lewis. "We are not sybarites in this glen, and our drinks are the drinks of simple folk. Do you remember Cranstoun? I once went stalking with him, and we had *pate-de-foie-gras* for luncheon away up on the side of a rugged mountain. That sort of thing sets my teeth on edge."

"Honest man!" cried George. "But here are your friends, and you had better stir yourself and make them welcome."

Five very cool and leisurely beings were coming up the hill-path, for, having driven to above the village, they had had an easy walk of scarcely half a mile. Lewis's eye sought out a slight figure behind the others, a mere gleam of pink and white. As she stepped out from the path to the heather his eye was quick to seize her exquisite grace. Other women arrayed themselves in loose and floating raiment, ribbons and what not; but here was one who knew her daintiness, and made no effort to cloak it. Trim, cool, and sweet, the coils of bright hair above the white frock catching the noon sun--surely a lady to pray for and toil for, one made for no facile wooing or easy conquest.

Lewis advanced to Mr. Stocks as soon as he had welcomed his aunt, and shook hands cordially. "We seem to have lost sight of each other during the last few days. I never congratulated you enough, but you probably understood that my head was full of other things. You fought splendidly, and I can't say I regret the issue. You will do much better than I ever could."

Mr. Stocks smiled happily. The wheel of his fortunes was bringing him very near the top. All the way up he had had Alice for a companion; and that young woman, happy from a wholly different cause, had been wonderfully gracious. He felt himself on Mr. Lewis Haystoun's level at last, and the baffling sense of being on a different plane, which he had always experienced in his company, was gone, he hoped, for ever. So he became frank and confidential, forgot the pomp of his talk and his inevitable principles, and assisted in laying lunch.

Lady Manorwater drove her nephew into a corner.

"Where have you been. Lewis, all these days? If you had been anybody else, I should have said you were sulking. I must speak to you seriously. Do you know that Alice has been breaking her heart for you? I won't have the poor child made miserable, and though I don't in the least want you to marry her, yet; I cannot have you playing with her."

Lewis had grown suddenly very red.

"I think you are mistaken," he said stiffly. "Miss Wishart does not care a straw for me. If she is in love with anybody, it is with Stocks."

"I am much older than you, my dear, and I should know better. I may as well confess that I hoped it would be Mr. Stocks, but I can't disbelieve my own eyes. The child becomes wretched whenever she hears your name."

"You are making me miserably unhappy, because I can't believe a word of it. I have made a howling fool of myself lately, and I can't be blind to what she thinks of me."

Lady Manorwater looked pathetic. "Is the great Lewis ashamed of himself?"

"Not a bit. I would do it again, for it is my nature to, as the hymn says. I am cut all the wrong way, and my mind is my mind, you know. But I can't expect Miss Wishart to take that point of view."

His aunt shook a hopeless head. "Your moral nature is warped, my dear. It has always been the same since you were a very small boy at Glenavelin, and read the Holy War on the hearthrug. You could never be made to admire Emmanuel and his captains, but you set your heart on the reprobates Jolly and Griggish. But get away and look after your guests, sir."

Lunch came just in time to save five hungry men from an undignified end. The Glenavelin party looked on with amusement as the ravenous appetites were satisfied. Mr. Stocks, in a huge good humour, talked discursively of sport. He inquired concerning the morning's bag, and called up reminiscences of friends who had equalled or exceeded it. Lewis was uncomfortable, for he felt that in common civility Mr. Stocks should have been asked to shoot. He could not excuse himself with the plea of an unintentional omission, for he had heard reports of the gentleman's wonderful awkwardness with a gun, and he had not found it in his heart to spoil the sport of five keen and competent hands.

He dared not look at Alice, for his aunt's words had set his pulses beating hotly. For the last week he had wrestled with himself, telling his heart that this lady was beyond his ken for ever and a day, for he belonged by nature to the clan of despondent lovers. Before, she had had all the icy reserve, he all the fervours. The hint of some spark of fire behind the snows of her demeanour filled him with a delirious joy. Every movement of her body pleased him, every word which she spoke, the blitheness of her air and the ready kindness. The pale, pretty Afflint girls, with their wit and their confidence, seemed old and womanly compared with Alice. Let simplicity be his goddess henceforth-- simplicity and youth.

The Pool of Ness is a great, black cauldron of clear water, with berries above and berries below, and high crags red with heather. There you may find shade in summer, and great blaeberries and ripening rowans in the wane of August. These last were the snare for Alice, who was ever an adventurer. For the moment she was the schoolgirl again, and all sordid elderly cares were tossed to the wind. She teased Doctor Gracey to that worthy's delight, and she bade George and Arthur fetch and carry in a way that made them her slaves for life. Then she unbent to Mr. Stocks and made him follow her out on a peninsula of rock, above which hung a great cluster of fruit. The unfortunate politician was not built for this kind of exercise, and slipped and clung despairingly to every root and cleft. Lewis followed aimlessly: her gaiety did not fit with his mood; and he longed to have her to himself and know his fortune.

He passed the panting Stocks and came up with the errant lady.

"For heaven's sake be careful, Miss Wishart," he cried in alarm. "That's an ugly black swirl down there."

The girl laughed in his face.

"Isn't the place glorious!" she cried. "It's as cool as winter, and oh! the colours of that hillside. I'm going up to that birk-tree to sit. Do you think I can do it?"

"I am coming up after you," said Lewis.

She stopped and regarded it with serious eyes. "It's hard, but I'm going to try. It's 'harder than the Midburn that I climbed up on the day I saw you fishing."

She remembered! Joy caught at his heart, and he laughed so gladly that Alice turned round to look at him. Something in his eyes made her turn her head away and scan the birk-tree again.

Then suddenly there was a slip of soil, a helpless clutch at fern and heather, a cry of terror, and he was alone on the headland. The black swirl was closing over the girl's head.

He had been standing rapt in a happy fancy, his thoughts far in a world of their own, and his eyes vacant of any purpose. Startled to alertness, he still saw vaguely, and for a second stood irresolute and wondering. Then came another splash, and a heavy body flung itself into the pool from lower down the rock. He knew the black head and the round shoulders of Mr. Stocks.

The man caught the girl as she struggled to get out of the swirl and with strong ugly strokes began to make for shore. Lewis stood with a sick heart, slow to realize the horror which had overtaken him. She was out of danger, though the man was swimming badly; dismally he noted the fact of his atrocious swimming. But this was the hero; he had stood irresolute. The thought burned him like a hot iron.

Half a dozen pairs of hands relieved the swimmer of his burden. Alice was little the worse, a trifle pale, very draggled and unhappy, and utterly tired. Lady Manorwater wept over her and kissed her, and hailed the dripping Stocks as her preserver. Lewis alone stood back. He satisfied himself that she was unhurt, and then, on the plea of getting the carriage, set off down the glen with a very grey, quivering face.

CHAPTER XIII

THE PLEASURES OF A CONSCIENCE

It was half-way down the glen that the full ignominy of his position came on Lewis with the shock of a thunder-clap. A hateful bitterness against her preserver and the tricks of fate had been his solitary feeling, till suddenly he realized the part he had played, and saw himself for a naked coward. Coward he called himself-without reflection; for in such a moment the mind thinks in crude colours and bold lines of division. He set his teeth in his lip, and with a heart sinking at the shameful thought stalked into the farm stables where the Glenavelin servants were.

He could not return to the Pool. Alice was little hurt, so anxiety was needless; better let him leave Mr. Stocks to enjoy his heroics in peace. He would find an excuse; meanwhile, give him quiet and solitude to digest his bitterness. He cursed himself for the unworthiness of his thoughts. What a pass had he come to when he grudged a little *kudos* to a rival, grudged it churlishly, childishly. He flung from him the self-reproach. Other people would wonder at his ungenerousness, and his sulky ill-nature. They would explain by the first easy discreditable reason. What eared he for their opinion when he knew the far greater shame in his heart?

For as he strode up the woodland path to Etterick the wrappings of surface passion fell off from his view of the past hour, and he saw the bald and naked ribs of his own incapacity. It was a trivial incident to the world, but to himself a momentous self-revelation. He was a dreamer, a weakling, a fool. He had hesitated in a crisis, and another had taken his place. A thousand incidents of ready courage in past sport and travel were forgotten, and on this single slip the terrible indictment was founded. And the reason is at hand; this weakness had at last drawn near to his life's great passion.

He found a deserted house, but its solitude was too noisy for his unrest. Bidding the butler tell his friends that he had gone up the hill, he crossed the sloping lawns and plunged into the thicket of rhododendrons. Soon he was out on the heather, with the great slopes, scorched with the heat, lying still and fragrant before him. He felt sick and tired, and flung himself down amid the soft brackens.

It was the man's first taste of bitter mental anguish. Hitherto his life had been equable and pleasant; his friends had adored him; the world had flattered him; he had been at peace with his own soul. He had known his failings, but laughed at them cavalierly; he stood on a different platform from the struggling, conscience-stricken herd. Now he had in very truth been flung neck and crop from the pedestal of his self-esteem; and he lay groaning in the dust of abasement.

Wratislaw guessed with a friend's instinct his friend's disquietude, and turned his steps to the hill when he had heard the butler's message. He had known something of Lewis's imaginary self-upbraidings, and he was prepared for them, but he was not prepared for the grey and wretched face in the lee of the pinewood. A sudden suspicion that Lewis had been guilty of some real dishonour flashed across his mind for the moment, only to be driven out with scorn.

"Lewie, my son, what the deuce is wrong with you?" he cried.

The other looked at him with miserable eyes.

"I am beginning to find out my rottenness."

Wratislaw laughed in spite of himself. "What a fool to go making psychological discoveries on such a day! Is it all over the little misfortune at the pool?"

Tragedy grew in Lewis's eyes. "Don't laugh, old chap. You don't know what I did. I let her fall into the water, and then I stood staring and let another man-- the other man--save her."

"Well, and what about that? He had a better chance than you. You shouldn't grudge him his good fortune."

"Good Lord, man, you don't think it's that that's troubling me! I felt murderous, but it wasn't on his account."

"Why not?" asked the older man drily. "You love the girl, and he's in the running with you. What more?"

Lewis groaned. "How can I talk about loving her when my love is such a trifling thing that it doesn't nerve me to action? I tell you I love her body and soul. I live for her. The whole world is full of her. She is never a second out of my thoughts. And yet I am so little of a man that I let her come near death and never try to save her."

"But, confound it, man, it may have been mere absence of mind. You were always an extraordinarily plucky chap." Wratislaw spoke irritably, for it seemed to him sheer folly.

Lewis looked at him imploringly. "Can you not understand?" he cried.

Wratislaw did understand, and suddenly. The problem was subtler than he had thought. Weakness was at the core of it, weakness revealed in self-deception and self-accusation alike, the weakness of the finical dreamer, the man with the unrobust conscience. But the weakness which Lewis arraigned himself on was the very obvious failing of the diffident and the irresolute. Wratislaw tried the path of boisterous encouragement.

"Get up, you old fool, and come down to the house. You a coward! You are simply a romancer with an unfortunate knack of tragedy." The man must be laughed out of this folly. If he were not he would show the self-accusing front to the world, and the Manorwaters, Alice, Stocks--all save his chosen intimates-- would credit him with a cowardice of which he had no taint.

Arthur and George, resigned now to the inevitable lady, had seen in the incident only the anxiety of a man for his beloved, and just a hint of the ungenerous in his treatment of Mr. Stocks. They were not prepared for the silent tragic figure which Wratislaw brought with him.

Arthur had a glint of the truth, but the obtuse George saw nothing. "Do you know that you are going to have the Wisharts for neighbours for a couple of months yet? Old Wishart has taken Glenavelin from the end of August."

This would have been pleasant hearing at another time, but now it simply drove home the nail of his bitter reflections. Alice would be near him, a terrible reproach-she, the devotee of strength and competence. He could not win her, and it is characteristic of the man that he had ceased to think of Mr. Stocks as his rival. He would lose her to no rival; to his ragged incapacity alone would his ill fortune be due.

He struggled to act the part of the cheerful host, and Wratislaw watched his efforts grimly. He ate little at dinner, showed no desire to smoke, and played billiards so badly that Wratislaw, an execrable player, won the first and last game of his life. The victor took him out of doors thereafter to walk on the moonlit, fragrant lawn.

"You are taking things to heart," said he.

"And I'm blessed if I can understand you. To me it's sheer mania."

"And to me it's the last link in a chain. I have suspected myself for long, now I know myself and-ugh! the knowledge is a hideous thing."

Wratislaw stood regarding his companion seriously. "I wonder what will happen to you, Lewie. Life is serious enough without inventing a crotchety virtue to make it miserable."

"Can't you understand me, Tommy? It isn't that I'm a cad, it's that I am a coward. I couldn't be a cad supposing I tried. These things are a matter chiefly of blood and bone, and I am not made that way. But God help me! I am a coward. I can't fight worth twopence. Look at my performance a fortnight ago. The ordinary gardener's boy can beat me at making love. I am full of generous impulses and sentiments, but what's the use of them? Everything grows cold and I am a dumb icicle when it comes to action. I knew all this before, but I thought I had kept my bodily courage. I've had a good enough training, and I used to have pluck."

"But you don't mean to tell me that it was funk that kept you out of the pool to-day?" cried the impatient Wratislaw.

"How do I know that it wasn't?" came the wretched answer.

Wratislaw turned on his heel and made to go back.

"You're an infernal idiot, Lewie, and an infernal child. Thank heaven! your friends know you better than you know yourself."

The next morning it was a different man who came down to breakfast. He had lost his haggard air, and seemed to have forgotten the night's episode.

"Was I very rude to everybody last night?" he asked. "I have a vague recollection of playing the fool."

"You were particularly rude about yourself," said Wratislaw.

The young man laughed. "It's a way I have sometimes. It's an awkward thing when a man's foes are of his own household."

The others seemed to see a catch in his mirth, a ring as of something hollow. He opened some letters, and looked up from one with a twitching face and a curious droop of the eyelids. "Miss Wishart is all right," he said. "My aunt says that she is none the worse, but that Stocks has caught a tremendous cold. An unromantic ending!"

The meal ended, they wandered out to the lawn to smoke, and Wratislaw found himself standing with a hand on his host's shoulder. He noticed something distraught in his glance and air.

"Are you fit again to-day?" he asked.

"Quite fit, thanks," said Lewis, but his face belied him. He had forgiven himself the incident of yesterday, but no proof of a non sequitur could make him relinquish his dismal verdict. The wide morning landscape lay green and soothing at his feet. Down in the glen men were winning the bog-hay; up on the hill slopes they were driving lambs; the Avelin hurried to the Gled, and beyond was the great ocean and the infinite works of man. The whole brave bustling world was astir, little and great ships hasting out of port, the soldier scaling the breach, the adventurer travelling the deserts. And he, the fool, had no share in this braggart heritage. He could not dare to look a man straight in the face, for like the king in the old fable he had lost his soul.

CHAPTER XIV

A GENTLEMAN IN STRAITS

The fall of the leaf found Etterick very full of people, and new dwellers in Glenavelin. The invitations were of old standing, but Lewis found their fulfilment a pleasant trick of Fortune's. To keep a bustling household in good spirits leaves small room for brooding, and he was famous for his hospitality. The partridges were plentiful that year, and a rainless autumn had come on the heels of a fine summer. So life went pleasantly with all, and the master of the place cloaked a very sick heart under a ready good-humour.

His thoughts were always on Glenavelin, and when he happened to be near it he used to look with anxious eyes for a slim figure which was rarely out of his fancy. He had not seen Alice since the accident, save for one short minute, when riding from Gledsmuir he had passed her one afternoon at the Glenavelin gates. He had earnestly desired to stop, but his curious cowardice had made him pass with a lifted hat and a hasty smile. Could he have looked back, he might have seen the girl watching him out of sight with tearful eyes. To himself he was the hopeless lover, and she the scornful lady, while she in her own eyes was the unhappy girl for whom the soldier in the song shakes his bridle reins and cries an eternal adieu.

Matters did not improve when the Manorwaters left and Mr. Wishart himself came down, bringing with him Stocks, a certain Mr. Andrews and his wife, and an excellent young man called Thompson. All were pleasant people, with the manners which the world calls hearty, well-groomed, presentable folk, who enjoyed this life and looked forward to a better.

Mr. Wishart explored the place thoroughly the first evening, and explained that he was thankful indeed that he had been led to take it. He was a handsome man with a worn, elderly face, a square jaw and somewhat weary eyes. It is given to few men to make a great fortune and not bear the signs of it on their persons.

"I expect you enjoyed staying with Lady Manorwater, Alice?" Mrs. Andrews declared at dinner. "They are very plain people, aren't they, to be such great aristocrats?

"I suppose so," said the girl listlessly.

"I once met Lady Manorwater at Mrs. Cookson's at afternoon tea. I thought she was badly dressed. You know Manorwater, don't you, George?" said the lady to her husband, with the boldness which comes from the use of a peer's name without the handle.

"Oh yes, I know him well. I have met him at the Liberal Club dinners, and I was his chairman once when he spoke on Irish affairs. A delightful man!"

"I suppose they would have a pleasant house-party when you were here, my dear?" asked the lady. "And of course you had the election. What fun! And what a victory for you, Mr. Stocks! I hear you beat the greatest landowner in the district."

Mr. Stocks smiled and glanced at Alice. The girl flushed; she could not help it; and she hated Mr. Stocks for his look.

Her father spoke for the first time. "What is the young man like, Mr. Stocks? I hear he is very proud and foolish, the sort of over-educated type which the world has no use for."

"I like him," said Mr. Stocks dishonestly. "He fought like a gentleman."

"These people are so rarely gentlemen," said Mrs. Andrews, proud of her high attitude. "I suppose his father made his money in coal and bought the land from some poor dear old aristocrat. It is so sad to think of it. And that sort of person is always over-educated, for you see they have not the spirit of the old families and they bury themselves in books." Mrs. Andrews's father had kept a crockery shop, but his daughter had buried the memory.

Mr. Wishart frowned. The lady had been asked down for her husband's sake, and he did not approve of this chatter about family. Mr. Stocks, who was about to explain the Haystoun pedigree, caught his host's eye and left the dangerous subject untouched.

"You said in your letters that they had been kind to you at this young man's place. We must ask him down here to dinner, Alice. Oh, and that reminds me I found a letter from him to-day asking me to shoot. I don't go in for that sort of thing, but you young fellows had better try it."

Mr. Stocks declined, said he had given it up. Mr. Thompson said, "Upon my word I should like to," and privately vowed to forget the invitation. He distrusted his prowess with a gun.

"By the by, was he not at the picnic when you saved my daughter's life? I can never thank you enough, Stocks. What should I have done without my small girl?"

"Yes, he was there. In fact he was with Miss Alice at the moment she slipped."

He may not have meant it, but the imputation was clear, and it stirred one fiery expostulation. "Oh, but he hadn't time before Mr. Stocks came after me," she began, and then feeling it ungracious towards that gentleman to make him share a possibility of heroism with another, she was silent. More, a lurking fear which had never grown large enough for a suspicion, began to catch at her heart. Was it possible that Lewis had held back?

For a moment the candle-lit room vanished from her eyes. She saw the warm ledge of rock with the rowan berries above. She saw his flushed, eager face--it was her last memory before she had fallen. Surely never--never was there cowardice in those eyes!

Mrs. Andrews's vulgarities and her husband's vain repetitions began to pall upon the anxious girl. The young Mr. Thompson talked shrewdly enough on things of business, and Mr. Stocks abated something of his pomposity and was honestly amiable. These were her own people, the workers for whom she had craved. And yet--were they so desirable? Her father's grave, keen face pleased her always, but what of the others? The radiant gentlewomen whom she had met with the Manorwaters seemed to belong to another world than this of petty social struggling and awkward ostentation. And the men! Doubtless they were foolish, dilettanti, barbarians of sport, half-hearted and unpractical! And she shut her heart to any voice which would defend them.

Lewis drove over to dine some four days later with dismal presentiments. The same hopeless self-contempt which had hung over him for weeks was still weighing on his soul. He dreaded the verdict of Alice's eyes, and in a heart which held only kindness he looked for a cold criticism. It was this despair which made his position hopeless He would never take his chance; there could be no opportunity for the truth to become clear to both; for in his plate-armour of despair he was shielded against the world. Such was his condition to the eyes of a friend; to himself he was the common hopeless lover who sighed for a stony mistress.

He noticed changes in Glenavelin. Businesslike leather pouches stood in the hall, and an unwontedly large pile of letters lay on a table. The drawing-room was the same as ever, but in the dining-room an escritoire had been established which groaned under a burden of papers. Mr. Wishart puzzled and repelled him. It was a strong face, but a cold and a stupid one, and his eyes had the glassy hardness of the man without vision. He was bidden welcome, and thanked in a tactless way for his kindness to Mr. Wishart's daughter. Then he was presented to Mrs. Andrews, and his courage sank as he bowed to her.

At table the lady twitted him with graceful badinage. "Alice and you must have had a gay time, Mr. Haystoun. Why, you've been seeing each other constantly for months. Have you become great friends?" She exerted herself, for, though he might be a parvenu, he was undeniably handsome.

Mr. Stocks explained that Mr. Haystoun had organized wonderful picnic parties. The lady clapped her many-ringed hands, and declared that he must repeat the experiment. "For I love picnics," she said, "I love the simplicity and the fresh air and the rippling streams. And washing up is fun, and it is such a great chance for you young men." And she cast a coy glance over her shoulder.

"Do you live far off, Mr. Haystoun?" she asked repeatedly. "Four miles? Oh, that's next door. We shall come and see you some day. We have just been staying with the Marshams--Mr. Marsham, you know, the big cotton people. Very vulgar, but the house is charming. It was so exciting, for the elections were on, and the Hestons, who are the great people in that part of the country, were always calling. Dear Lady Julia is so clever. Did you ever meet Mr. Marsham, by any chance?"

"Not that I remember. I know the Hestons of course. Julia is my cousin."

The lady was silenced. "But I thought," she murmured. "I thought--they were--" She broke off with a cough.

"Yes, I spent a good many of my school holidays at Heston."

Alice broke in with a question about the Manorwaters. The youthful Mr. Thompson, who, apart from his solicitor's profession, was a devotee of cricket, asked in a lofty way if Mr. Haystoun cared for the game.

"I do rather. I'm not very good, but we raised an eleven this year in the glen which beat Gledsmuir."

The notion pleased the gentleman. If a second match could be arranged he might play and show his prowess. In all likelihood this solemn and bookish laird, presumably brought up at home, would be a poor enough player.

"I played a lot at school," he said. "In fact I was in the Eleven for two years and I played in the Authentics match, and once against the Eton Ramblers. A strong lot they were."

"Let me see. Was that about seven years ago? I seem to remember."

"Seven years ago," said Mr. Thompson. "But why? Did you see the match?"

"No, I wasn't in the match; I had twisted my ankle, jumping. But I captained the Ramblers that season, so I remember it."

Respect grew large in Mr. Thompson's eyes. Here were modesty and distinction equally mated. The picture of the shy student had gone from his memory.

"If you like to come up to Etterick we might get up a match from the village," said Lewis courteously. "Ourselves with the foresters and keepers against the villagers wouldn't be a bad arrangement."

To Alice the whole conversation struck a jarring note. His eye kindled and he talked freely on sport. Was it not but a new token of his incurable levity? Mr. Wishart, who had understood little of the talk, found in this young man strange stuff to shape to a politician's ends. Contrasted with the gravity of Mr. Stocks, it was a schoolboy beside a master.

"I have been reading," he said slowly, "reading a speech of the new Under-Secretary for Foreign Affairs. I cannot understand the temper of mind which it illustrates. He talks of the Bosnian war, and a brave people struggling for freedom, as if it were merely a move in some hideous diplomatists' game. A man of that sort cannot understand a moral purpose."

"Tommy--I mean to say Mr. Wratislaw--doesn't believe in Bosnian freedom, but you know he is a most ardent moralist."

"I do not understand," said Mr. Wishart drily.

"I mean that personally he is a Puritan, a man who tries every action of his life by a moral standard. But he believes that moral standards vary with circumstances."

"Pernicious stuff, sir. There is one moral law. There is one Table of Commandments."

"But surely you must translate the Commandments into the language of the occasion. You do not believe that 'Thou shalt not kill' is absolute in every case?"

"I mean that except in the God-appointed necessity of war, and in the serving of criminal justice, killing is murder."

"Suppose a man goes travelling," said Lewis with abstracted eyes, "and has a lot of native servants. They mutiny, and he shoots down one or two. He saves his life, he serves, probably, the ends of civilization. Do you call that murder?"

"Assuredly. Better, far better that he should perish in the wilderness than that he should take the law into his own hands and kill one of God's creatures."

"But law, you know, is not an absolute word."

Mr. Wishart scented danger. "I can't argue against your subtleties, but my mind is clear; and I can respect no man who could think otherwise."

Lewis reddened and looked appealingly at Alice. She, too, was uncomfortable. Her opinions sounded less convincing when stated dogmatically by her father.

Mr. Stocks saw his chance and took it.

"Did you ever happen to be in such a crisis as you speak of, Mr. Haystoun? You have travelled a great deal."

"I have never had occasion to put a man to death," said Lewis, seeing the snare and scorning to avoid it.

"But you have had difficulties?"

"Once I had to flog a couple of men. It was not pleasant, and worst of all it did no good."

"Irrational violence seldom does," grunted Mr. Wishart.

"No, for, as I was going to say, it was a clear case where the men should have been put to death. They had deserved it, for they had disobeyed me, and by their disobedience caused the death of several innocent people. They decamped shortly afterwards, and all but managed to block our path. I blame myself still for not hanging them."

A deep silence hung over the table. Mr. Wishart and the Andrews stared with uncomprehending faces. Mr. Stocks studied his plate, and Alice looked on the speaker with eyes in which unwilling respect strove with consternation.

Only the culprit was at his ease. The discomfort of these good people for a moment amused him. Then the sight of Alice's face, which he wholly misread, brought him back to decent manners.

"I am afraid I have shocked you," he said simply. "If one knocks about the world one gets a different point of view."

Mr. Wishart restrained a flood of indignation with an effort. "We won't speak on the subject," he said. "I confess I have my prejudices."

Mr. Stocks assented with a smile and a sigh. In the drawing-room afterwards Lewis was presented with the olive-branch of peace. He had to attend Mrs. Andrews to the piano and listen to her singing of a sentimental ballad with the face of a man in the process of enjoyment. Soon he pleaded the four miles of distance and the dark night, and took his leave. His spirits had in a measure returned. Alice had not been gracious, but she had shown no scorn. And her spell at the first sight of her was woven a thousand-fold over his heart.

He found her alone for one moment in the hall.

"Alice--Miss Wishart, may I come and see you? It is a pity such near neighbours should see so little of each other."

His hesitation made him cloak a despairing request in the garb of a conventional farewell.

The girl had the sense to pierce the disguise. "You may come and see us, if you like, Mr. Haystoun. We shall be at home all next week."

"I shall come very soon," he cried, and he was whirled away from the light; with the girl's face framed in the arch of the doorway making a picture for his memory.

When the others had gone to bed, Stocks and Mr. Wishart sat up over a last pipe by the smoking-room fire.

The younger man moved uneasily in his chair. He had something to say which had long lain on his mind, and he was uncertain of its reception.

"You have been for a long time my friend, Mr. Wishart," he began. "You have done me a thousand kindnesses, and I only hope I have not proved myself unworthy of them."

Mr. Wishart raised his eyebrows at the peculiar words. "Certainly you have not," he said. "I regard you as the most promising by far of the younger men of my acquaintance, and any little services I may have rendered have been amply repaid me."

The younger man bowed and looked into the fire.

"It is very kind of you to speak so," he said. "I have been wondering whether I might not ask for a further kindness, the greatest favour which you could confer upon me. Have you made any plans for your daughter's future?"

Mr. Wishart sat up stiffly on the instant. "You mean?" he said.

"I mean that I love Alice . . . your daughter . . . and I wish to make her my wife. If you will give me your consent, I will ask her."

"But--but," said the old man, stammering. "Does the girl know anything of this?"

"She knows that I love her, and I think she will not be unkind."

"I don't know that I object," said Mr. Wishart after a long pause. "In fact I am very willing, and I am very glad that you had the good manners to speak to me first. Yes, upon my word, sir, I am pleased. You have had a creditable career, and your future promises well. My girl will help you, for though I say it, she will not be ill-provided for. I respect your character and I admire your principles, and I give you my heartiest good wishes."

Mr. Stocks rose and held out his hand. He felt that the interview could not be prolonged in the present fervour of gratitude.

"Had it been that young Haystoun now," said Mr. Wishart, "I should never have given my consent. I resolved long ago that my daughter should never marry an idle man. I am a plain man, and I care nothing for social distinctions."

But as Mr. Stocks left the room the plain man glanced after him, and sitting back suffered a moment's reflection. The form of this worker contrasted in his mind with the figure of the idler who had that evening graced his table. A fool, doubtless, but a fool with an air and a manner! And for one second he allowed himself to regret that he was to acquire so unromantic a son-in-law.

CHAPTER XV

The NEMESIS OF A COWARD

Two days later the Andrews drove up the glen to Etterick, taking with them the unwilling Mr. Wishart. Alice had escaped the ordeal with some feigned excuse, and the unfortunate Mr. Thompson, deeply grieving, had been summoned by telegram from cricket to law. The lady had chattered all the way up the winding moorland road, crying out banalities about the pretty landscape, or questioning her very ignorant companions about the dwellers in Etterick. She was full of praises for the house when it came in view; it was "quaint," it was "charming," it was everything inappropriate. But the amiable woman's prattle deserted her when she found herself in the cold stone hall with the great portraits and the lack of all modern frippery. It was so plainly a man's house, so clearly a place of tradition, that her pert modern speech seemed for one moment a fatuity.

It was an off-day for the shooters, and so for a miracle there were men in the drawing-room at tea-time. The hostess for the time was an aunt of Lewis's, a certain Mrs. Alderson, whose husband (the famous big-game hunter) had but recently returned from the jaws of a Zambesi lion. George's sister, Lady Clanroyden, a tall, handsome girl in a white frock, was arranging flowers in a bowl, and on the sill of the open window two men were basking in the sun. From the inner drawing-room there came an echo of voices and laughter. The whole scene was sunny and cheerful, youth and age, gay frocks and pleasant faces amid the old tapestry and mahogany of a moorland house.

Mr. Andrews sat down solemnly to talk of the weather with the two men, who found him a little dismal. One--he of the Zambesi lion episode--was grizzled, phlegmatic, and patient, and in no way critical of his company. So soon he was embarked on extracts from his own experience to which Mr. Andrews, who had shares in some company in the neighbourhood, listened with flattering attention. Mrs. Alderson set herself to entertain Mr. Wishart, and being a kindly, simple person, found the task easy. They were soon engaged in an earnest discussion of unsectarian charities.

Lady Clanroyden, with an unwilling sense of duty, devoted herself to Mrs. Andrews. That simpering matron fell into a vein of confidences and in five brief minutes had laid bare her heart. Then came the narrative of her recent visit to the Marshams, and the inevitable mention of the Hestons.

"Oh, you know the Hestons?" said Lady Clanroyden, brightening.

"Very well indeed." The lady smiled, looking round to make sure that Lewis was not in the room.

"Julia is here, you know. Julia, come and speak to your friends."

A dark girl in mourning came forward to meet the expansive smile of Mrs. Andrews. Earnestly the lady hoped that she remembered the single brief meeting on which she had built a fictitious acquaintance, and was reassured when the newcomer shook hands with her pleasantly. Truth to tell, Lady Julia had no remembrance of her face, but was too good-natured to be honest.

"And how is your dear mother? I was so sorry to hear from a mutual friend that she had been unwell." How thankful she was that she read each week various papers which reported people's doings!

A sense of bewilderment lurked in her heart. Who was this Lewis Haystoun who owned such a house and such a kindred? The hypothesis of money made in coal seemed insufficient, and with much curiosity she set herself to solve the problem.

"Is Mr. Haystoun coming back to tea?" she asked by way of a preface.

"No, he has had to go to Gledsmuir. We are all idle this afternoon, but he has a landowner's responsibilities."

"Have his family been here long? I seem never to have heard the name."

Lady Clanroyden looked a little surprised. "Yes, they have been rather a while. I forget how many centuries, but a good many. It was about this place, you know, that the old ballad of 'The Riding of Etterick' was made, and a Haystoun was the hero."

Mrs. Andrews knew nothing about old ballads, but she feigned a happy reminiscence.

"It is so sad his being beaten by Mr. Stocks," she declared. "Of course an old county family should provide the members for a district. They have the hearts of the people with them."

"Then the hearts of the people have a funny way of revealing themselves," Lady Clanroyden laughed. "I'm not at all sorry that Lewie was beaten. He is the best man in the world, but one wants to shake him up. His motto is 'Thole,' and he gets too few opportunities of 'tholing.'"

"You all call him 'Lewie,'" commented the lady. "How popular he must be!"

Mabel Clanroyden laughed. "I have known him ever since I was a small girl in a short frock and straight-brushed hair. He was never anything else than Lewie to his friends. Oh, here is my wandering brother and my only son returned," and she rose to catch up a small, self-possessed boy of some six years, who led the flushed and reluctant George in tow.

The small boy was very dirty, ruddy and cheerful. He had torn his blouse, and scratched his brow, and the crown of his straw hat had parted company with the brim.

"George," said his sister severely, "have you been corrupting the manners of my son? Where have you been?"

The boy--he rejoiced in the sounding name of Archibald--slapped a small leg with a miniature whip, and counterfeited with great skill the pose of the stable-yard. He slowly unclenched a smutty fist and revealed three separate shillings.

"I won um myself," he explained.

"Is it highway robbery?" asked his mother with horrified eyes. "Archibald, have you stopped a coach, or held up a bus or anything of the kind?"

The child unclenched his hand again, beamed on his prize, smiled knowingly at the world, and shut it.

"What has the dreadful boy been after? Oh, tell me, George, please. I will try to bear it."

"We fell in with a Sunday-school picnic along in the glen, and Archie made me take him there. And he had tea--I hope the little chap won't be ill, by the by. And he made a speech or a recitation or something of the sort. Nobody understood it, but it went down like anything."

"And do you mean to say that the people gave him money, and you allowed him to take it?" asked an outraged mother.

"He won it," said George. "Won it in fair fight. He was second in the race under twelve, and first in the race under ten. They gave him a decent handicap, and he simply romped home. That chap can run, Mabel. He tried the sack race, too, but the first time he slipped altogether inside the thing and had to be taken out, yelling. But he stuck to it like a Trojan, and at the second shot he got started all right, and would have won it if he hadn't lost his head and rolled down a bank. He isn't scratched much, considering he fell among whins. That also explains the state of his hat."

"George, you shall never, never, as long as I live, take my son out with you again. It is a wonder the poor child escaped with his life. You have not a scrap of feeling. I must take the boy away or he will shame me before everybody. Come and talk to Mrs. Andrews, George. May I introduce my brother, Mr. Winterham?"

George, who wanted to smoke, sat down unwillingly in the chair which his sister had left. The lady, whose airs and graces were all for men, put on her most bewitching manner.

"Your sister and I have just been talking about this exquisite place, Mr. Winterham. It must be delightful to live in such a centre of old romance. That lovely 'Riding of Etterick' has been running in my head all the way up."

George privately wondered at the confession. The peculiarly tragic and ghastly fragments which made up "The Riding of Etterick," seemed scarcely suited to haunt a lady's memory.

"Had you a long drive?" he asked in despair for a topic.

"Only from Glenavelin."

He awoke to interest. "Are you staying at Glenavelin just now? The Wisharts are in it, are they not? We were a great deal about the place when the Manorwaters were there."

"Oh yes. I have heard about Lady Manorwater from Alice Wishart. She must be a charming woman; Alice cannot speak enough about her."

George's face brightened. "Miss Wishart is a great friend of mine, and a most awfully good sort."

"And as you are a great friend of hers I think I may tell you a great secret," and the lady patted him playfully. "Our pretty Alice is going to be married."

George was thoroughly roused to attention. "Who is the man?" he asked sharply.

"I think I may tell you," said Mrs. Andrews, enjoying her sense of importance. "It is Mr. Stocks, the new member."

George restrained with difficulty a very natural oath. Then he looked at his informant and saw in her face only silliness and truth. For the good woman had indeed persuaded herself of the verity of her fancy. Mr. Stocks had told her that he had her father's consent and good wishes, and misinterpreting the girl's manner she had considered the affair settled.

It was unfortunate that Mr. Wishart at this moment showed such obvious signs of restlessness that the lady rose to take her leave, otherwise George might have learned the truth. After the Glenavelin party had gone he wandered out to the lawn, pulling his moustache in vast perplexity and cursing the twisted world. He had no guess at Lewis's manner of wooing; to him it had seemed the simple, straightforward love which he thought beyond resistance. And now, when he learned of this melancholy issue, he was sore at heart for his friend.

He was awakened from his reverie by Lewis himself, who, having ridden straight to the stables, was now sauntering towards the house. A trim man looks at his best in riding clothes, and Lewis was no exception. He was flushed with sun and motion, his spirits were high, for all the journey he had been dreaming of a coming meeting with Alice, and the hope which had suddenly increased a thousand-fold. George marked his mood, and with a regret at his new role caught him by the arm and checked him.

"I say, old man, don't go in just yet. I want to tell you something, and I think you had better hear it now."

Lewis turned obediently, amazed by the gravity of his friend's face.

"Some people came up from Glenavelin this afternoon and among them a Mrs. Andrews, whom I had a talk to. She told me that Al--Miss Wishart is engaged to that fellow Stocks."

Lewis's face whitened and he turned away his eyes. He could not credit it. Two days ago she had been free; he could swear it; he remembered her eyes at parting. Then came the thought of his blindness, and in a great horror of self-mistrust he seemed to see throughout it all his criminal folly. He, poor fool, had been pleasing himself with dreams of a meeting, when all the while the other man had been the real lover. She had despised him, spared not a thought for him save as a pleasing idler; and he--that he should ever have ventured for one second to hope! Curiously enough, for the first time he thought of Stocks with respect; to have won the girl seemed in itself the proof of dignity and worth.

"Thanks very much for telling me. I am glad I know. No, I don't think I'll go into the house yet."

The days passed and Alice waited with anxious heart for the coming of the very laggard Lewis. To-day he will come, she said each morning; and evening found her--poor heart!--still expectant. She told herself a thousand times that it was sheer folly. He meant nothing, it was a mere fashion of speech; and then her heart would revolt and bid common sense be silent. He came indeed with some of the Etterick party on a formal call, but this was clearly not the fulfilment of his promise. So the girl waited and despaired, while the truant at Etterick was breaking his heart for the unattainable.

Mr. Stocks, having won the official consent, conducted his suit with commendable discretion. Suit is the word for the performance, so full was it of elaborate punctilios. He never intruded upon her unhappiness. A studied courtesy, a distant thoughtfulness were his only compliments. But when he found her gayer, then would he strive with subtle delicacies of manner to make clear the part he desired to play.

The girl saw his kindness and was grateful. In the revulsion against the Andrews he seemed a link with the more pleasant sides of life, and soon in her despair and anger his modest merits took heroic proportions in her eyes. She forgot her past dislike; she thought only of this, the simple good man, contrasted with the showy and fickle-hearted--true metal against glittering tinsel. His very weaknesses seemed homely and venial. He was of her own world, akin to the things which deep down in her soul she knew she must love to the last. It is to the credit of the man's insight that he saw the mood and took pains to foster it.

Twice he asked her to marry him. The first time her heart was still sore with disappointment and she refused--yet half-heartedly.

He waited his time and when the natural cheerfulness of her temper was beginning to rise, he again tried his fortune.

"I cannot," she cried. "I cannot. I like you very much, but oh, it is too much to ask me to marry you."

"But I love you with all my heart, Alice." And the honesty of his tone and the distant thought of a very different hope brought the tears to her eyes.

He had forgotten all pompous dreams and the stilted prospects with which he had aforetime hoped to beguile his wife. The man was plain and simple now, a being very much on fire with an honest passion. He may have left her love-cold, but he touched the sympathy which in a true woman is love's nearest neighbour. Before she knew herself she had promised, and had been kissed respectfully and tenderly by her delighted lover. For a moment she felt something like joy, and then, with a dreadful thought of the baselessness of her pleasure, walked slowly homewards by his side.

The next morning Alice rose with a dreary sense of the irrevocable. A door seemed to have closed behind her, and the future stretched before her in a straight dusty path with few nooks and shadows. This was not the blithe morning of betrothal she had looked for. The rapturous outlook on life which she had dreamed of was replaced by a cold and business-like calculation of profits. The rose garden of the "god unconquered in battle" was exchanged for a very shoddy and huckstering paradise.

Mrs. Andrews claimed her company all the morning, and with the pertinacity of her kind soon guessed the very obvious secret. Her gushing congratulations drove the girl distracted. She praised the good Stocks, and Alice drank in the comfort of such words with greedy ears. From one young man she passed to another, and hung lovingly over the perfections of Mr. Haystoun. "He has the real distinction, dear," she cried, "which you can never mistake. It only belongs to old blood and it is quite inimitable. His friends are so charming, too, and you can always tell a man by his people. It is so pleasant to fall in with old acquaintances again. That dear Lady Clanroyden promised to come over soon. I quite long to see her, for I feel as if I had known her for ages."

After lunch Alice fled the house and sought her old refuge--the hills. There she would find the deep solitude for thought. She was not broken-hearted, though she grieved now and again with a blind longing of regret. But she was confused and shaken; the landmarks of her vision seemed to have been removed, and she had to face the grim narrowing-down of hopes which is the sternest trial for poor mortality.

Autumn's hand was lying heavy on the hillsides. Bracken was yellowing, heather passing from bloom, and the clumps of wild-wood taking the soft russet and purple of decline. Faint odours of wood smoke seemed to flit over the moor, and the sharp lines of the hill fastnesses were drawn as with a graving-tool against the sky. She resolved to go to the Midburn and climb up the cleft, for the place was still a centre of memory. So she kept for a mile to the Etterick road, till she came in view of the little stone bridge where the highway spans the moorland waters.

There had been intruders in Paradise before her. Broken bottles and scraps of paper were defacing the hill turf, and when she turned to get to the water's edge she found the rushy coverts trampled on every side. From somewhere among the trees came the sound of singing--a silly music-hall catch. It was a sharp surprise, and the girl, in horror at the profanation, was turning in all haste to leave.

But the Fates had prepared an adventure. Three half-tipsy men came swinging down the slope, their arms linked together, and bowlers set rakishly on the backs of their heads. They kept up the chorus of the song which was being sung elsewhere, and they suited their rolling gait to the measure.

"For it ain't Maria," came the tender melody; and the reassuring phrase was repeated a dozen times. Then by ill-luck they caught sight of the astonished Alice, and dropping their musical efforts they hailed her familiarly. Clearly they were the stragglers of some picnic from the town, the engaging type of gentleman who on such occasions is drunk by midday. They were dressed in ill-fitting Sunday clothes, great flowers beamed from their button-holes, and after the fashion of their kind their waistcoats were unbuttoned for comfort. The girl tried to go back by the way she had come, but to her horror she found that she was intercepted. The three gentlemen commanded her retreat.

They seemed comparatively sober, so she tried entreaty. "Please, let me pass," she said pleasantly. "I find I have taken the wrong road."

"No, you haven't, dearie," said one of the men, who from a superior neatness of apparel might have been a clerk. "You've come the right road, for you've met us. And now you're not going away." And he came forward with a protecting arm.

Alice, genuinely frightened, tried to cross the stream and escape by the other side. But the crossing was difficult, and she slipped at the outset and wet her ankles. One of the three lurched into the water after her, and withdrew with sundry oaths.

The poor girl was in sad perplexity. Before was an ugly rush of water and a leap beyond her strength; behind, three drunken men, their mouths full of endearment and scurrility. She looked despairingly to the level white road for the Perseus who should deliver her.

And to her joy the deliverer was not wanting. In the thick of the idiot shouting of the trio there came the clink-clank of a horse's feet and a young man came over the bridge. He saw the picture at a glance and its meaning; and it took him short time to be on his feet and then over the broken stone wall to the waterside. Suddenly to the girl's delight there appeared at the back of the roughs the inquiring, sunburnt face of Lewis.

The men turned and stared with hanging jaws. "Now, what the dickens is this?" he cried, and catching two of their necks he pulled their heads together and then flung them apart.

The three seemed sobered by the apparition. "And what the h-ll is your business?" they cried conjointly; and one, a dark-browed fellow, doubled his fists and advanced.

Lewis stood regarding them with a smiling face and very bright, cross eyes. "Are you by way of insulting this lady? If you weren't drunk, I'd teach you manners. Get out of this in case I forget myself."

For answer the foremost of the men hit out. A glance convinced Lewis that there was enough sobriety to make a fight of it. "Miss Wishart . . . Alice," he cried, "come back and go down to the road and see to my horse, please. I'll be down in a second."

The girl obeyed, and so it fell out that there was no witness to that burn-side encounter. It was a complex fight and it lasted for more than a second. Two of the men had the grace to feel ashamed of themselves half-way through, and retired from the contest with shaky limbs and aching faces. The third had to be assisted to his feet in the end by his antagonist. It was not a good fight, for the three were pasty-faced, overgrown young men, in no training and stupid with liquor. But they pressed hard on Lewis for a little, till he was compelled in self-defence to treat them as fair opponents.

He came down the road in a quarter of an hour with a huge rent in his coat-sleeve and a small cut on his forehead. He was warm and breathless, still righteously indignant at the event, and half-ashamed of so degrading an encounter. He found the girl standing statue-like, holding the bridle-rein, and looking into the distance with vacant eyes.

"Are you going back to Glenavelin, Miss Wishart?" he asked. "I think I had better go with you if you will allow me."

Alice mutely assented and walked beside him while he led his horse. He could think of nothing to say. The whole world lay between them now, and there was no single word which either could speak without showing some trace of the tragic separation.

It was the girl who first broke the silence.

"I want to thank you with all my heart," she stammered. And then by an awkward intuition she looked in his face and saw written there all the hopelessness and longing which he was striving to conceal. For one moment she saw clearly, and then the crooked perplexities of the world seemed to stare cruelly in her eyes. A sob caught her voice, and before she was conscious of her action she laid a hand on Lewis's arm and burst into tears.

The sight was so unexpected that it deprived him of all power of action. Then came the fatally easy solution that it was but reaction of over-strained nerves. Always ill at ease in a woman's presence, a woman's tears reduced him to despair. He stroked her hair gently as he would have quieted a favourite horse.

"I am so sorry that these brutes have frightened you. But here we are at Glenavelin gates."

And all the while his heart was crying out to him to clasp her in his arms, and the words which trembled on his tongue were the passionate consolations of a lover.

CHAPTER XVI

A MOVEMENT OP THE POWERS

At Mrs. Montrayner's dinner parties a world of silent men is sandwiched between a *monde* of chattering women. The hostess has a taste for busy celebrities who eat their dinner without thought of the cookery, and regard their fair neighbours much as the diners think of the band in a restaurant. She chose her company with care, and if at her table there was not the busy clack of a fluent conversation, there was always the possibility of *bons mots* and the off-chance of a State secret. So to have dined with the Montrayners became a boast in a small social set, and to the unilluminate the Montrayner banquets seemed scarce less momentous than Cabinet meetings.

Wratislaw found himself staring dully at a snowy bank of flowers and looking listlessly at the faces beyond. He was extremely worried, and his grey face and sunken eyes showed the labour he had been passing through. The country was approaching the throes of a crisis, and as yet the future was a blind alley to him. There was an autumn session, and he had been badgered all the afternoon in the Commons; his even temper had been perilously near its limits, and he had been betrayed unconsciously into certain ineptitudes which he knew would grin in his face on the morrow from a dozen leading articles. The Continent seemed on the edge of an outbreak; in the East especially, Russia by a score of petty acts had seemed to foreshadow an incomprehensible policy. It was a powder-barrel waiting for the spark; and he felt dismally that the spark might come at any moment from some unlooked-for quarter of the globe. He ran over in his mind the position of foreign affairs. All seemed vaguely safe; and yet he was conscious that all was vaguely unsettled. The world was on the eve of one of its cyclic changes, and unrest seemed to make the air murky.

He tried to be polite and listened attentively to the lady on his right, who was telling him the latest gossip about a certain famous marriage. But his air was so manifestly artificial that she turned to the presumably more attractive topic of his doings.

"You look ill," she said--she was one who adopted the motherly air towards young men, which only a pretty woman can use. "Are they over-working you in the House?"

"Pretty fair," and he smiled grimly. "But really I can't complain. I have had eight hours' sleep in the last four days, and I don't think Beauregard could say as much. Some day I shall break loose and go to a quiet place and sleep for a week. Brittany would do--or Scotland."

"I was in Scotland last week," she said. "I didn't find it quiet. It was at one of those theatrical Highland houses where they pipe you to sleep and pipe you to breakfast. I used to have to sit up all night by the fire and read Marius the Epicurean, to compose myself. Did you ever try the specific?"

"No," he said, laughing. "I always soothe my nerves with Blue-books."

She made a mouth at the thought. "And do you know I met such a nice man up there, who said you were a great friend of his? His name was Haystoun."

"Do you remember his Christian name?" he asked.

"Lewis," she said without hesitation.

He laughed. "He is a man who should only have one name and that his Christian one. I never heard him called 'Haystoun' in my life. How is he?"

"He seemed well, but he struck me as being at rather a loose end. What is wrong with him? You know him well and can tell me. He seems to have nothing to do; to have fallen out of his niche, you know. And he looks so extraordinarily clever."

"He *is* extraordinarily clever. But if I undertook to tell you what was wrong with Lewie Haystoun, I should never get to the House to-night. The vitality of a great family has run to a close in him. He is strong and able, and yet, unless the miracle of miracles happens, he will never do anything. Two hundred years ago he might have led some mad Jacobite plot to success. Three hundred and he might have been another Raleigh. Six hundred, and there would have been a new crusade. But as it is, he is out of harmony with his times; life is too easy and mannered; the field for a man's courage is in petty and recondite things, and Lewie is not fitted to understand it. And all this, you see, spells a kind of cowardice: and if you have a friend who is a hero out of joint, a great man smothered in the wrong sort of civilization, and all the while one who is building up for himself with the world and in his own heart the reputation of a coward, you naturally grow hot and bitter."

The lady looked curiously at the speaker. She had never heard the silent politician speak so earnestly before.

"It seems to me a clear case of *chercher la femme*," said she.

"That," said Wratislaw with emphasis, "is the needle-point of the whole business. He has fallen in love with just the wrong sort of woman. Very pretty, very good, a demure puritanical little Pharisee, clever enough, too, to see Lewie's merits, too weak to hope to remedy them, and too full of prejudice to accept them. There you have the makings of a very pretty tragedy."

"I am so sorry," said the lady. She was touched by this man's anxiety for his friend, and Mr. Lewis Haystoun, whom she was never likely to meet again, became a figure of interest in her eyes. She turned to say something more, but Wratislaw, having unburdened his soul to some one, and feeling a little relieved, was watching his chief's face further down the table. That nobleman, hopelessly ill at ease, had given up the pretence of amiability and was now making frantic endeavours to send mute signals across the flowers to his under secretary.

The Montrayner guests seldom linger. Within half an hour after the ladies left the table Beauregard and Wratislaw were taking leave and hurrying into their greatcoats.

"You are going down to the House," said the elder man, "and I'll come too. I want to have some talk with you. I tried to catch your eye at dinner to get you to come round and deliver me from old Montrayner, for I had to sit on his right hand and couldn't come round to you. Heigho-ho! I wish I was a Trappist."

The cab had turned out of Piccadilly into St. James's Street before either man spoke again. The tossing lights of a windy autumn evening were shimmering on the wet pavement, and faces looked spectral white in the morris-dance of shine and shadow. Wratislaw, whose soul was sick for high, clean winds and the great spaces of the moors, was thinking of Glenavelin and Lewis and the strong, quickening north. His companion was furrowing his brow over some knotty problem in his duties.

In Pall Mall there was a lull in the noise, but neither seemed disposed to talk.

"We had better wait till we get to the House," said Beauregard. "We must have peace, for I have got the most vexatious business to speak about." And again he wrinkled his anxious brows and stared in front of him.

They entered a private room where the fire had burned itself out, and the lights fell on heavy furniture and cheerless solitude. Beauregard spread himself out in an arm-chair, and stared at the ceiling. Wratislaw, knowing his chief's manners, stood before the blackened grate and waited.

"Fetch me an atlas--that big one, and find the map of the Indian frontier." Wratislaw obeyed and stretched the huge folio on the table.

The elder man ran his forefinger in a circle.

"There--that wretched radius is the plague of my life. Our reports stop short at that line, and reliable information begins again some hundreds of miles north. Meanwhile--between?" And he shrugged his shoulders.

"I got news to-day in a roundabout way from Taghati. That's the town just within the Russian frontier there. It seems that the whole country is in a ferment. The hill tribes are out and the Russian frontier line is threatened. So they say. I have the actual names of the people who are making the row. Russian troops are being massed along the line there. The whole place, you know, has been for long a military beehive and absurdly over-garrisoned, so there is no difficulty about the massing. The difficulty lies in the reason. Three thousand square miles or so of mountain cannot be so dangerous. One would think that the whole Afghan nation was meditating a descent on the Amu Daria." He glanced up at his companion, and the two men saw the same anxiety in each other's eyes.

"Anything more of Marka?" asked Wratislaw.

"Nothing definite. He is somewhere in the Pamirs, up to some devilry or other. Oh, by the by, there is something I have forgotten. I found out the other day that our gentleman had been down quite recently in south-west Kashmir. He was Arthur Marker at the time, the son of a German count and a Scotch mother, you understand. Immensely popular, too, among natives and Europeans alike. He went south from Bardur, and apparently returned north by the Punjab. At Bardur, Logan and Thwaite were immensely fascinated, Gribton remained doubtful. Now the good Gribton is coming home, and so he will have the place for a happy hunting-ground."

Wratislaw was puffing his under-lip in deep thought. "It is a sweet business," he said. "But what can we do? Only wait?"

"Yes, one could wait if Marka were the only disquieting feature. But what about Taghati and the Russian activity? What on earth is going on or about to go on in this square inch of mountain land to make all the pother? If it is a tribal war on a first-class scale then we must know about it, for it is in the highest degree our concern too. If it is anything else, things look more than doubtful. All the rest I don't mind. It's open and obvious, and we are on the alert. But that little bit of frontier there is so little known and apparently so remote that I begin to be afraid of trouble in that direction. What do you think?"

Wratislaw shook his head. He had no opinion to offer.

"At any rate, you need fear no awkward questions in the House, for this sort of thing cannot be public for months."

"I am wondering whether somebody should not go out. Somebody quite unofficial and sufficiently clever."

"My thought too," said Beauregard. "The pinch is where to get our man from. I have been casting up possibilities all day, and this one is too clever, another too dull, another too timid, and another too hare-brained."

Wratislaw seemed sunk in a brown study.

"Do you remember my telling you once about my friend Lewis Haystoun?" he asked.

"I remember perfectly. What made him get so badly beaten? He ought to have won."

"That's part of my point," said the other. "If I knew him less well than I do I should say he was the man cut out by Providence for the work. He has been to the place, he knows the ropes of travelling, he is exceedingly well-informed, and he is uncommonly clever. But he is badly off colour. The thing might be the saving of him, or the ruin--in which case, of course, he would also be the ruin of the thing."

"As risky as that?" Beauregard asked. "I have heard something of him, but I thought it merely his youth. What's wrong with him?"

"Oh, I can't tell. A thousand things, but all might be done away with by a single chance like this. I tell you what I'll do. After to-night I can be spared for a couple of days. I feel rather hipped myself, so I shall get up to the north and see my man. I know the circumstances and I know Lewis. If the two are likely to suit each other I have your authority to give him your message?"

"Certainly, my dear Wratislaw. I have all the confidence in the world in your judgment. You will be back the day after to-morrow?"

"I shall only be out of the House one night, and I think the game worth it. I need not tell you that I am infernally anxious both about the business and my friend. It is just on the cards that one might be the solution of the other."

"You understand everything?"

"Everything. I promise you I shall be exacting enough. And now I had better be looking after my own work."

Beauregard stared after him as he went out of the room and remained for a few minutes in deep thought. Then he deliberately wrote out a foreign telegram form and rang the bell.

"I fancy I know the man," he said to himself. "He will go. Meantime I can prepare things for his passage." The telegram was to the fugitive Gribton at Florence, asking him to meet a certain Mr. Haystoun at the Embassy in Paris within a week for the discussion of a particular question.

CHAPTER XVII

THE BRINK OF THE RUBICON

The next evening Wratislaw drove in a hired dogcart up Glenavelin from Gledsmuir just as a stormy autumn twilight was setting in over the bare fields. A wild back-end had followed on the tracks of a marvellous summer. Though it was still October the leaves lay heaped beneath the hedgerows, the bracken had yellowed to a dismal hue of decay, and the heather had turned from the purple of its flower to the grey-blue of its passing. Rain had fallen, and the long road-side pools were fired by the westering sun. Glenavelin looked crooked and fantastic in the falling shadows, and two miles farther the high lights of Etterick rose like a star in the bosom of the hills. Seen after many weeks' work in the bustle and confinement of town, the solitary, shadow-haunted world soothed and comforted.

He found Lewis in his room alone. The place was quite dark for no lamp was lit, and only a merry fire showed the occupant. He welcomed his friend with crazy vehemence, pushing him into a great armchair, offering a dozen varieties of refreshment, and leaving the butler aghast with contradictory messages about dinner.

"Oh, Tommy, upon my soul, it is good to see you here! I was getting as dull as an owl."

"Are you alone?" Wratislaw asked.

"George is staying here, but he has gone over to Glenaller to a big shoot. I didn't care much about it, so I stayed at home. He will be back to-morrow."

Lewis's face in the firelight seemed cheerful and wholesome enough, but his words belied it. Wratislaw wondered why this man, who had been wont to travel to the ends of the earth for good shooting, should deny himself the famous Glenaller coverts.

At dinner the lamplight showed him more clearly, and the worried look in his eyes could not be hidden. He was listless, too, his kindly, boisterous manner seemed to have forsaken him, and he had acquired a great habit of abstracted silence. He asked about recent events in the House, commenting shrewdly enough, but without interest. When Wratislaw in turn questioned him on his doings, he had none of the ready enthusiasm which had been used to accompany his talk on sport. He gave bare figures and was silent.

Afterwards in his own sanctum, with drawn curtains and a leaping fire, he became more cheerful. It was hard to be moody in that pleasant room, with the light glancing from silver and vellum and dark oak, and a thousand memories about it of the clean, outdoor life. Wratislaw stretched his legs to the blaze and watched the coils of blue smoke mounting from his pipe with a feeling of keen pleasure. His errand was out of the focus of his thoughts.

It was Lewis himself who recalled him to the business.

"I thought of coming down to town," he said. "I have been getting out of spirits up here, and I wanted to be near you."

"Then it was an excellent chance which brought me up to-night. But why are you dull? I thought you were the sort of man who is sufficient unto himself, you know."

"I am not," he said sharply. "I never realized my gross insufficiency so bitterly."

"Ah!" said Wratislaw, sitting up, "love?

"Did you happen to see Miss Wishart's engagement in the papers?"

"I never read the papers. But I have heard about this: in fact, I believe I have congratulated Stocks."

"Do you know that she ought to have married me?" Lewis cried almost shrilly. "I swear she loved me. It was only my hideous folly that drove her from me."

"Folly?" said Wratislaw, smiling. "Folly? Well you might call it that. I have come up 'ane's errand,' as your people hereabouts say, to talk to you like a schoolmaster, Lewie. Do you mind a good talking-to?"

"I need it," he said. "Only it won't do any good, because I have been talking to myself for a month without effect. Do you know what I am, Tommy?"

"I am prepared to hear," said the other.

"A coward! It sounds nice, doesn't it? I am a shirker, a man who would be drummed out of any regiment."

"Rot!" said Wratislaw. "In that sort of thing you have the courage of your kind. You are the wrong sort of breed for common shirking cowards. Why, man, you might get the Victoria Cross ten times over with ease, as far as that goes. Only you wouldn't, for you are something much more subtle and recondite than a coward."

It was Lewis's turn for the request. "I am prepared to hear," he said.

"A fool! An arrant, extraordinary fool! A fool of quality and parts, a fool who is the best fellow in the world and who has every virtue a man can wish, but at the same time a conspicuous monument of folly. And it is this that I have come to speak about."

Lewis sat back in his chair with his eyes fixed on the glowing coal.

"I want you to make it all plain," he said slowly. "I know it all already; I have got the dull, dead consciousness of it in my heart, but I want to hear it put into words." And he set his lips like a man in pain.

"It is hard," said Wratislaw, "devilish hard, but I've got to try." He knocked out the ashes from his pipe and leaned forward.

"What would you call the highest happiness, Lewie?" he asked.

"The sense of competence," was the answer, given without hesitation.

"Right. And what do we mean by competence? Not success! God knows it is something very different from success! Any fool may be successful, if the gods wish to hurt him. Competence means that splendid joy in your own powers and the approval of your own heart, which great men feel always and lesser men now and again at favoured intervals. There are a certain number of things in the world to be done, and we have got to do them. We may fail--it doesn't in the least matter. We may get killed in the attempt--it matters still less. The things may not altogether be worth doing--it is of very little importance. It is ourselves we have got to judge by. If we are playing our part well, and know it, then we can thank God and go on. That is what I call happiness."

"And I," said Lewis.

"And how are you to get happiness? Not by thinking about it. The great things of the world have all been done by men who didn't stop to reflect on them. If a man comes to a halt and analyses his motives and distrusts the value of the thing he strives for, then the odds are that his halt is final. You strive to strive and not to attain. A man must have that direct, practical virtue which forgets itself and sees only its work. Parsons will tell you that all virtue is self-sacrifice, and they are right, though not in the way they mean. It may all seem a tissue of contradictions. You must not pitch on too fanciful a goal, nor, on the other hand, must you think on yourself. And it is a contradiction which only resolves itself in practice, one of those anomalies on which the world is built up."

Lewis nodded his head.

"And the moral of it all is that there are two sorts of people who will never do any good on this planet. One is the class which makes formulas and shallow little ideals its gods and has no glimpse of human needs and the plain issues of life. The other is the egotist whose eye is always filled with his own figure, who investigates his motives, and hesitates and finicks, till Death knocks him on the head and there is an end of him. Of the two give me the second, for even a narrow little egotistical self is better than a formula. But I pray to be delivered from both."

"'Then who shall stand if Thou, O Lord, dost mark iniquity?'" Lewis quoted.

"There are two men only who will not be ashamed to look their work in the face in the end--the brazen opportunist and the rigid Puritan. Suppose you had some desperate frontier work to get through with and a body of men to pick for it, whom would you take? Not the ordinary, colourless, respectable being, and still less academic nonentities! If I had my pick, my companions should either be the narrowest religionists or frank, unashamed blackguards. I should go to the Calvinists and the fanatics for choice, but if I could not get them then I should have the rankers. For, don't you see, the first would have the fear of God in them, and that somehow keeps a man from fearing anything else. They would do their work because they believed it to be their duty. And the second would have the love of the sport in them, and they should also be made to dwell in the fear of me. They would do their work because they liked it, and liked me, and I told them to do it."

"I agree with you absolutely," said Lewis. "I never thought otherwise."

"Good," said Wratislaw. "Now for my application. You've had the misfortune to fall between the two stools, Lewie. You're too clever for a Puritan and too good for a ranker. You're too finicking and high-strung and fanciful for a prosaic world. You think yourself the laughing philosopher with an infinite appreciation of everything, and yet you have not the humour to stand aside and laugh at yourself."

"I am a coward, as I have told you," said the other dourly.

"No, you are not. But you can't bring yourself down to the world of compromises, which is the world of action. You have lost the practical touch. You muddled your fight with Stocks because you couldn't get out of touch with your own little world in practice, however you might manage it in theory. You can't be single-hearted. Twenty impulses are always pulling different ways with you, and the result is that you become an unhappy, self-conscious waverer."

Lewis was staring into the fire, and the older man leaned forward and put his hand very tenderly on his shoulder.

"I don't want to speak about the thing which gives you most pain, old chap; but I think you have spoiled your chances in the same way in another matter-the most important matter a man can have to do with, though it ill becomes a cynical bachelor like myself to say it."

"I know," said Lewis dismally.

"You see it is the Nemesis of your race which has overtaken you. The rich, strong blood of you Haystouns must be given room or it sours into moodiness. It is either a spoon or a spoiled horn with you. You are capable of the big virtues, and just because of it you are extraordinarily apt to go to the devil. Not the ordinary devil, of course, but to a very effective substitute. You want to be braced and pulled together. A war might do it, if you were a soldier. A religious enthusiasm would do it, if that were possible for you. As it is, I have something else, which I came up to propose to you."

Lewis faced round in an attitude of polite attention. But his eyes had no interest in them.

"You know Bardur and the country about there pretty well?"

Lewis nodded.

"Also I once talked to you about a man called Marka. Do you remember?"

"Yes, of course I do. The man who went north from Bardur the week before I turned up there?"

"Well, there's trouble brewing thereabouts. You know the Taghati country up beyond the Russian line. Things are in a ferment there, great military preparations and all the rest of it, and the reason, they say, is that the hill-tribes in the intervening No-man's-land are at their old games. Things look very ugly abroad just now, and we can't afford to neglect anything when a crisis may be at the door. So we want a man to go out there and find out the truth."

Lewis had straightened himself and was on his feet before Wratislaw had done. "Upon my word," he cried, "if it isn't what I expected! We have been far too sure of the safety of that Kashmir frontier. You mean, of course, that there may be a chance of an invasion?"

"I mean nothing. But things look ugly enough in Europe just now, and Asia would naturally be the starting-point."

Lewis made some rapid calculations in his head which he jotted on the wood of the fireplace. "It would take a week to get from Bardur to Taghati by the ordinary Kashmir rate of travelling, but of course the place is unknown and it might take months. One would have to try it?"

"I can only give you the bare facts. If you decide to go, Beauregard will give you particulars in town."

"When would he want to know?"

"At once. I go back to-morrow morning, and I must have your answer within three days. You would be required to start within a week. You can take time and quiet to make up your mind."

"It's a great chance," said Lewis. "Does Beauregard think it important?"

"Of the highest importance. Also, of course it is dangerous. The travelling is hard, and you may be knocked on the head at any moment as a spy."

"I don't mind that," said the other, flushing. "I've been through the same thing before."

"I need not say the work will be very difficult. Remember that your errand will not be official, so in case of failure or trouble we could not support you. We might even have to disclaim all responsibility. In the event of success, on the other hand, your fortune is something more than made."

"Would you go?" came the question.

"No," said Wratislaw, "I shouldn't."

"But if you were in my place?"

"I should hope that I would, but then I might not have the courage. I am giving you the brave man's choice, Lewie. You will be going out to uncertainty and difficulty and extreme danger. On the other hand, I believe in my soul it will harden you into the man you ought to be. Lord knows I would rather have you stay at home!"

The younger man looked up for a second and saw something in Wratislaw's face which made him turn away his eyes. The look of honest regret cut him to the heart. Those friends of his, of whom he was in nowise worthy, made the burden of his self-distrust doubly heavy.

"I will tell you within three days," he said hoarsely. "God bless you, Tommy. I don't deserve to have a man like you troubling himself about me."

It was his one spoken tribute to their friendship; and both, with the nervousness of honest men in the presence of emotion, hastened to change the subject.

CHAPTER XVIII

THE FURTHER BRINK

Wratislaw left betimes the next morning, and a long day faced Lewis with every hour clamouring for a decision. George would be back by noon, and before his return he must seek quiet and the chances of reflection. He was happy with a miserable fluctuating happiness. Of a sudden his horizon was enlarged, but as he gazed it seemed to narrow again. His mind was still unplumbed; somewhere in its depths might lie the shrinking and unwillingness which would bind him to the dreary present.

He went out to the autumn hills and sought the ridge which runs for miles on the lip of the glen. It was a grey day, with snow waiting in cloud-banks in the north sky and a thin wind whistling through the pines. The scene matched his humour. He was in love for the moment with the stony and stormy in life. He hungered morbidly for ill-fortune, something to stamp out the ease in his soul, and weld him into the form of a man.

He had got his chance and the rest lay with himself. It was a chance of high adventure, a great mission, a limitless future. At the thought the old fever began to rise in his blood. The hot, clear smell of rock and sand, the brown depths of the waters, the far white peaks running up among the stars, all spoke to him with the long-remembered call. Once more he should taste life, and, alert in mind and body, hold up his chin among his fellows. It would be a contest of wits, and for all his cowardice this was not the contest he shrank from.

And then there came back on him, like a flood, the dumb misery of incompetence which had weighed on heart and brain. The hatred of the whole struggling, sordid crew, all the cant and ugliness and ignorance of a mad world, his weakness in the face of it, his fall from common virtue, his nerveless indolence--all stung him like needle points, till he cried out in agony. Anything to deliver his soul from such a bondage, and in his extreme bitterness his mind closed with Wratislaw's offer.

He felt--and it is a proof of his weakness--a certain nameless feeling of content when he had once forced himself into the resolution. Now at least he had found a helm and a port to strain to. As his fancy dwelt upon the mission and drew airy pictures of the land, he found to his delight a boyish enthusiasm arising. Old simple pleasures seemed for the moment dear. There was a zest for toils and discomforts, a tolerance of failure, which had been aforetime his chief traveller's heritage.

And then as he came to the ridge where the road passes from Glenavelin to Glen Adler, he stopped as in duty bound to look at the famous prospect. You stand at the shedding of two streams; behind, the green and woodland spaces of the pastoral Avelin; at the feet, a land of stones and dwarf junipers and naked rifts in the hills, with white-falling waters and dark shadows even at midday. And then, beyond and afar, the lines of hill-land crowd upon each other till the eye is lost in a mystery of grey rock and brown heather and single bald peaks rising sentinel-like in the waste. The grey heavens lent a chill eeriness to the dim grey distances; the sharp winds, the forerunners of snow, blew over the moors like blasts from a primeval night.

By an odd vagary of temper the love of these bleak hills blazed up fiercely in his heart. Never before had he felt so keenly the nameless glamour of his own heritage. He had not been back six months and yet he had come to accept all things as matters of course, the beauty of the place, its sport, its memories. Rarely had he felt that intimate joy in it which lies at the bottom of all true souls. There is a sentiment which old poets have made into songs and called the "Lilt of the Heather," and which is knit closer to man's heart than love of wife or kin or his own fair fortune. It had not come to him in the time of the hills' glory, but now on the brink of winter the far-off melancholy of the place and its infinite fascination seemed to clutch at his heart-strings. It was his own land, the place of his fathers; and now he must sever himself from it and carry only a barren memory.

And yet he felt no melancholy. Rather it was the immortal gaiety of the wanderer, to whom the homeland is dearest as a memory, who pitches his camp by waters of Babylon and yet as ever the old word on his lip, the old song in his ear, and the kindly picture in his heart. Strange that it is the little races who wander farthest and yet have the eternal home-sickness! And yet not strange, for to the little peoples, their land, bare and uncouth and unfriendly for the needs of life, must be more the ideal, the dream, than the satisfaction. The lush countries give corn and wine for their folks, the little bare places afford no more than a spiritual heritage. Yet spiritual it is, and for two men who in the moment of their extremity will think on meadow, woodland, or placid village, a score will figure the windy hill, the grey lochan, and the mournful sea.

For the moment he felt a self-pity which he cast from him. To this degradation at least he should never come. But as the thought of Alice came up ever and again, his longing for her seemed to be changed from hot pain to a chastened regret. The red hearth-fire was no more in his fancy. The hunger for domesticity had gone, and the girl was now less the wife he had desired than the dream of love he had vainly followed. As he came back across the moors, for the first time for weeks his jealous love left him at peace. His had been a fanciful Sylvia, "holy, fair, and wise"; and what if mortal Sylvia were unkind, there was yet comfort in this elusive lady of his memories.

He found George at the end of a second breakfast, a very ruddy, happy young man hunting high and low for a lost tobacco-jar.

"Oh, first-class," he said in answer to Lewis's question. "Out and out the best day's shooting I've had in my life. You were an ass not to come, you know. A lot of your friends there, tremendously disappointed too, and entrusted me with a lot of messages for you which I have forgotten."

His companion's high spirits infected Lewis and he fell into cheery gossip. Then he could contain the news no more.

"I had Tommy up last night on a flying visit. He says that Beauregard wants me to go out to Kashmir again. There has been some threatening of a row up there, and he thinks that as I know the place I might be able to get good information."

"Official?" asked George.

"Practically, yes; but in theory it's quite off my own bat, and they are good enough to tell me that they will not acknowledge responsibility. However, it's a great chance and I am going."

"Good," said the other, and his face and voice had settled into gravity. "Pretty fair sport up in those parts, isn't there?"

"Pretty fair? it's about the best in the world. Your ordinary man who goes the grand tour comes home raving about the sport in the Himalayan foothills, and it's not to be named with this."

"Good chance too of a first-rate row, isn't there? Natives troublesome, and Russia near, and that sort of thing?" George's manner showed a growing enthusiasm.

"A rather good chance. It is about that I'm going, you know."

"Then if you don't mind, I am coming with you."

Lewis stared, incredulous.

"It's quite true. I am serious enough. I am doing nothing at the Bar, and I want to travel, proper travelling, where you are not coddled with railways and hotels."

"But it's hideously risky, and probably very arduous and thankless. You will tire of it in a week."

"I won't," said George, "and in any case I'll make my book for that. You must let me come, Lewie. I simply couldn't stand your going off alone."

"But I may have to leave you. There are places where one can go when two can't."

"When you come to that sort of place I'll stay behind. I'll be quite under your orders."

"Well, at any rate take some time to think over it."

"Bless you, I don't want time to think over it," cried George. "I know my own mind. It's the chance I've been waiting on for years."

"Thanks tremendously then, my dear chap," said Lewis, very ill at ease. "It's very good of you. I must wire at once to Tommy."

"I'll take it down, if you like. I want to try that new mare of yours in the dog-cart."

When his host had left the room George forgot to light his pipe, but walked instead to the window and whistled solemnly. "Poor old man," he said softly to himself, "it had to come to this, but I'm hanged if he doesn't take it like a Trojan." And he added certain striking comments on the ways of womankind and the afflictions of life, which, being expressed in Mr. Winterham's curious phraseology, need not be set down.

Alice had gone out after lunch to walk to Gledsmuir, seeking in the bitter cold and the dawning storm the freshness which comes from conflict. All the way down the glen the north wind had stung her cheeks to crimson and blown stray curls about her ears; but when she left the little market-place to return she found a fine snow powdering the earth, and a haze creeping over the hills which threatened storm. A mile of the weather delighted her, but after that she grew weary. When the fall thickened she sought the shelter of a way-side cottage, with the purpose of either sending to Glenavelin for a carriage or waiting for the off-chance of a farmer's gig.

By four o'clock the snow showed no sign of clearing, but fell in the same steady, noiseless drift. The mistress of the place made the girl tea and dispatched her son to Glenavelin. But the errand would take time, for the boy was small, and Alice, ever impatient, stood drumming on the panes, watching the dreary weather with a dreary heart. The goodwife was standing at the door on the look-out for a passing gig, and her cry brought the girl to attention.

"I see a machine comin'! I think it's the Etterick dowg-cairt. Ye'll get a drive in it."

Alice had gone to the door, and lo! through the thick fall a dog-cart came into view driven by a tall young man. He recognized her at once, and drew up.

"Hullo, Miss Wishart! Storm-stayed? Can I help you?"

The girl looked distrustfully at the very restless horse and he caught her diffidence.

"Don't be afraid. 'What I don't know about 'oases ain't worth knowin',''" he quoted with a laugh; and leaning forward he prepared to assist her to mount.

There was nothing for it but to accept, and the next minute she found herself in the high seat beside him. Her wraps, sufficient for walking, were scarcely sufficient for a snowy drive, and this, to his credit, the young man saw. He unbuttoned his tweed shooting-cape, and gravely put it round her. A curious dainty figure she made with her face all bright with wind, framed in the great grey cloak.

The horse jibbed for a second and then swung along the wild road with the vigorous ease of good blood skilfully handled. George was puzzling his brain all the while as to how he should tell his companion something which she ought to know. The strong drift and the turns of the road claimed much of his attention, so it is possible that he blurted out his news somewhat baldly.

"Do you know, Miss Wishart, that Lewis Haystoun and I are going off next week? Abroad, you know."

The girl, who had been enjoying the ecstasy of swift motion through the bitter weather, glanced up at him with pain in her eyes. .

"Where?" she asked.

"To the Indian frontier. We are going to be special unpaid unofficial members of the Intelligence Department."

She asked the old, timid woman's question about danger.

"It's where Lewis was before. Only, you see, things have got into a mess thereabouts, and the Foreign Office has asked him to go out again. By the by, you mustn't tell any one about this, for it's in strict confidence."

The words were meaningless, and yet they sent a pang through her heart. Had he no guess at her inmost feelings? Could he think that she would talk to

Mr. Stocks of a thing which was bound up for her with all the sorrow and ecstasy of life?

He looked down and saw that her face had paled and that her mouth was drawn with some emotion. A sudden gleam of light seemed to break in upon him.

"Are you sorry?" he asked half-unwittingly.

For answer the girl turned her tragic eyes upon him, tried to speak, and faltered. He cursed him-self for a fool and a brute, and whipped up an already over-active horse, till it was all but unmanageable. It was a wise move, for it absorbed his attention and gave the poor child at his side a chance to recover her composure.

They came to Glenavelin gates and George turned in. "I had better drive you to the door, in this charming weather," he said. The sight of the pale little face had moved him to deep pity. He cursed his blindness, the blindness of a whole world of fools, and at the same time, with the impotence of the honest man, he could only wait and be silent.

At the door he stopped to unbutton his cape from her neck, and even in his nervousness he felt the trembling of her body. She spoke rapidly and painfully.

"I want you to take a message from me to--to--Lewis. Tell him I must see him. Tell him to come to the Midburn foot, to-morrow in the afternoon. Oh, I am ashamed to ask you, but you must tell him." And then without thanks or good-bye she fled into the house.

CHAPTER XIX

THE BRIDGE OF BROKEN HEARTS

Listless leaves were tossing in the light wind or borne downward in the swirl of the flooded Midburn, to the weary shallows where they lay, beached high and sodden, till the frost nipped and shrivelled their rottenness into dust. A bleak, thin wind it was, like a fine sour wine, searching the marrow and bringing no bloom to the cheek. A light snow powdered the earth, the grey forerunner of storms.

Alice stood back in the shelter of the broken parapet. The highway with its modern crossing-place was some hundreds of yards up stream, but here, at the burn mouth, where the turbid current joined with the cold, glittering Avelin, there was a grass-grown track, and an ancient, broken-backed bridge. There were few passers on the high-road, none on this deserted way; but the girl in all her loneliness shrank back into the shadow. In these minutes she endured the bitter mistrust, the sore hesitancy, of awaiting on a certain but unknown grief.

She had not long to wait, for Lewis came down the Avelin side by a bypath from Etterick village. His alert gait covered his very real confusion, but to the girl he seemed one who belonged to an alien world of cheerfulness. He could not know her grief, and she regretted her coming.

His manners were the same courteous formalities. The man was torn with emotion, and yet he greeted her with a conventional ease.

"It was so good of you, Miss Wishart, to give me a chance to come and say good-bye. My going is such a sudden affair, that I might have had no time to come to Glenavelin, but I could not have left without seeing you."

The girl murmured some indistinct words. "I hope you will have a good time and come back safely," she said, and then she was tongue-tied.

The two stood before each other, awkward and silent--two between whom no word of love had ever been spoken, but whose hearts were clamouring at the iron gates of speech.

Alice's face and neck were dyed crimson, as the impossible position dawned on her mind. No word could break down the palisade, of form. Lewis, his soul a volcano, struggled for the most calm and inept words. He spoke of the weather, of her father, of his aunt's messages.

Then the girl held out her hand.

"Good-bye," she said, looking away from him.

He held it for a second. "Good-bye, Miss Wishart," he said hoarsely. Was this the consummation of his brief ecstasy, the end of months of longing? The steel hand of fate was on him and he turned to leave.

He turned when he had gone three paces and came back. The girl was still standing by the parapet, but she had averted her face towards the wintry waters. His step seemed to fall on deaf ears, and he stood beside her before she looked towards him.

Passion had broken down his awkwardness. He asked the old question with a shaking voice. "Alice," he said, "have I vexed you?"

She turned to him a pale, distraught face, her eyes brimming over with the sorrow of love, the passionate adventurous longing which claims true hearts for ever.

He caught her in his arms, his heart in a glory of joy.

"Oh, Alice, darling," he cried. "What has happened to us? I love you, I love you, and you have never given me a chance to say it."

She lay passive in his arms for one brief minute and then feebly drew back.

"Sweetheart," he cried. "Sweetheart! For I will call you sweetheart, though we never meet again. You are mine, Alice. We cannot help ourselves."

The girl stood as in a trance, her eyes caught and held by his face.

"Oh, the misery of things," she said half-sobbing. "I have given my soul to another, and I knew it was not mine to give. Why, oh why, did you not speak to me sooner? I have been hungering for you and you never came."

A sense of his folly choked him.

"And I have made you suffer, poor darling! And the whole world is out of joint for us!"

The hopeless feeling of loss, forgotten for a moment, came back to him. The girl was gone from him for ever, though a bridge of hearts should always cross the chasm of their severance.

"I am going away," he said, "to make reparation. I have my repentance to work out, and it will be bitterer than yours, little woman. Ours must be an austere love."

She looked at him till her pale face flushed and a sad exultation woke in her eyes.

"You will never forget?" she asked wistfully, confident of the answer.

"Forget!" he cried. "It is my only happiness to remember. I am going away to be knocked about, dear. Wild, rough work, but with a man's chances!"

For a moment she let another thought find harbour in her mind. Was the past irretrievable, the future predetermined? A woman's word had an old right to be broken. If she went to him, would not he welcome her gladly, and the future might yet be a heritage for both?

The thought endured but a moment, for she saw how little simple was the crux of her destiny. The two of them had been set apart by the fates; each had salvation to work out alone; no facile union would ever join them. For him there was the shaping of a man's path; for her the illumination which only sorrows and parting can bring. And with the thought she thought kindly of the man to whom she had pledged her word. It was but a little corner of her heart he could ever possess; but doubtless in such matters he was not ambitious.

Lewis walked by her side down the by-path towards Glenavelin. Tragedy muffled in the garments of convention was there, not the old picturesque Tragic with sword and cloak and steel for the enemy, but the silent Tragic which pulls at the heart-strings.

"The summer is over," she said. "It has been a cruel summer, but very bright."

"Romance with the jarring modern note which haunts us all to-day," he said. "This upland country is confused with bustling politics, and pastoral has been worried to death by sickness of heart. You cannot find the old peaceful life without."

"And within?" she asked.

"That is for you and me to determine, dear. God grant it. I have found my princess, like the man in the fairy-tale, but I may not enter the kingdom."

"And the poor princess must sit and mope in her high stone tower? It is a hard world for princesses."

"Hard for the knights, too, for they cannot come back and carry off their ladies. In the old days it used to be so, but then simplicity has gone out of life."

"And the princess waits and watches and cries herself to sleep?

"And the knight goes off to the World's End and never forgets."

They were at Glenavelin gates now, and stood silent against the moment of parting. She flew to his arms, for a second his kisses were on her lips, and then came the sundering. A storm of tears was in her heart, but with dry eyes she said the words of good-bye. Meanwhile from the hills came a drift of snow, and a dreary wind sang in the pines the dirge of the dead summer, the plaint of long farewells.

PART II

CHAPTER XX

THE EASTERN ROAD

If you travel abroad in certain seasons you will find that a type predominates among the travellers. From Dover to Calais, from Calais to Paris, there is an unnatural eagerness on faces, an unrest in gait, a disorder in dress which argues worry and haste. And if you inquire further, being of a speculative turn, you will find that there is something in the air. The papers, French and English, have ugly headlines and mystic leaders. Disquiet is in the atmosphere, each man has a solution or a secret, and far at the back sits some body of men who know that a crisis is near and square their backs for it. The journalist is sick with work and fancied importance; the diplomat's hair whitens with the game which he cannot understand; the statesman, if he be wise, is in fear, knowing the meaning of such movements, while, if he be foolish, he chirps optimistically in his speeches and is applauded in the press. There are grey faces at the seats of the money-changers, for war, the scourge of small cords, seems preparing for the overturning of their tables, and the castigation of their persons.

Lewis and George rang the bell in the Faubourg St. Honoré on a Monday afternoon, and asked for Lord Rideaux. His lordship was out, but, if they were the English gentlemen who had the appointment with M. Gribton, Monsieur would be with them speedily.

Lewis looked about the heavily furnished ante-room with its pale yellow walls and thick, green curtains, with the air of a man trying to recall a memory. "I came over here with John Lambert, when his father had the place. That was just after I left Oxford. Gad, I was a happy man then. I thought I could do anything. They put me next to Madame de Ravignet because of my French, and because old Ankerville declared that I ought to know the cleverest woman in Europe. Séry, the man who was Premier last year, came and wrung my hand afterwards, said my fortune was assured because I had impressed the Ravignet, and no one had ever done it before except Bismarck. Ugh, the place is full of ghosts Poor old John died a year after, and here am I, far enough, God knows, from my good intentions."

A servant announced "Monsieur Gribton," and a little grizzled man hobbled in, leaning heavily on a stick. He wore a short beard, and in his tanned face two clever grey eyes twinkled sedately. He shook hands gravely when Lewis introduced George, but his eyes immediately returned to the former's face. "You look a fit pair," he said. "I am instructed to give you all the help in my power, but I should like to know your game. It isn't sport this time, is it, Haystoun? Logan is still talking about his week with you. Well, well, we can do things at our leisure. I have letters to write, and then it will be dinner-time, when we can talk. Come to the club at eight, 'Cercle des Voyageurs,' corner of Rue Neuve de St. Michel. I expect you belong, Haystoun; and anyway I'll be there."

He bowed them out with his staccato apologies, and the two returned to their hotel to dress. Two hours later they found Gribton warming his hands in the smoking-room of the Cercle, a fussy and garrulous gentleman, eager for his dinner. He pointed out such people as he knew, and was consumed with curiosity about the others. Lewis wandered about the room before he sat down, shaking hands with several and nodding to many.

"You seem to know the whole earth," said Gribton.

"I suppose that a world of acquaintance is the only reward of slackness," Lewis said, laughing. "It's a trick I have. I never forget a face and I honestly like to see people again."

George pulled his long moustache. "It's simply hideous the way one is forgotten. It's all right for the busy people, for they shift their sets with their fortune, but for drones like me it's the saddest thing in life. Before we came away, Lewie, I went up for a day to Oxford to see about some things, and stopped a night there. I haven't been down long, and yet I knew nobody at the club except the treasurer, and he had nothing to say to me except to ask after you. I went to dinner with the dons at the high table, and I nearly perished of the blues. Little Riddell chirped about my profession, and that bounder Jackson, who was of our year, pretended that he had been your bosom friend. I got so bored that I left early and wandered back to the club. Somebody was making a racket in our old rooms in the High, windows open, you know, and singing. I stopped to look at them, and then they started, 'Willie brewed a peck o' maut,' and, 'pon my soul, I had to come away. Couldn't stand it. It reminded me so badly of you and Arthur and old John Lambert, and all the honest men that used to be there. It was infernally absurd that I should have got so sentimental, but that wasn't the worst of it. For I met Tony and he made me come round to a dinner, and there I found people I didn't know from Adam drinking the old toasts we started. Gad, they had them all. 'Las Palmas,' 'The Old Guard,' 'The Wandering Scot,' and all the others. It made me feel as low as an owl, and when I got back to the club and saw poor old John's photograph on the wall, I tell you I went to bed in the most wretched melancholy."

Lewis stared open-mouthed at George, the irrepressible, in this new attitude. He, as the hardened traveller, had had little more than a decent pang of home-sickness. His regret was far deeper and more real than the sentimental article of commerce, and he could afford to be almost gay while George sat in the depths.

"I'm coming home, and I'm not happy; you young men are going out, and you have got the blues. There's no pleasing weak humanity. I say, Haystoun, who's that old man?" Gribton's jovial looks belied his words.

Lewis mentioned a name for his host's benefit. The room was emptying rapidly, for the Cercle dined early.

"Now for business," said Gribton, when a waiter had brought the game course, and they sat in the midst of a desert of linen and velvet. "I have given the thing up, but I spent twenty of my best years at Bardur. So, as I am instructed to do all in my power to aid you, I am ready. First, is it sport?

"Partly," said George, but Lewis's head gave denial.

"Because, if it is, I am not the best man. Well, then, is it geographical? For if it is, there is much to be done."

"Partly," said Lewis.

"Then I take it that the residue is political. You are following the popular avenue to politics, I suppose. Leave the 'Varsity very raw, knock about in an unintelligent way for three or four years on some frontier, then come home, go into the House, and pose as a specialist in foreign affairs. I should have thought you had too much humour for that."

"Only, you see, I have been there before. I am merely going back upon my tracks to make sure. I go purely as an adventurer, hoping to pick up some valuable knowledge, but prepared to fail."

Gribton helped himself to champagne. "That's better. Now I know your attitude, we can talk like friends. Better come to the small smoking-room. They've got a '51 brandy here which is beyond words. Have some for a liqueur."

In the smoking-room Gribton fussed about coffee and cigars for many minutes ere he settled down. Then, when he could gaze around and see his two guests in deep armchairs, each smoking and comfortable, he returned to his business.

"I don't mind telling you a secret," he said, "or rather it's only a secret here, for once you get out there you will find 'Gribton's view,' as they call it, well enough known and very much laughed at. I've always been held up to ridicule as an alarmist about that Kashmir frontier, and especially about that Bardur country. Take the whole province. It's well garrisoned on the north, but below that it is all empty and open. The way into the Punjab is as clear as daylight for a swift force, and the way to the Punjab is the way to India."

Lewis rose and went to a rack on the wall. "Do you mind if I get down maps? These French ones are very good." He spread a sheet of canvas on the table, thereby confounding all Gribton's hospitable manoeuvring.

"There," said Gribton, his eyes now free from drowsiness, and clear and bright, "that's the road I fear."

"But these three inches are unknown," said Lewis. "I have been myself as far as these hills."

Gribton looked sharply up. "You don't know the place as I know it. I've never been so far, but I know the sheep-skinned devils who come across from Turkestan. I tell you that place isn't the impenetrable craggy desert that the Government of India thinks it. There's a road there of some sort, and if you're worth your salt you'll find it out."

"I know," said Lewis. "I am going to try."

"There's another thing. For the last three years all that north part of Kashmir, and right away south-west to the Punjab borders, has been honoured with visits from plausible Russian gentlemen who may come down by the ordinary caravan routes, or, on the other hand, may not. They turn up quite suddenly with tooth-brushes and dressing-cases, and they can't have come from the south. They fool around in Bardur, and then go down to Gilgit, and, I suppose, on to the Punjab. They've got excellent manners, and they hang about the clubs and give dinners and charm the whole neighbourhood. Logan is their bosom friend, and Thwaite declares that their society reconciles him to the place. Then they go away, and the place keeps on the randan for weeks after."

"Do you know a man called Marker by any chance?" Lewis asked.

Gribton looked curiously at the speaker. "Have you actually heard about him? Yes, I know him, but not very well, and I can't say I ever cared for him. However, he is easily the most popular man in Bardur, and I daresay is a very good fellow. But you don't call him Russian. I thought he was sort of half a Scotsman."

"Very likely he is," said Lewis. "I happen to have heard a good deal about him. But what ails you at him?"

"Oh, small things," and the man laughed. "You know I am getting elderly and cranky, and I like a man to be very fair and four-square. I confess I never got to the bottom of the chap. He was a capital sportsman, good bridge-player, head like a rock for liquor, and all that; but I'm hanged if he didn't seem to me to be playing some sort of game. Another thing, he seemed to me a terribly cold-blooded devil. He was always slapping people on the back and calling them 'dear old fellows,' but I happened to see a small interview once between him and one of his servants. Perhaps I ought not to mention it, but the thing struck me unpleasantly. It was below the club verandah, and nobody happened to be about except myself, who was dozing after lunch. Marker was rating a servant in some Border tongue--Chil, it sounded like; and I remember wondering how he could have picked it up. I saw the whole thing through a chink in the floor, and I noticed that the servant's face was as grey as a brown hillman's can be. Then the fellow suddenly caught his arm and twisted it round, the man's face working with pain, though he did not dare to utter a sound. It was an ugly sight, and when I caught a glimpse of Marker's face, 'pon my soul, those straight black eyebrows of his gave him a most devilish look."

"What's he like to look at?" George asked.

"Oh, he's rather tall, very straight, with a sort of military carriage, and he has one of those perfect oval faces that you sometimes see. He has most remarkable black eyes and very neat, thin eyebrows. He is the sort of man you'd turn round to look at if you once passed him in the street; and if you once saw him smile you'd begin to like him. It's the prettiest thing I've ever seen."

"I expect I'll run across him somewhere," said Lewis, "and I want badly to know him. Would you mind giving me an introduction?"

"Charmed!" said Gribton. "Shall I write it now?" And sitting down at a table he scribbled a few lines, put them in an envelope, and gave it to Lewis.

"You are pretty certain to know him when you see him, so you can give him that line. You might run across him anywhere from Hyderabad to Rawal Pinch, and in any case you'll hear word of him in Bardur. He's the man for your purpose; only, as I say, I never liked him. I suspect a loop somewhere."

"What are Logan and Thwaite like?" Lewis asked.

"Easy-going, good fellows. Believe in God and the British Government, and the inherent goodness of man. I am rather the other way, so they call me a cynic and an alarmist."

"But what do you fear?" said George. "The place is well garrisoned."

"I fear four inches in that map of unknown country," said Gribton shortly. "The people up there call it a 'God-given rock-wall,' and of course there is no force to speak of just near it. But a tribe of devils incarnate, who call themselves the Bada-Mawidi, live on its skirts, and there must be a road through it. It isn't the caravan route, which goes much farther east and is plain enough. But I know enough of the place to know that every man who comes over the frontier to Bardur does not come by the high-road."

"But what could happen? Surely Bardur is strongly garrisoned enough to block any secret raid."

"It isn't bad in its way, if the people were not so slack and easy. They might rise to scratch, but, on the other hand, they might not, and once past Bardur you have the open road to India, if you march quick enough."

"Then you have no man sufficiently adventurous there to do a little exploring?"

"None. They care only about shooting, and there happens to be little in those rocks. Besides, they trust in God and the Government of India. I didn't, so I became unpopular, and was voted a bore. But the work is waiting for you young men."

Gribton rose, yawned, and stretched himself. "Shall I tell you any more?"

"I don't think so," said Lewis, smiling; "I fancy I understand, and I am sure we are obliged to you. Hadn't we better have a game?"

They went to the billiard-room and played two games of a hundred up, both of which George, who had the idler's knack in such matters, won with ease. Gribton played so well that he became excessively good-humoured.

"I almost wish I was going out again if I had you two as company. We don't get the right sort out there. Our globe-trotters all want to show their cleverness, or else they are merely fools. You will find it miserably dull. Nothing but bad claret and cheap champagne at the clubs, a cliquey set of English residents, and the sort of stock sport of which you tire in a month. That's what you may expect our frontier towns to be like."

"And the neighbourhood?" said Lewis, with lifted eyebrows.

"Oh, the neighbourhood is wonderful enough; but our people there are too slack and stale to take advantage of it. It is a peaceful frontier, you know, and men get into a rut as easily there as elsewhere. The country's too fat and wealthy, and people begin to forget the skeleton up among the rocks in the north."

"What are the garrisons like?"

"Good people, but far too few for a serious row, and just sufficiently large to have time hang on their hands. Our friends the Bada-Mawidi now and then wake them up. I see from the *Temps* that a great stirring of the tribes in the Southern Pamirs is reported. I expect that news came overland through Russia. It's the sort of canard these gentry are always getting up to justify a massing of troops on the Amu Daria in order that some new governor may show his strategic skill. I daresay you may find things a little livelier than I found them."

As they went towards the Faubourg St. Honoré a bitter Paris north-easter had begun to drift a fine powdered snow in their eyes. Gribton shivered and turned up the collar of his fur coat. "Ugh, I can't stand this. It makes me sick to be back. Thank your stars that you are going to the sun and heat, and out of this hideous grey weather."

They left him at the Embassy, and turned back to their hotel.

"He's a useful man," said Lewis, "he has given us a cue; life will be pretty well varied out there for you and me, I fancy."

Then, as they entered a boulevard, and the real sweep of the wind met their faces, both men fell strangely silent. To George it was the last word of the north which they were leaving, and his recent home-sickness came back and silenced him. But to Lewis, his mind already busy with his errand, this sting of wind was the harsh disturber which carried him back to a lonely home in a cold, upland valley. It was the wintry weather which was his own, and Alice's face, framed in a cloak, as he had seen it at the Broken Bridge, rose in the gallery of his heart. In a moment he was disillusioned. Success, enterprise, new lands and faces seemed the most dismal vexation of spirit. With a very bitter heart he walked home, and, after the fashion of his silent kind, gave no sign of his mood save by a premature and unreasonable retirement to bed.

CHAPTER XXI

IN THE HEART OF THE HILLS

All around was stone and scrub, rising in terraces to the foot of sheer cliffs which opened up here and there in nullahs and gave a glimpse of great snow hills behind them. On one of the flat ridge-tops a little village of stunted, slaty houses squatted like an ape, with a vigilant eye on twenty gorges. Thin, twisting paths led up to it, and before, on the more clement slopes, some fields of grain were tilled as our Aryan forefathers tilled the soil on the plains of Turkestan. The place was at least 8,000 feet above the sea, so the air was highland, clear and pleasant, save for the dryness which the great stone deserts forced upon the soft south winds. You will not find the place marked in any map, for it is a little beyond even the most recent geographer's ken, but it is none the less a highly important place, for the nameless village is one of the seats of that most active and excellent race of men, the Bada-Mawidi, who are so old that they can afford to look down on their neighbours from a vantage-ground of some thousands of years. It is well known that when God created the earth He first fashioned this tangle of hill land, and set thereon a primitive Bada-Mawidi, the first of the clan, who was the ancestor, in the thousandth degree, of the excellent Fazir Khan, the present father of the tribe.

The houses clustered on the scarp and enclosed a piece of well-beaten ground and one huge cedar tree. Sounds came from the near houses, but around the tree itself the more privileged sat in solemn conclave. Food and wine were going the round, for the Maulai kohammedans have no taboos in eating and drinking. Fazir Khan sat smoking next the tree trunk, a short, sinewy man with a square, Aryan face, clear-cut and cruel. His chiefs were around him, all men of the same type, showing curiously fair skins against their oiled black hair. A mullah sat cross-legged, his straggling beard in his lap, repeating some crazy charm to himself and looking every now and again with anxious eyes to the guest who sat on the chief's right hand.

The guest was a long, thin man, clad in the Cossacks' fur lined military cloak, under which his untanned riding-boots showed red in the moonlight. He was still busy eating goat's flesh, cheese and fruits, and drinking deeply from the sweet Hunza wine, like a man who had come far and fast. He ate with the utmost disregard of his company. He might have been a hunter supping alone in the solitary hills for all the notice he took of the fifty odd men around him.

By and by be finished, pulled forth a little silver toothpick from an inner pocket, and reached a hand for the long cherry-wood pipe which had been placed beside him. He lit it, and blew a few clouds into the calm air.

"Now, Fazir Khan," he said, "I am a new man, and we shall talk. First, have you done my bidding?"

"Thy bidding has been done," said the great man sulkily. "See, I am here with my chiefs. All the twenty villages of my tribe have been warned, and arms have been got from the fools at Bardur. Also, I have the Yarkand powder I was told of, to give the signals on the hills. The Nazri Pass road, which we alone know, has been widened. What more could man do?"

"That is well," said the other. "It is well for you and your people that you have done this. Your service shall not be forgotten. Otherwise--"

"Otherwise?" said the Fazir Khan, his hand travelling to his belt at the sound of a threat.

The man laughed. "You know the tale," he said. "Doubtless your mother told you it when you clutched at her breast. Some day a great white people from the north will come down and swallow up the disobedient. That day is now at hand. You have been wise in time. Therefore I say it is well."

The stranger spoke with perfect coolness. He looked round curiously at the circle of dark faces and laughed quietly to himself. The chief stole one look at him and then said something to a follower.

"I need not speak of the reward," said the stranger. "You are our servants, and duty is duty. But I have authority for saying that we shall hold your work in mind when we have settled our business."

"What would ye be without us?" said the chief in sudden temper. "What do ye know of the Nazri gates or the hill country? What is this talk of duty, when ye cannot stir a foot without our aid?"

"You are our servants, as I said before," said the man curtly. "You have taken our gold and our food. Where would you be, outlaws, vagrants that you are, hated of God and man, but for our help? Your bodies would have rotted long ago on the hills. The kites would be feeding on your sons; your women would be in the Bokhara market. We have saved you a dozen times from the vengeance of the English. When they wished to come up and burn you out, we have put them past the project with smooth words. We have fed you in famine, we have killed your enemies, we have given you life. You are freemen indeed in the face of the world, but you are our servants."

Fazir Khan made a gesture of impatience. "That is as God may direct it," he said. "Who are ye but a people of yesterday, while the Bada-Mawidi is as old as the rocks. The English were here before you, and we before the English. It is right that youth should reverence age."

"That is one proverb," said the man, "but there are others, and in especial one to the effect that the man without a sword should bow before his brother who has one. In this game we are the people with the sword, my friends."

The hillman shrugged his shoulders. His men looked on darkly, as if little in love with the stranger's manner of speech.

"It is ill working in the dark," he said at length. "Ye speak of this attack and the aid you expect from us, but we have heard this talk before. One of your people came down with some followers in my father's time, and his words were the same, but lo! nothing has yet happened."

"Since your father's time things have changed, my brother. Then the English were very much on the watch, now they sleep. Then there were no roads, or very bad ones, and before an army could reach the plains the whole empire would have been wakened. Now, for their own undoing, they have made roads up to the very foot of yon mountains, and there is a new railway down the Indus through Kohistan waiting to carry us into the heart of the Punjab. They seek out inventions for others to enjoy, as the Koran says, and in this case we are to be the enjoyers."

"But what if ye fail?" said the chief. "Ye will be penned up in that Hunza valley like sheep, and I, Fazir Khan, shall be unable to unlock the door of that sheepfold."

"We shall not fail. This is no war of rock-pigeons, my brothers. Our agents are in every town and village from Bardur to Lahore. The frontier tribes, you among the rest, are rising in our favour. There is nothing to stop us but isolated garrisons of Gurkhas and Pathans, with a few overworked English officers at their head. In a week we shall command the north of India, and if we hold the north, in another week we shall hold Calcutta and Bombay."

The chief nodded his head. Such far-off schemes pleased his fancy, but only remotely touched his interest. Calcutta was beyond his ken, but he knew Bardur and Gilgit.

"I have little love for the race," he said. "They hanged two of my servants who ventured too near the rifle-room, and they shot my son in the back when we raided the Chitralis. If ye and your friends cross the border I will be with you. But meantime, till that day, what is my duty?"

"To wait in patience, and above all things to let the garrisons alone. If we stir up the hive in the valleys they may come and see things too soon for our success. We must win by secrecy and surprise. All is lost if we cannot reach the railway before the Punjab is stirring."

The mullah had ceased muttering to himself. He scrambled to his feet, shaking down his rags over his knees, a lean, crazy apparition of a man with deep-set, smouldering eyes.

"I will speak," he cried. "Ye listen to the man's words and ye are silent, believing all things. Ye are silent, my children, because ye know not. But I am old and I have seen many things, and these are my words. Ye speak of pushing out the English from the land. Allah knows I love not the breed! I spit upon it, I thirst for the heart of every man, woman, and child, that I might burn them in the sight of all of you. But I have heard this talk before. When I was a young priest at Kufaz, there was word of this pushing out of the foreigner, and I rejoiced, being unwise. Then there was much fighting, and at the end more English came up the valleys and, before we knew, we were paying tribute. Since then many of our people have gone down from the mountains with the same thought, and they have never returned. Only the English and the troops have crept nearer. Now this stranger talks of his Tsar and how an army will come through the passes, and foreigner will fight with foreigner. This talk, too, I have heard. Once there came a man with a red beard who spoke thus, and he went down to Bardur, and lo! our men told me that they saw him hanged there for a warning. Let foreigner war on foreigner if they please, but what have we to do in the quarrel, my children? Ye owe nothing to either."

The stranger regarded the speaker with calm eyes of amusement.

"Nothing," said he, "except that we have fed you and armed you. By your own acts you are the servants of my master."

The mullah was rapidly working himself into a frenzy. He swung his long bony arms across his breast and turned his face skywards. "Ye hear that, my children. The free people, the Bada-Mawidi, of whose loins sprang Abraham the prophet, are the servants of some foreign dog in the north. If ye were like your fathers, ye would have long ago ere this wiped out the taunt in blood."

The man sat perfectly composed, save that his right hand had grasped a revolver. He was playing a bold game, but he had played it before. And he knew the man he had to deal with.

"I say again, you are my master's servants by your own confession. I did not say his slaves. You are a free people, but you will serve a greater in this affair. As for this dog who blasphemes, when we have settled more important matters we will attend to him."

The mullah was scarcely a popular member of his tribe, for no one stirred at the call. The stranger sat watching him with very bright, eager eyes. Suddenly the priest ceased his genuflexions, there was a gleam of steel among his rags, then something bright flashed in the air. It fell short, because at the very moment of throwing, a revolver had cracked out in the silence, and a bullet had broken two of his fingers. The man flung himself writhing on the ground, howling forth imprecations.

The stranger looked half apologetically at the chief, whose glum demeanour had never relaxed. "Sorry," he said; "it had to be done in self-defence. But I ask your pardon for it."

Fazir Khan nodded carelessly. "He is a disturber of peace, and to one who cannot fight a hand matters little. But, by Allah, ye northerners shoot quick."

The stranger relinquished the cherry-wood pipe and filled a meerschaum from a pouch which he carried in the pocket of his cloak. He took a long drink from the loving-cup of mulled wine which was passing round.

"Your mad priest has method in his folly," he said. "It is true that we are attacking a great people; therefore the more need of wariness for you and me, Fazir Khan. If we fail there will be the devil to pay for you. The English will shift their frontier-line beyond the mountains, and there will be no more lifting of women and driving of cattle for the Bada-Mawidi. You will all be sent to school, and your guns will be taken from you."

The chief compressed his attractive features into a savage scowl. "That may not be in my lifetime," he said. "Besides, are there no mountains all around? In five hours I shall be in China, and in a little more I might be beyond the Amu. But why talk of this? The accursed English shall not escape us, I swear by the hilt of my sword and the hearts of my fathers."

A subdued murmur of applause ran around the circle.

"You are men after my own heart," said the stranger. "Meanwhile, a word in your own ear, Fazir Khan. Dare you come to Bardur with me?"

The chief made a gesture of repugnance. "I hate that place of mud and lime. The blood of my people cries on me when I enter the gates. But if it is your counsel I will come with you."

"I wish to assure myself that the place is quiet. Our success depends upon the whole country being unsuspicious and asleep. Now if word has got to the south, and worse still to England, there will be questions asked and vague instructions sent up to the frontier. We shall find a stir among the garrisons, and perhaps some visitors in the place. And at the very worst we might find some fool inquiring about the Nazri Pass. There was once a man in Bardur who did, but people laughed at him and he has gone."

"Where?" asked the chief.

"To England. But he was a harmless man, and he is too old to have any vigour."

As the darkness grew over the hills the fires were brightened and the curious game of *khoti* was played in groups of six. The women came to the house-doors to sit and gossip, and listened to the harsh laughter of their lords from beside the fires. A little after midnight, when the stars were picked out in the deep, velvet sky, Fazir Khan and the stranger, both muffled to the ears, stole beyond the street and scrambled down the perilous path-ways to the south.

CHAPTER XXII

THE OUTPOSTS

Towards the close of a wet afternoon two tongas discharged Lewis, George, two native servants, and a collection of gun-cases in the court-yard of the one hotel in Bardur. They had made a record journey up country, stopping to present no letters of introduction, which are the thieves of time. Now, as Lewis found himself in the strait valley, with the eternal snows where the sky should be, and sniffed the dry air from the granite walls, he glowed with the pleasure of recollection.

The place was the same as ever. The same medley of races perambulated the streets. Sheep-skinned Central Asians and Mongolian merchants from Yarkand still displayed their wares and their cunning; Hunza tribesmen, half-clad Chitralis, wild-eyed savages from Yagistan mingled in the narrow stone streets with the civilized Persian and Turcoman from beyond the mountains. Kashmir sepoys, an untidy race, still took their ease in the sun, and soldiers of South India from the Imperial Service Troops showed their odd accoutrements and queer race mixtures. The place looked and smelled like a kind of home, and Lewis, with one eye on the gun-cases and one on the great hills, forgot his heart-sickness and had leisure for the plain joys of expectation.

"I am going to get to work at once," he said, when he had washed the dust out of his eyes and throat. "I shall go and call on the Logans this very minute, and I expect we shall see Thwaite and some of the soldiers at the club to-night." So George, much against his will, was compelled to don a fresh suit and suffer himself to be conducted to the bungalow of the British Resident.

The Sahib was from home, at Gilgit, but Madame would receive the strangers. So the two found themselves in a drawing-room aggressively English in its air, shaking hands with a small woman with kind eyes and a washed-out complexion.

Mrs. Logan was unaffectedly glad to see them. She had that trick of dominating her surroundings which English ladies seem to bear to the uttermost ends of the globe. There, in that land of snows and rock, with savage tribesmen not thirty miles away, and the British frontier-line something less than fifty, she gave them tea and talked small talk with the ease and gusto of an English country home.

"It's the most unfortunate thing in the world," she cried. "If you had only wired, Gilbert would have stayed, but as it is he has gone down to Gilgit about some polo ponies, and won't be back for two days. Things are so humdrum and easy-going up here that one loses interest in one's profession. Gilbert has nothing to do except arrange with the foreman of the coolies who are making roads, and hold stupid courts, and consult with Captain Thwaite and the garrison people. The result is that the poor man has become crazy about golf, and wastes all his spare money on polo ponies. You can have no idea what a godsend a new face is to us poor people. It is simply delightful to see you again,

Mr. Haystoun. You left us about sixteen months ago, didn't you? Did you enjoy going back?"

Lewis said yes, with an absurd sense of the humour of the question. The lady talked as if home had been merely an interlude, instead of the crisis of his life.

"And what did you do? And whom did you see? Please tell me, for I am dying for a gossip."

"I have been home in Scotland, you know. Looking after my affairs and idling. I stood for Parliament and got beaten."

"Really! How exciting! Where is your home in Scotland, Mr. Haystoun? You told me once, but I have forgotten. You know I have no end of Scotch relatives."

"It's in rather a remote part, a place called Etterick, in Glenavelin."

"Glenavelin, Glenavelin," the lady repeated. "That's where the Manorwaters live, isn't it?"

"My uncle," said Lewis.

"I had a letter from a friend who was staying there in the summer. I wonder if you ever met her. A Miss Wishart. Alice Wishart?"

Lewis strove to keep any extraordinary interest out of his eyes. This voice from another world had broken rudely in upon his new composure.

"I knew her," he said, and his tone was of such studied carelessness that Mrs. Logan looked up at him curiously.

"I hope you liked her, for her mother was a relation of my husband, and when I have been home the small Alice has always been a great friend of mine. I wonder if she has grown pretty. Gilbert and I used to bet about it on different sides. I said she would be very beautiful some day."

"She is very beautiful," said Lewis in a level voice, and George, feeling the thin ice, came to his friend's rescue. He could at least talk naturally of Miss Wishart.

"The Wisharts took the place, you know, Mrs. Logan, so we saw a lot of them. The girl was delightful, good sportswoman and all that sort of thing, and capital company. I wonder she never told us about you. She knew we were coming out here, for I told her, and she was very interested."

"Yes, it's odd, for I suppose she had read Mr. Haystoun's book, where my husband comes in a good deal. I shall tell her about seeing you in my next letter. And now tell me your plans."

Lewis's face had begun to burn in a most compromising way. Those last days in Glenavelin had risen again before the eye of his mind and old wounds were reopened. The thought that Alice was not yet wholly out of his life, that the new world was not utterly severed from the old, affected him with a miserable delight. Mrs. Logan became invested with an extraordinary interest. He pulled himself together to answer her question.

"Oh, our errand is much the same as last time. We want to get all the sport we can, and if possible to cross the mountains into Turkestan. I am rather keen on geographical work just now, and there's a bit of land up here which wants exploring."

The lady laughed. "That sounds like poor dear Mr. Gribton. I suppose you remember him? He left here in the summer, but when he lived in Bardur he had got that northern frontier-line on the brain. He was a horrible bore, for he would always work the conversation round to it sooner or later. I think it was really Mr. Gribton who made people often lose interest in these questions. They had to assume an indolent attitude in pure opposition to his fussiness."

"When will your husband be home?" Lewis asked.

"In two days, or possibly three. I am so sorry about it. I'll wire at once, but it's a slow journey, especially if he is bringing ponies. Of course you want to see him before you start. It's such a pity, but Bardur is fearfully empty of men just now. Captain Thwaite has gone off after ibex, and though I think he will be back to-morrow, I am afraid he will be too late for my dance. Oh, really, this is lucky. I had forgotten all about it. Of course you two will come. That will make two more men, and we shall be quite a respectable party. We are having a dance to-morrow night, and as the English people here are so few and uncertain in their movements we can't afford to miss a chance. You *must* come. I've got the Thwaites and the Beresfords and the Waltons, and some of the garrison people who are down on leave. Oh, and there's a man coming whom you must know. A Mr. Marker, a most delightful person. I don't think you met him before, but you must have heard my husband talk about him. He is the very man for your purpose. Gilbert says he knows the hills better than any of the Hunza tribesmen, and that he is the best sportsman he ever met. Besides, he is such an interesting person, very much a man of the world, you know, who has been everywhere and knows everybody."

Lewis congratulated himself on his luck. "I should like very much to come to the dance, and I especially want to meet Mr. Marker."

"He is half Scotch, too," said the lady. "His mother was a Kirkpatrick or some name like that, and he actually seems to talk English with a kind of Scotch accent. Of course that may be the German part of him. He is a Pomeranian count or something of the sort, and very rich. You might get him to go with you into the hills."

"I wish we could," said Lewis falsely. His curiosity was keenly excited.

"Why does he come up here such a lot?" George asked.

"I suppose because he likes to 'knock about,' as you call it. He is a tremendous traveller. He has been into Tibet and all over Turkestan and Persia. Gilbert says that he is the wonder of the age."

"Is he here just now?"

"No, I don't think so. I know he is coming to-morrow, because he wrote me about it, and promised to come to my dance. But he is a very busy man, so I don't suppose he will arrive till just before. He wrote me from Gilgit, so he may find Gilbert there and bring him up with him."

Marker, Marker. The air seemed full of the strange name. Lewis saw again Wratislaw's wrinkled face when he talked of him, and remembered his words.

"You were within an ace of meeting one of the cleverest men living, a cheerful being in whom the Foreign Office is more interested than in any one else in the world." Wratislaw had never been in the habit of talking without good authority. This Marker must be indeed a gentleman of parts.

Then conversation dwindled. Lewis, his mind torn between bitter memories and the pressing necessities of his mission, lent a stupid ear to Mrs. Logan's mild complaints, her gossip about Bardur, her eager questions about home. George manfully took his place, and by a fortunate clumsiness steered the flow of the lady's talk from Glenavelin and the Wisharts. Lewis spoke now and then, when appealed to, but he was busy thinking out his own problem. On the morrow night he should meet Marker, and his work would reveal itself. Meanwhile he was in the dark, the flimsiest adventurer on the wildest of errands. This easy, settled place, these Englishmen whose minds held fast by polo and games, these English ladies who had no thought beyond little social devices to relieve the monotony of the frontier, all seemed to make a mockery of his task. He had fondly imagined himself going to a certainty of toil and danger; to his vexation this certainty seemed to be changing into the most conventional of visits to the most normal of places. But to-morrow he should see Marker; and his hope revived at the prospect.

"It is so pleasant seeing two fresh fellow-countrymen," Mrs. Logan was saying. "Do you know, you two people look quite different from our men up here. They are all so dried up and tired out. Our complexions are all gone, and our eyes have got that weariness of the sun in them which never goes away even when we go home again. But you two look quite keen and fresh and enthusiastic. You mustn't mind compliments from an old woman, but I wish our own people looked as nice as you. You will make us all homesick."

A native servant entered, more noiseless and more dignified than any English footman, and announced another visitor. Lewis lifted his head, and saw the lady rise, smiling, to greet a tall man who had come in with the frankness of a privileged acquaintance. "How do you do, Mr. Marker?" he heard. "I am so glad to see you. We didn't dare to expect you till to-morrow. May I introduce two English friends, Mr. Haystoun and Mr. Winterham?"

And so the meeting came about in the simplest way. Lewis found himself shaking hands cordially with a man who stood upright, quite in the English fashion, and smiled genially on the two strangers. Then he took the vacant chair by Mrs. Logan, and answered the lady's questions with the ease and kindliness of one who knows and likes his fellow-creatures. He deplored Logan's absence, grew enthusiastic about the dance, and produced from a pocket certain sweetmeats, not made in Kashmir, for the two children. Then he turned to George and asked pleasantly about the journey. How did they find the roads from Gilgit? He hoped they would get good sport, and if he could be of any service, would they command him? He had heard of Lewis's former visit, and, of course, he had read his book. The most striking book of travel he had seen for long. Of course he didn't agree with certain things, but each man for his own view; and he should like to talk over the matter with Mr. Haystoun. Were they staying long? At Galetti's of course? By good luck that was also his headquarters. And so he talked pleasingly, in the style of a lady's drawing-room, while Lewis, his mind consumed with interest, sat puzzling out the discords in his face.

"Do you know, Mr. Marker, we were talking about you before you came in. I was telling Mr. Haystoun that I thought you were half Scotch. Mr. Haystoun, you know, lives in Scotland."

"Do you really? Then I am a thousand times delighted to meet you, for I have many connections with Scotland. My grandmother was a Scotswoman, and though I have never been in your beautiful land, yet I have known many of your people. And, indeed, I have heard of one of your name who was a friend of my father's--a certain Mr. Haystoun of Etterick."

"My father," said Lewis.

"Ah, I am so pleased to hear. My father and he met often in Paris, when they were attached to their different embassies. My father was in the German service."

"Your mother was Russian, was she not?" Lewis asked tactlessly, impelled by he knew not what motive.

"Ah, how did you know?" Mr. Marker smiled in reply, with the slightest raising of the eyebrows. "I have indeed the blood of many nationalities in my veins. Would that I were equally familiar with all nations, for I know less of Russia than I know of Scotland. We in Germany are their near neighbours, and love them, as you do here, something less than ourselves."

He talked English with that pleasing sincerity which seems inseparable from the speech of foreigners, who use a purer and more formal idiom than ourselves. George looked anxiously towards Lewis, with a question in his eyes, but finding his companion abstracted, he spoke himself.

"I have just arrived," said the other simply; "but it was from a different direction. I have been shooting in the hills, getting cool air into my lungs after the valleys. Why, Mrs. Logan, I have been down to Rawal Pindi since I saw you last, and have been choked with the sun. We northerners do not take kindly to glare and dust."

"But you are an old hand here, they tell me. I wish you'd show me the ropes, you know. I'm very keen, but as ignorant as a babe. What sort of rifles do they use here? I wish you'd come and look at my ironmongery." And George plunged into technicalities.

When Lewis rose to leave, following unwillingly the convention which forbids a guest to stay more than five minutes after a new visitor has arrived, Marker crossed the room with them. "If you're not engaged for to-night, Mr. Haystoun, will you do me the honour to dine with me? I am alone, and I think we might manage to find things to talk about." Lewis accepted gladly, and with one of his sweetest smiles the gentleman returned to Mrs. Logan's side.

CHAPTER XXIII

THE DINNER AT GALETTI'S

"I Have heard of you so much," Mr. Marker said, "and it was a lucky chance which brought me to Bardur to meet you." They had taken their cigars out to the verandah, and were drinking the strong Persian coffee, with a prospect before them of twinkling town lights, and a mountain line of rock and snow. Their host had put on evening clothes and wore a braided dinner-jacket which gave the faintest touch of the foreigner to his appearance. At dinner he had talked well of a score of things. He had answered George's questions on sport with the readiness of an expert; he had told a dozen good stories, and in an easy, pleasant way he had gossiped of books and places, people and politics. His knowledge struck both men as uncanny. Persons of minute significance in Parliament were not unknown to him, and he was ready with a theory or an explanation on the most recondite matters. But coffee and cigars found him a different man. He ceased to be the enthusiast, the omnivorous and versatile inquirer, and relapsed into the ordinary good fellow, who is no cleverer than his neighbours.

"We're confoundedly obliged to you," said George. "Haystoun is keen enough, but when he was out last time he seems to have been very slack about the sport."

"Sort of student of frontier peoples and politics, as the newspapers call it. I fancy that game is, what you say, 'played out' a little nowadays. It is always a good cry for alarmist newspapers to send up their circulation by, but you and I, my friend, who have mixed with serious politicians, know its value."

George nodded. He liked to be considered a person of importance, and he wanted the conversation to get back to ibex.

"I speak as of a different nation," Marker said, looking towards Lewis. "But I find the curse of modern times is this mock-seriousness. Some centuries ago men and women were serious about honour and love and religion. Nowadays we are frivolous and sceptical about these things, but we are deadly in earnest about fads. Plans to abolish war, schemes to reform criminals, and raise the condition of woman, and supply the Bada-Mawidi with tooth-picks are sure of the most respectful treatment and august patronage."

"I agree," said Lewis. "The Bada-Mawidi live there?" And he pointed to the hill line.

Marker nodded. He had used the name inadvertently as an illustration, and he had no wish to answer questions on the subject.

"A troublesome tribe, rather?" asked Lewis, noticing the momentary hesitation.

"In the past. Now they are quiet enough."

"But I understood that there was a ferment in the Pamirs. The other side threatened, you know." He had almost said "your side," but checked himself.

"Ah yes, there are rumours of a rising, but that is further west. The Bada-Mawidi are too poor to raise two swords in the whole tribe. You will come across them if you go north, and I can recommend them as excellent beaters."

"Is the north the best shooting quarter?" asked Lewis with sharp eyes. "I am just a little keen on some geographical work, and if I can join both I shall be glad. Due north is the Russian frontier?

"Due north after some scores of the most precipitous miles in the world. It is a preposterous country. I myself have been on the verge of it, and know it as well as most. The geographical importance, too, is absurdly exaggerated. It has never been mapped because there is nothing about it to map, no passes, no river, no conspicuous mountain, nothing but desolate, unvaried rock. The pass to Yarkand goes to the east, and the Afghan routes are to the west. But to the north you come to a wall, and if you have wings you may get beyond it. The Bada-Mawidi live in some of the wretched nullahs. There is sport, of course, of a kind, but not perhaps the best. I should recommend you to try the more easterly hills."

The speaker's manner was destitute of all attempt to dissuade, and yet Lewis felt in some remote way that this man was trying to dissuade him. The rock-wall, the Bada-Mawidi, whatever it was, something existed between Bardur and the Russian frontier which this pleasant gentleman did not wish him to see.

"Our plans are all vague," he said, "and of course we are glad of your advice."

"And I am glad to give it, though in many ways you know the place better than I do. Your book is the work of a very clever and observant man, if you will excuse my saying so. I was thankful to find that you were not the ordinary embryo-publicist who looks at the frontier hills from Bardur, and then rushes home and talks about invasion."

"You think there is no danger, then?"

"On the contrary, I honestly think that there is danger, but from a different direction. Britain is getting sick, and when she is sick enough, some people who are less sick will overwhelm her. My own opinion is that Russia will be the people."

"But is not that one of the old cries that you object to?" and Lewis smiled.

"It was; now it is ceasing to be a cry, and passing into a fact, or as much a fact as that erroneous form of gratuity, prophecy, can be. Look at Western Europe and you cannot disbelieve the evidence of your own eyes. In France you have anarchy, the vulgarest frivolity and the cheapest scepticism, joined with a sort of dull capacity for routine work. Germany, the very heart of it eaten out with sentiment, either the cheap military or the vague socialist brand. Spain and Italy shadows, Denmark and Sweden farces, Turkey a sinful anachronism."

"And Britain?" George asked.

"My Scotch blood gives me the right to speak my mind," said the man, laughing. "Honestly I don't find things much better in Britain. You were always famous for a dogged common sense which was never tricked with catch-words, and yet the British people seem to be growing nervous and ingenuous. The cult of abstract ideals, which has been the curse of the world since Adam, is as strong with you as elsewhere. The philosophy of 'gush' is good enough in its place, but it is the devil in politics."

"That is true enough," said Lewis solemnly. "And then you are losing grip. A belief in sentiment means a disbelief in competence and strength, and that is the last and fatalest heresy. And a belief in sentiment means a foolish scepticism towards the great things of life. There is none of the blood and bone left for honest belief. You hold your religion half-heartedly. Honest fanaticism is a thing intolerable to you. You are all mild, rational sentimentalists, and I would not give a ton of it for an ounce of good prejudice." George and Lewis laughed.

"And Russia?" they asked.

"Ah, there I have hope. You have a great people, uneducated and unspoiled. They are physically strong, and they have been trained by centuries of serfdom to discipline and hardships. Also, there is fire smouldering somewhere. You must remember that Russia is the stepdaughter of the East. The people are northern in the truest sense, but they have a little of Eastern superstition. A rational, sentimental people live in towns or market gardens, like your English country, but great lonely plains and forests somehow do not agree with that sort of creed. That slow people can still believe freshly and simply, and some day when the leader arrives they will push beyond their boundaries and sweep down on Western Europe, as their ancestors did thirteen hundred years ago. And you have no walls of Rome to resist them, and I do not think you will find a Charlemagne. Good heavens! What can your latter-day philosophic person, who weighs every action and believes only in himself, do against an unwearied people with the fear of God in their hearts? When that day comes, my masters, we shall have a new empire, the Holy Eastern Empire, and this rotten surface civilization of ours will be swept off. It is always the way. Men get into the habit of believing that they can settle everything by talk, and fancy themselves the arbiters of the world, and then suddenly the great man arrives, your Caesar or Cromwell, and clears out the talkers."

"I've heard something like that before. In fact, on occasions I have said it myself. It's a pretty idea. How long do you give this *Volkerwanderung* to get started?"

"It will not be in our time," said the man sadly. "I confess I am rather anxious for it to come off. Europe is a dull place at present, given up to Jews and old women. But I am an irreclaimable wanderer, and it is some time since I have been home. Things may be already changing."

"Scarcely," said Lewis. "And meantime where is this Slav invasion going to begin? I suppose they will start with us here, before they cross the Channel?"

"Undoubtedly. But Britain is the least sick of the crew, so she may be left in peace till the confirmed invalids are destroyed. At the best it will be a difficult work. Our countrymen, you will permit the name, my friends, have unexpected possibilities in their blood. And even this India will be a hard nut to crack. It is assumed that Russia has but to find Britain napping, buy a passage from the more northerly tribes, and sweep down on the Punjab. I need not tell you how impossible such a land invasion is. It is my opinion that when the time comes the attack will be by sea from some naval base on the Persian Gulf. It is a mere matter of time till Persia is the Tsar's territory, and then they may begin to think about invasion."

"You think the northern road impossible! I suppose you ought to know."

"I do, and I have some reason for my opinion. I know Afghanistan and Chitral as few Europeans know it."

"But what about Bardur, and this Kashmir frontier? I can understand the difficulties of the Khyber, but this Kashmir road looks promising."

Marker laughed a great, good-humoured, tolerant, incredulous laugh. "My dear sir, that's the most utter nonsense. How are you to bring an army over a rock wall which a chamois hunter could scarcely climb? An invading army is not a collection of winged fowl. I grant you Bardur is a good starting-point if it were once reached. But you might as well think of a Chinese as of a Russian invasion from the north. It would be a good deal more possible, for there is a road to Yarkand, and respectable passes to the north-east. But here we are shut off from the Oxus by as difficult a barrier as the Elburz. Go up and see. There is some shooting to be had, and you will see for yourself the sort of country between here and Taghati."

"But people come over here sometimes."

"Yes, from the south, or by Afghanistan."

"Not always. What about the Korabaut Pass into Chitral? Ianoff and the Cossacks came through it."

"That's true," said the man, as if in deep thought. "I had forgotten, but the band was small and the thing was a real adventure."

"And then you have Gromchevtsky. He brought his people right down through the Pamirs."

For a second the man's laughing ease deserted him. He leaned his head forward and peered keenly into Lewis's face. Then, as if to cover his discomposure, he fell into the extreme of bluff amusement. The exaggeration was plain to both his hearers.

"Oh yes, there was poor old Gromchevtsky. But then you know he was what you call 'daft,' and one never knew how much to believe. He had hatred of the English on the brain, and he went about the northern valleys making all sorts of wild promises on the part of the Tsar. A great Russian army was soon to come down from the hills and restore the valleys to their former owners. And then, after he had talked all this nonsense, and actually managed to create some small excitement among the tribesmen, the good fellow disappeared. No man knows where he went. The odd thing is that I believe he has never been heard of again in Russia to this day. Of course his mission, as he loved to call it, was perfectly unauthorized, and the man himself was a creature of farce. He probably came either by the Khyber or the Korabaut Pass, possibly even by the ordinary caravan-route from Yarkand, but felt it necessary for his mission's sake to pretend he had found some way through the rock barrier. I am afraid I cannot allow him to be taken seriously."

Lewis yawned and reached out his hand for the cigars. "In any case it is merely a question of speculative interest. We shall not fall just yet, though you think so badly of us."

"You will not fall just yet," said Marker slowly, "but that is not your fault. You British have sold your souls for something less than the conventional mess of pottage. You are ruled in the first place by money-bags, and the faddists whom they support to blind your eyes. If I were a young man in your country with my future to make, do you know what I would do? I would slave in the Stock Exchange. I would spend my days and nights in the pursuit of fortune, and, by heaven, I would get it. Then I would rule the market and break, crush, quietly and ruthlessly, the whole gang of Jew speculators and vulgarians who would corrupt a great country. Money is power with you, and I should attain it, and use it to crush the leeches who suck our blood."

"Good man," said George, laughing. "That's my way of thinking. Never heard it better put."

"I have felt the same," said Lewis. "When I read of 'rings' and 'corners' and 'trusts' and the misery and vulgarity of it all, I have often wished to have a try myself, and see whether average brains and clean blood could not beat these fellows on their own ground."

"Then why did you not?" asked Marker. "You were rich enough to make a proper beginning."

"I expect I was too slack. I wanted to try the thing, but there was so much that was repulsive that I never quite got the length of trying. Besides, I have a bad habit of seeing both sides of a question. The ordinary arguments seemed to me weak, and it was too much fag to work out an attitude for oneself."

Marker looked sharply at Lewis, and George for a moment saw and contrasted the two faces. Lewis's keen, kindly, humorous, cultured, with strong lines ending weakly, a face over-bred, brave and finical; the other's sharp, eager, with the hungry wolf-like air of ambition, every line graven in steel, and the whole transfused, as it were, by the fire of the eyes into the living presentment of human vigour.

It was the eternal contrast of qualities, and for a moment in George's mind there rose a delight that two such goodly pieces of manhood should have found a meeting-ground.

"I think, you know, that we are not quite so bad as you make out," said Lewis quietly. "To an outsider we must appear on the brink of incapacity, but then it is not the first time we have produced that impression. You will still find men who in all their spiritual sickness have kept something of that restless, hard-bitten northern energy, and that fierce hunger for righteousness, which is hard to fight with. Scores of people, who can see no truth in the world and are sick with doubt and introspection and all the latter-day devils, have yet something of pride and honour in their souls which will make them show well at the last. If we are going to fall our end will not be quite inglorious."

Marker laughed and rose. "I am afraid I must leave you now. I have to see my servant, for I am off to-morrow. This has been a delightful meeting. I propose that we drink to its speedy repetition."

They drank, clinking glasses in continental fashion, and the host shook hands and departed.

"Good chap," was George's comment. "Put us up to a wrinkle or two, and seemed pretty sound in his politics. I wish I could get him to come and stop with me at home. Do you think we shall run across him again?"

Lewis was looking at the fast vanishing lights of the town. "I should think it highly probable," he said.

CHAPTER XXIV

THE TACTICS OF A CHIEF

There is another quarter in Bardur besides the English one. Down by the stream side there are narrow streets built on the scarp of the rock, hovels with deep rock cellars, and a wonderful amount of cubic space beneath the brushwood thatch. There the trader from Yarkand who has contraband wares to dispose of may hold a safe market. And if you were to go at nightfall into this quarter, where the foot of the Kashmir policeman rarely penetrates, you might find shaggy tribesmen who have been all their lives outlaws, walking unmolested to visit their friends, and certain Jewish gentlemen, members of the great family who have conquered the world, engaged in the pursuit of their unlawful calling.

Marker speedily left the broader streets of the European quarter, and plunged down a steep alley which led to the stream. Half way down there was a lane to the left in the line of hovels, and, after stopping a moment to consider, he entered this. It was narrow and dark, but smelt cleanly enough of the dry granite sand. There were little dark apertures in the huts, which might have been either doors or windows, and at one of these he stopped, lit a match, and examined it closely. The result was satisfactory; for the man, who had hitherto been crouching, straightened himself up and knocked. The door opened instantaneously, and he bowed his tall head to enter a narrow passage. This brought him into a miniature courtyard, about thirty feet across, above which gleamed a patch of violet sky, sown with stars. Below a door on the right a light shone, and this he pushed open, and entered a little room.

The place was richly furnished, with low couches and Persian tables, and on the floor a bright matting. The short, square-set man sitting smoking on the divan we have already met at a certain village in the mountains. Fazir Khan, descendant of Abraham, and father and chief of the Bada-Mawidi, has a nervous eye and an uneasy face to-night, for it is a hard thing for a mountaineer, an inhabitant of great spaces, to sit with composure in a trap-like room in the citadel of a foe who has many acts of rape and murder to avenge on his body. To do Fazir Khan justice he strove to conceal his restlessness under the usual impassive calm of his race. He turned his head slightly as Marker entered, nodded gravely over the bowl of his pipe, and pointed to the seat at the far end of the divan.

"It is a dark night," he said. "I heard you stumbling on the causeway before you entered. And I have many miles to cover before dawn."

Marker nodded. "Then you must make haste, my friend. You must be in the hills by daybreak, for I have some errands I want you to do for me. I have to-night been dining with two strangers, who have come up from the south."

The chief's eyes sparkled. "Do they suspect?"

"Nothing in particular, everything in general. They are English. One was here before and got far up into your mountains. He wrote a clever book when he returned, which made people think. They say their errand is sport, and it may be. On the other hand I have a doubt. One has not the air of the common sportsman. He thinks too much, and his eyes have a haggard look. It is possible that they are in their Government's services and have come to reconnoitre."

"Then we are lost," said Fazir Khan sourly. "It was always a fool's plan, at the mercy of any wandering Englishman."

"Not so," said Marker. "Nothing is lost, and nothing will be lost. But I fear these two men. They do not bluster and talk at random like the others. They are so very quiet that they may mean danger."

"They must remain here," said the chief. "Give me the word, and I will send one of my men to hough their horses and, if need be, cripple themselves."

Marker laughed. "You are an honest fool, Fazir Khan. That sort of thing is past now. We live in the wrong times and places for it. We cannot keep them here, but we must send them on a goose-chase. Do you understand?"

"I understand nothing. I am a simple man and my ways are simple, and not as yours."

"Then attend to my words, my friend. Our expedition must be changed and made two days sooner. That will give these two Englishmen three days only to checkmate it. Besides, they are ignorant, and to-morrow is lost to them, for they go to a ball at the Logan woman's. Still, I fear them with two days to work in. If they go north, they are clever and suspicious, and they may see or fancy enough to wreck our plans. They may have the way barred, and we know how little would bar the way."

"Ten resolute men," said the chief. "Nay, I myself, with my two sons, would hold a force at bay there."

"If that is true, how much need is there to be wary beforehand! Since we cannot prevent these men from meddling, we can give them rope to meddle in small matters. Let us assume that they have been sent out by their Government. They are the common make of Englishmen, worshipping a god which they call their honour. They will do their duty if they can find it out. Now there is but one plan, to create a duty for them which will take them out of the way."

The chief was listening with half-closed eyes. He saw new trouble for himself and was not cheerful.

"Do you know how many men Holm has with him at the Forza camp?"

"A score and a half. Some of my people passed that way yesterday, when the soldiers were parading."

"And there are two more camps?"

"There are two beyond the Nazri Pass, on the fringe of the Doorab hills. We call the places Khautmi-sa and Khautmi-bana, but the English have their own names for them."

Marker nodded.

"I know the places. They are Gurkha camps. The officers are called Mitchinson and St. John. They will give us little trouble. But the Forza garrison is too near the pass for safety, and yet far enough away for my plans." And for a moment the man's eyes were abstracted, as if in deep thought.

"I have another thing to tell of the Forza camp," the chief interrupted. "The captain, the man whom they call Holm, is sick, so sick that he cannot remain there. He went out shooting and came too near to dangerous places, so a bullet of one of my people's guns found his leg. He will be coming to Bardur to-morrow. Is it your wish that he be prevented?

"Let him come," said Marker. "He will suit my purpose. Now I will tell you your task, Fazir Khan, for it is time that you took the road. You will take a hundred of the Bada-Mawidi and put them in the rocks round the Forza camp. Let them fire a few shots but do no great damage, lest this man Holm dare not leave. If I know the man at all, he will only hurry the quicker when he hears word of trouble, for he has no stomach for danger, if he can get out of it creditably. So he will come down here to-morrow with a tale of the Bada-Mawidi in arms, and find no men in the place to speak of, except these two strangers. I will have already warned them of this intended rising, and if, as I believe, they serve the Government, they will let no grass grow below their feet till they get to Forza. Then on the day after let your tribesmen attack the place, not so as to take it, but so as to make a good show of fight and keep the garrison employed. This will keep these young men quiet; they will think that all rumours they may have heard culminate in this rising of yours, and they will be content, and satisfied that they have done their duty. Then, the day after, while they are idling at Forza, we will slip through the passes, and after that there will be no need for ruses."

The chief rose and pulled himself up to his full height. "After that," he said, "there will be work for men. God! We shall harry the valleys as our forefathers harried them, and we shall suck the juicy plains dry. You will give us a free hand, my lord?"

"Your hand shall be free enough," said Marker.

"But see that every word of my bidding is done. We fail utterly unless all is secret and swift. It is the lion attacking the village. If he crosses the trap gate safely he may ravage at his pleasure, but there is first the trap to cross. And now it is your time to leave."

The mountaineer tightened his girdle, and exchanged his slippers for deer-hide boots. He bowed gravely to the other and slipped out into the darkness of the court. Marker drew forth some plans and writing materials from his great-coat pocket and spread them before him on the table. It was a thing he had done a hundred times within the last week, and as he made his calculations again and traced his route anew, his action showed the tinge of nervousness to which the strongest natures at times must yield. Then he wrote a letter, and yawning deeply, he shut up the place and returned to Galetti's.

CHAPTER XXV

MRS. LOGAN'S BALL

When Lewis had finished breakfast next morning, and was sitting idly on the verandah watching the busy life of the bazaar at his feet, a letter was brought him by a hotel servant. "It was left for you by Marker Sahib, when he went away this morning. He sent his compliments to the sahibs and regretted that he had to leave too early to speak with them, but he left this note." Lewis broke the envelope and read:

DEAR MR. HAYSTOUN,

When I was thinking over our conversation last night, chance put a piece of information in my way which you may think fit to use. You know that I am more intimate than most people with the hill tribes. Well, let this be the guarantee of my news, but do not ask how I got it, for I cannot betray friends. Some of these, the Bada-Mawidi to wit, are meditating mischief. The Forza camp, which I think you have visited--a place some twenty miles off--is too near those villages to be safe. So to-morrow at latest they have planned to make a general attack upon it, and, unless the garrison were prepared, I should fear for the result, for they are the most cunning scoundrels in the world. What puzzles me is how they have ever screwed up the courage for such a move, for lately they were very much in fear of the Government. It appears as if they looked for backing from over the frontier. You will say that this proves your theory; but to me it merely seems as if some maniac of the Gromchevtsky type had got among them. In any case I wish something could be done. My duties take me away at once, and in a very different direction, but perhaps you could find some means of putting the camp on their guard. I should be sorry to hear of a tragedy; also I should be sorry to see the Bada-Mawidi get into trouble. They are foolish blackguards, but amusing.

Yours most sincerely,

ARTHUR MARKER.

Lewis read the strange letter several times through, then passed it to George. George read it with difficulty, not being accustomed to a flowing frontier hand. "Jolly decent of him, I call it," was his remark.

"I would give a lot to know what to make of it. The man is playing some game, but what the deuce it is I can't fathom."

"I suppose we had better get up to that Forza place as soon as we can."

"I think not," said Lewis.

"The man's honest, surely?

"But he is also clever. Remember who he is. He may wish to get us out of the way. I don't suppose that he can possibly fear us, but he may want the coast clear from suspicious spectators. Besides, I don't see the good of Forza. It is not the part of the hills I want to explore.

There can be no frontier danger there, and at the worst there can be nothing more than a little tribal disturbance. Now what on earth would Russia gain by moving the tribes there, except as a blind?"

"Still, you know, the man admits all that in his letter. And if the people up there are going to be in trouble we ought to go and give them notice."

"I'll take an hour to think over it, and then I'll go and see Thwaite. He was to be back this morning."

Lewis spread the letter before him. It was a simple, friendly note, giving him a chance of doing a good turn to friends. His clear course was to lay it before Thwaite and shift the responsibility for action to his shoulders. But he felt all the while that this letter had a personal application which he could not conceal. It would have been as easy for Marker to send the note to Thwaite, whom he had long known. But he had chosen to warn him privately. It might be a ruse, but he had no glimpse of the meaning. Or, again, it might be a piece of pure friendliness, a chance of unofficial adventure given by one wanderer to another. He puzzled it out, lamenting that he was so deep in the dark, and cursing his indecision. Another man would have made up his mind long ago; it was a ruse, therefore let it be neglected and remain in Bardur with open eyes; it was good faith and a good chance, therefore let him go at once. But to Lewis the possibilities seemed endless, and he could find no solution save the old one of the waverer, to wait for further light.

He found Thwaite at breakfast, just returned from his travels.

"Hullo, Haystoun. I heard you were here. Awfully glad to see you. Sit down, won't you, and have some breakfast." The officer was a long man, with a thin, long face, a reddish moustache, and small, blue eyes.

"I came to ask you questions, if you don't mind. I have the regular globe-trotter's trick of wanting information. What's the Forza camp like? Do you think that the Bada-Mawidi, supposing they stir again, would be likely to attack it?"

"Not a bit of it. That was the sort of thing that Gribton was always croaking about. Why, man, the Bada-Mawidi haven't a kick in them. Besides, they are very nearly twenty miles off and the garrison's a very fit lot. They're all right. Trust them to look after themselves." "But I have been hearing stories of Bada-Mawidi risings which are to come off soon."

"Oh, you'll always hear stories of that sort. All the old women in the neighbourhood purvey them."

"Who are in charge at Forza?"

"Holm and Andover. Don't care much for Holm, but Andy is a good chap. But what's this new interest of yours? Are you going up there?

"I'm out here to shoot and explore, you know, so Forza comes into my beat. Thanks very much. See you to-night, I suppose."

Lewis went away dispirited and out of temper. He had been pitchforked among easy-going people, when all the while mysterious things, dangerous things, seemed to hang in the air. He had not the material for even the first stages of comprehension. No one suspected, every one was satisfied; and at the same time came those broken hints of other things. He felt choked and muffled, wrapped in the cotton-wool of this easy life; and all the afternoon he chafed at his own impotence and the world's stupidity.

When the two travellers presented themselves at the Logans' house that evening, they were immediately seized upon by the hostess and compelled, to their amusement, to do her bidding. They were her discoveries, her new young men, and as such, they had their responsibilities. George, who liked dancing, obeyed meekly; but Lewis, being out of temper and seeing before him an endless succession of wearisome partners, soon broke loose, and accompanied Thwaite to the verandah for a cigar.

The man was ill at ease, and the sight of young faces and the sound of laughter vexed him with a sense of his eccentricity. He could never, like George, take the world as he found it. At home he was the slave of his own incapacity; now he was the slave of memories. He had come out on an errand, with a chance to recover his lost self-respect, and lo! he was as far as ever from attainment. His lost capacity for action was not to be found here, in the midst of this petty diplomacy and inglorious ease.

From the verandah a broad belt of lawn ran down to the edge of the north road. It lay shining in the moonlight like a field of snow with the highway a dark ribbon beyond it. Thwaite and Lewis walked down to the gate talking casually, and at the gate they stopped and looked down on the town. It lay a little to the left, the fort rising black before it, and the road ending in a patch of shade which was the old town gate. The night was very still, cool airs blew noiselessly from the hills, and a jackal barked hoarsely in some far-off thicket.

The men hung listlessly on the gate, drinking in the cool air and watching the blue cigar smoke wreathe and fade. Suddenly down the road there came the sound of wheels.

"That's a tonga," said Thwaite. "Wonder who it is."

"Do tongas travel this road?" Lewis asked.

"Oh yes, they go ten miles up to the foot of the rocks. We use them for sending up odds and ends to the garrisons. After that coolies are the only conveyance. Gad, I believe this thing is going to stop."

The thing in question, which was driven by a sepoy in bright yellow pyjamas, stopped at the Logans' gate. A peevish voice was heard giving directions from within.

"It sounds like Holm," said Thwaite, walking up to it, "and upon my soul it is Holm. What on earth are you doing here, my dear fellow?"

"Is that you, Thwaite?" said the voice. "I wish you'd help me out. I want Logan to give me a bed for the night. I'm infernally ill."

Lewis looked within and saw a pale face and bloodshot eyes which did not belie the words.

"What is it?" said Thwaite. "Fever or anything smashed?"

"I've got a bullet in my leg which has got to be cut out. Got it two days ago when I was out shooting. Some natives up in the rocks did it, I fancy. Lord, how it hurts." And the unhappy man groaned as he tried to move.

"That's bad," said Thwaite sympathetically. "The Logans have got a dance on, but we'll look after you all right. How did you leave things in Forza?"

"Bad. I oughtn't to be here, but Andy insisted. He said I would only get worse and crock entirely. Things look a bit wild up there just now. There has been a confounded lot of rifle-stealing, and the Bada-Mawidi are troublesome. However, I hope it's only their fun."

"I hope so," said Thwaite. "You know Haystoun, don't you?"

"Glad to meet you," said the man. "Heard of you. Coming up our way? I hope you will after I get this beastly leg of mine better."

"Thwaite will tell you I have been cross-examining him about your place. I wanted badly to ask you about it, for I got a letter this morning from a man called Marker with some news for you."

"What did he say?" asked Holm sharply.

"He said that he had heard privately that the Bada-Mawidi were planning an attack on you to-morrow or the day after."

"The deuce they are," said Holm peevishly, and Thwaite's face lengthened.

"And he told me to find some way of letting you know."

"Then why didn't you tell me earlier?" said Thwaite. "Marker should know if anybody does. We should have kept Holm up there. Now it's almost too late. Oh, this is the devil!"

Lewis held his peace. He had forgotten the solidity of Marker's reputation.

"What's the chances of the place?" Thwaite was asking. "I know your numbers and all that, but are they anything like prepared?"

"I don't know," said Holm miserably. "They might get on all right, but everybody is pretty slack just now. Andy has a touch of fever, and some of the men may get leave for shooting. I must get back at once."

"You can't. Why, man, you couldn't get half way. And what's more, I can't go. This place wants all the looking after it can get. A row in the hills means a very good possibility of a row in Bardur, and that is too dangerous a game. And besides myself there is scarcely a man in the place who counts. Logan has gone to Gilgit, and there's nobody left but boys."

"If you don't mind I should like to go," said Lewis shamefacedly.

"You," they cried. "Do you know the road?"

"I've been there before, and I remember it more or less. Besides, it is really my show this time. I got the warning, and I want the credit." And he smiled.

"The road's bound to be risky," said Thwaite thoughtfully. "I don't feel inclined to let you run your neck into danger like this."

Lewis was busy turning over the problem in his mind. The presence of the man Holm seemed the one link of proof he needed. He had his word that there were signs of trouble in the place, and that the Bada-Mawidi were ill at ease. Whatever game Marker was playing, on this matter he seemed to have spoken in good faith. Here was a clear piece of work for him. And even if it was fruitless it would bring him nearer to the frontier; his expedition to the north would be begun.

"Let me go," he said. "I came out here to explore the hills and I take all risks on my own head. I can give them Marker's message as well as anybody else."

Thwaite looked at Holm. "I don't see why he shouldn't. You're a wreck, and I can't leave my own place."

"Tell Andy you saw me," cried Holm. "He'll be anxious. And tell him to mind the north gate. If the fools knew how to use dynamite they might have it down at once. If they attack it can't last long, but then they can't last long either, for they are hard up for arms, and unless they have changed since last week they have no ammunition to speak of."

"Marker said it looked as if they were being put up to the job from over the frontier." "Gad, then it's my turn to look out," said Thwaite. "If it's the gentlemen from over the frontier they won't stop at Forza. Lord, I hate this border business, it's so hideously in the dark. But I think that's all rot. Any tribal row here is sure to be set down to Russian influence. We don't understand the joint possession of an artificial frontier," he added, with an air of quoting from some book.

"Did you get that from Marker?" Holm asked crossly. "He once said the same thing to me." His temper had suffered badly among the hills.

"We'd better get you to bed, my dear fellow," said Thwaite, looking down at him. "You look remarkably cheap. Would you mind going in and trying to find Mrs. Logan, Haystoun? I'll carry this chap in. Stop a minute, though. Perhaps he's got something to say to you."

"Mind the north gate . . . tell Andy I'm all right and make him look after himself . . . he's overworking . . . if you want to send a message to the other people you'd better send by Nazri . . . if the Badas mean business they'll shut up the road you go by. That's all. Good luck and thanks very much."

Lewis found Mrs. Logan making a final inspection of the supper-room. She ran to the garden, to find the invalid Holm in Thwaite's arms at the steps of the verandah. The sick warrior pulled off an imaginary cap and smiled feebly. "Oh, Mr. Holm, I'm so sorry. Of course we can have you. I'll put you in the other end of the house where you won't be so much troubled with the noise. You must have had a dreadful journey." And so forth, with the easy condolences of a kind woman.

When Thwaite had laid down his burden, he turned to Lewis.

"I wish we had another man, Haystoun. What about your friend Winterham? One's enough to do your work, but if the thing turns out to be serious, there ought to be some means of sending word. Andover will want you to stay, for they are short-handed enough."

"I'll get Winterham to go and wait for me somewhere. If I don't turn up by a certain time, he can come and look for me."

"That will do," said Thwaite, "though it's a stale job for him. Well, good-bye and good luck to you. I expect there won't be much trouble, but I wish you had told us in the morning."

Lewis turned to go and find George. "What a chance I had almost missed," was the word in his heart. The errand might be futile, the message a blind, but it was at least movement, action, a possibility.

CHAPTER XXVI

FRIEND TO FRIEND

He found George sitting down in the verandah after waltzing. His partner was a sister of Logan's, a dark girl whose husband was Resident somewhere in Lower Kashmir. The lady gave her hand to Lewis and he took the vacant seat on the other side.

He apologized for carrying off her companion, escorted her back to the ballroom, and then returned to satisfy the amazed George.

"I want to talk to you. Excuse my rudeness, but I have explained to Mrs. Tracy. I have a good many things I want to say to you."

"Where on earth have you been all night, Lewis? I call it confoundedly mean to go off and leave me to do all the heavy work. I've never been so busy in my life. Lots of girls and far too few men. This is the first breathing space I've had. What is it that you want?"

"I am going off this very moment up into the hills. That letter Marker sent me this morning has been confirmed. Holm, who commands up at the Forza fort, has just come down very sick, and he says that the Bada-Mawidi are looking ugly, and that we should take Marker's word. He wanted to go back himself but he is too ill, and Thwaite can't leave here, so I am going. I don't expect there will be much risk, but in case the rising should be serious I want you to do me a favour."

"I suppose I can't come with you," said George ruefully. "I know I promised to let you go your own way before we came out, but I wish you would let me stick by you. What do you want me to do?"

"Nothing desperate," said Lewis, laughing. "You can stay on here and dance till sunrise if you like. But to-morrow I want you to come up to a certain place at the foot of the hills which I will tell you about, and wait there. It's about half distance between Forza and the two Khautmi forts. If the rising turns out to be a simple affair I'll join you there to-morrow night and we can start our shooting. But if I don't, I want you to go up to the Khautmi forts and rouse St. John and Mitchinson and get them to send to Forza. Do you see?"

Lewis had taken out a pencil and began to sketch a rough plan on George's shirt cuff. "This will give you an idea of the place. You can look up a bigger map in the hotel, and Thwaite or any one will give you directions about the road. There's Forza, and there are the Khautmis about twenty miles west. Half-way between the two is that long Nazri valley, and at the top is a tableland strewn with boulders where you shoot mountain sheep. I've been there, and the road between Khautmi and Forza passes over it. I expect it is a very bad road, but apparently you can get a little Kashmir pony to travel it. To the north of that plateau there is said to be nothing but rock and snow for twenty miles to the frontier. That may be so, but if this thing turns out all right we'll look into the matter. Anyway, you have got to pitch your tent to-morrow on that tableland just above the head of the Nazri gully. With luck I should be able to get to you some time in the afternoon. If I don't turn up, you go off to Khautmi next morning at daybreak and give them my message. If I can't come myself I'll find a way to send word; but if you don't hear from me it will be fairly serious, for it will mean that the rising is a formidable thing after all. And that, of course, will mean trouble for everybody all round. In that case you'd better do what St. John and Mitchinson tell you. You're sure to be wanted."

George's face cleared. "That sounds rather sport. I'd better bring up the servants. They might turn out useful. And I suppose I'll bring a couple of rifles for you, in case it's all a fraud and we want to go shooting. I thought the place was going to be stale, but it promises pretty well now." And he studied the plan on his shirt cuff. Then an idea came to him.

"Suppose you find no rising. That will mean that Marker's letter was a blind of some sort. He wanted to get you out of the way or something. What will you do then? Come back here?"

"N--o," said Lewis hesitatingly. "I think Thwaite is good enough, and I should be no manner of use. You and I will wait up there in the hills on the off-chance of picking up some news. I swear I won't come back here to hang about and try and discover things. It's enough to drive a man crazy."

"It is rather a ghastly place. Wonder how the Logans thrive here. Odd mixture this. Strauss and hill tribes not twenty miles apart."

Lewis laughed. "I think I prefer the hill tribes. I am not in the humour for Strauss just now. I shall have to be off in an hour, so I am going to change. See you to-morrow, old man."

George retired to the ballroom, where he had to endure the reproaches of Mrs. Logan. He was an abstracted and silent partner, and in the intervals of dancing he studied his cuff. Miss A talked to him of polo, and Miss B of home; Miss C discovered that they had common friends, and Miss D that she had known his sister. Miss E, who was more observant, saw the cause of his distraction and asked, "What queer hieroglyphics have you got on your cuff, Mr. Winterham?"

George looked down in a bewildered way at his sleeve. "Where on earth have I been?" he asked in wonder. "That's the worst of being an absent-minded fellow. I've been scribbling on my cuff with my programme pencil."

Soon he escaped, and made his way down to the garden gate, where Thwaite was standing smoking. A *sais* held a saddled pony by the road-side. Lewis, in rough shooting clothes, was preparing to mount. From indoors came the jigging of a waltz tune and the sound of laughter, while far in the north the cliffs of the pass framed a dark blue cleft where the stars shone. George drew in great draughts of the cool, fresh air. "I wish I was coming with you," he said wistfully.

"You'll be in time enough to-morrow," said Lewis. "I wish you'd give him all the information you can about the place, Thwaite. He's an ignorant beggar. See that he remembers to bring food and matches. The guns are the only things I can promise he won't forget."

Then he rode off, the little beast bucking excitedly at the patches of moonlight, and the two men walked back to the house.

"Hope he comes back all right," said Thwaite.
"He's too good a man to throw away."

CHAPTER XXVII

THE ROAD TO FORZA

The road ran in a straight line through the valley of dry rocks, a dull, modern road, engineered and macadamized up to the edge of the hills. The click of hoofs raised echoes in the silence, for in all the great valley, in the chain of pools in the channel, the acres of sun-dried stone, the granite rocks, the tangle of mountain scrub, there seemed no life of bird or beast. It was a strange, deathly stillness, and overhead the purple sky, sown with a million globes of light, seemed so near and imminent that the glen for the moment was but a vast jewel-lit cavern, and the sky a fretted roof which spanned the mountains.

For the first time Lewis felt the East. Hitherto he had been unable to see anything in his errand but its futility. A stupider man, with a sharp, practical brain, would have taken himself seriously and come to Bardur with an intent and satisfied mind. He would have assumed the air of a diplomatist, have felt the dignity of his mission, and in success and failure have borne himself with self-confidence. But to Lewis the business which loomed serious in England, at Bardur took on the colour of comedy. He felt his impotence, he was touched insensibly by the easy content of the place. Frontier difficulties seemed matters for romance and comic opera; and Bardur resolved itself into an English suburb, all tea-parties and tennis. But at times an austere conscience jogged him to remembrance, and in one such fitful craving for action and enterprise he had found this errand. Now at last, astride the little Kashmir pony, with his face to the polestar and the hills, he felt the mystery of a strange world, and his work assumed a tinge of the adventurer. This was new, he told himself; this was romance. He had his eyes turned to a new land, and the smell of dry mountain sand and scrub, and the vault-like, imperial sky were the earnest of his inheritance. This was the East, the gorgeous, the impenetrable. Before him were the hill deserts, and then the great, warm plains, and the wide rivers, and then on and on to the cold north, the steppes, the icy streams, the untrodden forests. To the west and beyond the mountains were holy mosques, "shady cities of palm trees," great walled towns to which north and west and south brought their merchandise. And to the east were latitudes more wonderful, the uplands of the world, the impassable borders of the oldest of human cultures. Names rang in his head like tunes--Khiva, Bokhara, Samarkand, the goal of many boyish dreams born of clandestine suppers and the Arabian Nights. It was an old fierce world he was on the brink of, and the nervous frontier civilization fell a thousand miles behind him.

The white road turned to the right with the valley, and the hills crept down to the distance of a gun-shot. The mounting tiers of stone and brawling water caught the moonlight in waves, and now he was in a cold pit of shadow and now in a patch of radiant moonshine. It was a world of fantasy, a rousing world of wintry hill winds and sudden gleams of summer. His spirits rose high, and he forgot all else in plain enjoyment. Now at last he had found life, rich, wild, girt with marvels. He was beginning to whistle some air when his pony shied violently and fell back, and at the same moment a pistol-shot cracked out of a patch of thorn.

He turned the beast and rode straight at the thicket, which was a very little one. The ball had wandered somewhere into the void, and no harm was done, but he was curious about its owner. Up on the hillside he seemed to see a dark figure scrambling among the cliffs in the fretted moonlight.

It is unpleasant to be shot at in the dark from the wayside, but at the moment the thing pleased this strange young man. It seemed a token that at last he was getting to work. He found a rope stretched taut across the road, which accounted for the pony's stumble. Laughing heartily, he cut it with his knife, and continued, cheerful as before, but somewhat less fantastic. Now he kept a sharp eye on all wayside patches.

At the head of the valley the waters of the stream forked into two torrents, one flowing from the east in an open glen up which ran the road to Yarkand, the other descending from the northern hills in a wild gully. At the foot stood a little hut with an apology for stabling, where an old and dirty gentleman of the Hunza race pursued his calling till such time as he should attract the notice of his friends up in the hills and go to paradise with a slit throat.

Lewis roused the man with a violent knocking at the door. The old ruffian appeared with a sputtering lamp which might have belonged to a cave man, and a head of matted grey hair which suggested the same origin. He was old and suspicious, but at Lewis's bidding he hobbled forth and pointed out the stabling.

"The pony is to stay here till it is called for. Do you hear? And if Holm Sahib returns and finds that it is not fed he will pay you nothing. So good night, father. Sound sleep and a good conscience."

He turned to the twisting hill road which ran up from the light into the gloom of the cleft with all the vigour of an old mountaineer who has been long forced to dwell among lowlands. Once a man acquires the art of hill walking he will always find flat country something of a burden, and the mere ascent of a slope will have a tonic's power. The path was good, but perilous at the best, and the proximity of yawning precipices gave a zest to the travel. The road would fringe a pit of shade, black but for the gleam of mica and the scattered foam of the stream. It was no longer a silent world. Hawks screamed at times from the cliffs, and a multitude of bats and owls flickered in the depths. A continuous falling of waters, an infinite sighing of night winds, the swaying and tossing which is always heard in the midmost mountain solitudes, the crumbling of hill gravel and the bleat of a goat on some hill-side, all made a cheerful accompaniment to the scraping of his boots on the rocky road.

He remembered the way as if he had travelled it yesterday. Soon the gorge would narrow and he would be almost at the water's edge. Then the path turned to the right and wound into the heart of a side nullah, which at length brought it out on a little plateau of rocks. There the road climbed a long ridge till at last it reached the great plateau, where Forza, set on a small hilltop, watched thirty miles of primeval desert. The air was growing chilly, for the road climbed steeply and already it was many thousand feet above the sea. The curious salt smell which comes from snow and rock was beginning to greet his nostrils. The blood flowed more freely in his veins, and insensibly he squared his shoulders to drink in the cold hill air. It was of the mountains and yet strangely foreign, an air with something woody and alpine in the heart of it, an air born of scrub and snow-clad rock, and not of his own free spaces of heather. But it was hill-born, and this contented him; it was night-born, and it refreshed him. In a little the road turned down to the stream side, and he was on the edge of a long dark pool.

The river, which made a poor show in the broad channel at Bardur, was now, in this straitened place, a full lipping torrent of clear, green water. Lewis bathed his flushed face and drank, and it was as cold as snow. It stung his face to burning, and as he walked the heartsome glow of great physical content began to rise in his heart. He felt fit and ready for any work. Life was quick in his sinews, his brain was a weathercock, his strength was tireless. At last he had found a man's life. He had never had a chance before. Life had been too easy and sheltered; he had been coddled like a child; he had never roughed it except for his own pleasure. Now he was outside this backbone of the world with a task before him, and only his wits for his servant. Eton and Oxford, Eton and Oxford--so it had been for generations--an education sufficient to damn a race. Stocks was right, and he had all along been wrong; but now he was in a fair way to taste the world's iron and salt, and he exulted at the prospect.

It was hard walking in the nullah. In and out of great crevices the road wound itself, on the brink of stupendous waterfalls, or in the heart of a brushwood tangle. Soon a clear vault of sky replaced the out-jutting crags, and he came out on a little plateau where a very cold wind was blowing. The smell of snow was in the air, a raw smell like salt when carried on a north wind over miles of granite crags. But on the little tableland the moon was shining clearly. It was green with small cloud-berries and dwarf juniper, and the rooty fragrance was for all the world like an English bolt or a Highland pasture. Lewis flung himself prone and buried his face among the small green leaves. Then, still on the ground, he scanned the endless yellow distance. Mountains, serrated and cleft as in some giant's play, rose on every hand, while through the hollows gleamed the farther snow-peaks. This little bare plateau must be naked to any eye on any hill-side, and at the thought he got to his feet and advanced.

At first sight the place had looked not a mile long, but before he got to the farther slope he found that it was nearer two. The mountain air had given him extraordinary lightness, and he ran the distance, finding the hard, sandy soil like a track under his feet. The slope, when he had reached it, proved to be abrupt and boulder-strewn, and the path had an ugly trick of avoiding steepness by skirting horrible precipices. Luckily the moon was bright, and the man was an old mountaineer; otherwise he might have found a grave in the crevices which seamed the hill.

He had not gone far when he began to realize that he was not the only occupant of the mountain side. A whistle which was not a bird's seemed to catch his ear at times, and once, as he shrank back into the lee of a boulder, there was the sound of naked feet on the road before him. This was news indeed, and he crept very cautiously up the rugged path. Once, when in shelter, he looked out, and for a second, in a patch of moonlight, he saw a man with the loose breeches and tightened girdle of the hillmen. He was running swiftly as if to some arranged place of meeting.

The sight put all doubts out of his head. An attack on Forza was imminent, and this was the side from which least danger would be expected. If the enemy got there before him they would find an easy entrance. The thought made him quicken his pace. These scattered tribesmen must meet before they attacked, and there might still be time for him to get in front. His ears were sharp as a deer's to the slightest sound. A great joy in the game possessed him. When he crouched in the shelter of a granite boulder or sprawled among the scrub while the light footsteps of a tribesman passed on the road he felt that one point was scored to him in a game in which he had no advantages. He blessed his senses trained by years of sport to a keenness beyond a townsman's; his eye, which could see distances clear even in the misty moonlight; his ear, which could judge the proximity of sounds with a nice exactness. Twice he was on the brink of discovery. A twig snapped as he lay in cover, and he heard footsteps pause, and he knew that a pair of very keen eyes were scanning the brushwood. He blessed his lucky choice in clothes which had made him bring a suit so near the hue of his hiding-place. Then he felt that the eyes were averted, the footsteps died away, and he was safe. Again, as he turned a corner swiftly, he almost came on the back of a man who was stepping along leisurely before him. For a second he stopped, and then he was back round the corner, and had swung himself up to a patch of shadow on the crag-side. He looked down and saw his enemy clearly in the moonlight; a long, ferret-faced fellow, with a rifle hung on his back and an ugly crooked knife in his hand. The man looked round, sniffing the air like a stag, and then, satisfied that there was nothing to fear, turned and went on. Lewis, who had been sitting on a sharp jag of rock, swung an aching body to the ground and advanced circumspectly.

In an hour or two he came to the top of the slope and the beginning of the second tableland. A grey dimness was taking the place of the dark, and it had suddenly grown bitterly cold. Dawn in such high latitudes is not a thing of violent changes, but of slow and subtle gradations of light, of sudden, coy flushes of colour, of thin winds and bright fleeting hazes. He lay for a minute in the scrub of cloud-berries, the collar of his coat buttoned round his throat, and the morning wind, fresh from leagues of snow, blowing chill on his face. Behind was the slope alive with men who at any moment might emerge on the plateau. He waited for the sight of a figure, but none came; clearly the muster was not yet complete. A thought grew in his brain, and a sudden clearness in the air translated it into action; for in the hazy distance across the tableland he saw the walls of Forza fort.

The place could not be two miles off, and between it and him there was the smooth benty plateau. He might make a rush for it and cross unobserved. Even now the early sun was beginning to strike it. The yellow-grey walls stood out clear against the far line of mountains, and the wisp of colour which fluttered in the wind was clearly the British flag. The exceeding glory of the morning gave him a new vigour. Why should not he run with any tribesman of the lot? If he could but avoid the risk of a rifle bullet at the outset, he would have no fear of the issue.

He glanced behind him. The place seemed still, though far down there was a tinkle as of little stones falling. He stood up, straightened himself for one moment till he had filled his lungs with the clean air. Then he started to run quickly towards the fort.

The full orb of the sun topped the mountains and the dazzle was in his eyes from the first. If he covered the first half-mile unpursued he would be safe; otherwise he might expect a bullet. It was a comic feeling-the wide green heath, the fresh air, the easy vigour in his stride, the flush of the morning sun, and that awkward, nervous weakness in the small of his back where a bullet might be expected to find a lodgment.

He never looked back till he had gone what seemed to him the proper distance, and then he glanced hurriedly over his shoulder.

Two men had emerged from the scrub and stood on the edge of the slope. They were gazing intently at him, and suddenly one lifted a Snider to his shoulder and fired. The bullet burrowed in the sand to the right of him. Again he looked back and there they were--five of them now--crying out to him. Then with one accord they followed over the plateau.

It was now a clear race for life. He must keep beyond reasonable rifle-shot; otherwise a broken leg might bring him to a standstill. He cursed the deceptive clearness of the hill air which made it impossible for his unpractised eye to judge distances. The fort stood clear in every stone, but it might be miles off though it looked scarcely a thousand yards. Apparently it was still asleep, for no smoke was rising, and, strain his ears as he might, he could hear no sound of a sentry's walk. This looked awkward indeed for him. If the people were not awake to receive him, he would be potted against its wall as surely as a rat in a corner. He grew acutely nervous, and as he drew nearer he made the air hideous with shouts to wake the garrison. A clear race in the open he did not mind; but he had no stomach for a game of hide-and-seek around an unscalable wall with an active enemy.

Apparently the gentry behind him were growing despondent. Two rifle bullets, fired by running men, sang unsteadily in his wake. He was now so near that he could see the rough wooden gate and the pyramidal nails with which it was studded. He could guess the number of paces between him and safety. He was out of breath and a little tired, for the scramble up the nullah had not been a light one. Again he yelled frantically to the dead walls, beseeching their inmates to get out of bed and save his life.

There was still no sound from the sleeping fortress. He was barely a hundred yards off, and he saw now that the walls were too high to climb and that nothing remained but the gate. He picked up a stone and flung it against the woodwork. The din echoed through the empty place, but there was no sound of life. Just at the threshold there was a patch of shadow. It was his one way of escape, and as he reached the door and kicked and hammered at the wood, he cowered down in the shade, praying that his friends behind might be something less than sharpshooters.

The pursuit saw its chance, and running forward to get within easy range, proceeded to target practice. Lewis, kicking diligently at the door, was trying to draw himself into the smallest space, and his mind was far from comfortable. It needs good nerves to fill the position of a target with equanimity, and he was too tired to take it in good part. A disagreeable cold sweat stood on his brow, and his heart beat violently. Then a bullet did what all his knocking had failed to do, for it crashed into the woodwork and woke the garrison. He heard feet hurrying across a yard, and then it seemed to him that men were reconnoitring from the top of the wall. A second later--when the third bullet had buried itself in dust a foot beyond his head--the heavy gate was half opened and a man's hand assisted him to crawl inside.

He looked up to see a tall figure in pyjamas standing over him. "Now I wonder who the deuce you are?" it was saying.

"My name's Haystoun. H-a-y-s;" then he broke off and laughed. He had fallen into his old trick of spelling his name to the Oxford tradesmen when he was young and hated to have it garbled.

He looked up at the questioner again. "Bless me, Andy, so it's you."

The man gave a yell of delight. "Lewis, upon my soul. Who'd have thought it? It is a Providence. By Gad, I believe I'm just in time to save your life."

CHAPTER XXVIII

THE HILL-FORT

Lewis got to his feet and blinked at the morning sun across the yard.

"That was a near shave. Phew, I hate being a target for sharpshooting! These devils are your friends the Bada-Mawidi."

"The deuce they are," said Andover lugubriously. "I always knew it. I've told Holm a hundred times, and now here is the beggar away sick and I am left to pay the piper."

"I know. I met him in Bardur, and that's why I'm here. He told me to tell you to mind the north gate."

"More easily said than done. We're too few by half here if things get nasty. How was the chap looking?"

"Pretty miserable. Thwaite and I put him to bed. Then they sent me off here, for I've got news for you. You know a man called Marker?"

Andover nodded.

"I was dining with him the day before yesterday, and yesterday morning I got a note from him. He says that he has heard from some private source that the Bada-Mawidi were arming and proposed an attack on Forza to-day. He thinks they may have got their arms from the other side, you know. At any rate he asked me to try to let you hear, and when I saw Holm last night and heard that such a thing was possible, I came off at once. I suppose Marker is the sort of man who should know."

"What did Thwaite say?"

"He was keen that I should come at once. Do you think that it's a false alarm?"

"Oh, it will be genuine enough on Marker's part, but he may have been misinformed. What beats me is the attack by day. I know the Badas as I know my own name, and they're too few at the best to have any chance of rushing the place. Besides, they are poor fighters in the open. On the other hand they are devils incarnate in a night attack, as we used to find to our cost. You are sure he said to-day?"

"Sure. Some time this morning."

"Wonder what their game is. However, he ought to be right if anybody is, and we are much obliged to you for your trouble. You had a pretty hard time in the open, but how on earth did you get up the hill?"

"Deerstalking style. It was good sport. But for heaven's sake, Andy, give me breakfast, and tell me what you want me to do. I am under your orders now."

"You'd better feed and then sleep for a bit. If you don't mind I'll leave you, for I've got to be very busy. And poor old Holm looked pretty sick, did he? Well, I am glad he has been saved this affair anyhow."

A Sikh orderly brought Lewis breakfast. Beyond the tent door there was stir in the garrison. Men were deployed in the yard, Gurkhas mainly, with a few Kashmir sepoys, and the loud harsh voice of Andover was raised to give orders.

It was a hot still morning, with something thunderous in the air. Hot sulphurous clouds were massing on the western horizon, and the cool early breeze had gone. The whole place smelt of powder.

Half-way through the meal Andover returned, his lean face red with exertion. "I've got things more or less in order. They may easily starve us out, for we are wretchedly provisioned, but I don't think they'll get us with a rush. I wonder when the show is to commence." He drank some coffee, and then filled a pipe.

"I left a man at Nazri. If the thing turns out to be a small affair I am to meet him there to-night; but if I don't come he is to know that it is serious and go and warn the Khautmi people. You haven't a connection by any chance?"

"No. Wish we had. The heliograph is no good, and the telegraph is still under the consideration of some engineer man. But how do you propose to get to Nazri? It's only twelve miles, but they are mostly up on end."

"I did it when I was here before. It's easy enough if you have done any rock-climbing, and I can leave with the light. Besides, there's a moon."

Andover laughed. "You've turned over a new leaf, Lewis. Your energy puts us all to shame. I wish I had your physical gifts, my son. The worst of being long and lanky in a place like this is that you're always as stiff as a poker. I shall die of sciatica before I am forty. But upon my word it is queer meeting you here in the loneliest spot in creation. When I saw you in town before I came out, you were going into Parliament or some game of that kind. Then I heard that you had been out here, and gone back; and now for no earthly reason I waken up one fine morning to find you being potted at before my gate. You're as sudden as Marker, and a long chalk more mysterious."

Lewis looked grave. "I wish Marker were only as simple as me, or I as sudden as him. It's a gift not learned in a day. Anyhow I'm here, and we've got a day's sport before us. Hullo, the ball seems about to open." Little puffs of smoke and dust were rising from beyond the wall, and on the heavy air came the faint ping-ping of rifles.

Andover stretched himself elaborately. "Lord alive, but this is absurd. What do these beggars expect to do? They can't shell a fort with stolen expresses."

The two men went up to the edge of the wall and looked over the plateau. A hundred yards off stood a group of tribesmen formed in some semblance of military order, each with a smoking rifle in his hand. It was like a parody of a formation, and Andover after rubbing his eyes burst into a roar of laughter.

"The beggars must be mad. What in heaven's name do they expect to do, standing there like mummies and potting at a stone wall? There's two more companies of them over there. It isn't war, it's comic opera." And he sat down, still laughing, on the edge of a gun-case to put on the boots which his orderly had brought.

It was comic opera, but the tinge of melodrama was not absent. When a sufficient number of rounds had been fired, the tribesmen, as if acting on half-understood instructions from some prehistoric manual, slung their rifles on their shoulders and came on. The fire from the fort did not stop them, though it broke their line. In a minute they were clutching at every hand-grip and foothold on the wall, and Andover with a beaming face directed the disposition of his men.

Forza is built of great, rough stones, with ends projecting in places cyclopean-wise, which to an active man might give a foothold. The little garrison was at its posts, and picked the men off with carbines and revolvers, and in emergencies gave a brown chest the straight bayonet-thrust home. The tribesmen fought like fiends, scrambling up silently with long knives between their teeth, till a shot found them and they rolled back to die on the sand at the foot. Now and again a man would reach the parapet and spring down into the courtyard. Then it was the turn of Andover and Lewis to account for him, and they did not miss. One man with matted hair and beard was at Lewis's back before he saw him. A crooked knife had nearly found that young man's neck, but a lucky twisting aside saved him. He dodged his adversary up and down the yard till he got his pistol from his inner pocket. Then it was his turn to face about. The man never stopped and a ball took him between the eyes. He dropped dead as a stone, and his knife flying from his hand skidded along the sand till it stopped with a clatter on the stones. The sound in the hot sulphurous air grated horribly, and Lewis clapped his hands to his ears to find that he too had not come off scathless. The knife had cut the lobe, and, bleeding like a pig, he went in search of water.

The assailants seemed prepared to find paradise speedily, for they were not sparing with their lives. The attacking party was small, and apparently there was no reserve, for in all the wide landscape there was no sign of man. Then for no earthly reason the assault was at an end. One by one the men dropped back and disappeared from the plateau. There was no overt signal, no sound; but in a little the annoyed garrison were looking at vacancy and one another.

"This is the devil's own business," said Andover, rubbing his eyes. The men, too astonished to pick off stragglers, allowed the enemy to melt into space; then they set themselves down with rifles cuddled up to their chins, and stared at Andover.

"It beats me," said that disturbed man. "How many killed?"

"Seven," said a sergeant. "About five more wounded. None of us touched, barring a bullet in my boot, and two Johnnies slashed on the cheek. Seems to me as if the gen'lman, Mr. 'Aystoun, was 'it, though."

At the word Andover ran for his quarters, where he found his servant dressing Lewis's wounded ear. That young man with a face of great despair was inclining his head over a basin.

"What's the matter, Andy? Don't tell me the show has stopped. I thought they were game to go on for hours, and I was just coming to join you."

"They've gone, every mother's son of them. I told you it was comic opera all along. Seven of them have found the part too much for them, but the rest have cleared out like smoke. I give it up."

Lewis stared at the speaker, his brain busy with a problem. For a moment before the fight, and for a little during its progress he had been serenely happy.

He had done something hard and perilous; he had risked bullets; he had brought authentic news of a real danger. He was happily at peace with himself; the bland quiet of conscience which he had not felt for months had given him the vision of a new life. But the danger had faded away in smoke; and here was Andover with a mystified face asking its meaning.

"I swear that those fellows never had the least intention of beating us. There were far too few of them for one thing. They looked like criminals fighting under sentence, you know, like the Persian fellows. It was more like some religious ceremony than a fight. The whole thing is beyond me, but I think no harm's done. Hang it, I wish Holm were here. He's a depressing beggar, but he takes responsibility off my shoulders."

The dead men were buried as quickly and decently as the place allowed of. Things were generally cleaned up, and by noon the little fort was as spick as if the sound of a rifle had never been heard within its walls. Lewis and Andover had the midday meal in a sort of gun-room which looked over the edge of the plateau to a valley in the hills. It had been arranged and furnished by a former commandant who found in the view a repetition of the one in a much-loved Highland shooting-box. Accordingly it was comfortable and homelike beyond the average of frontier dwellings. Outside a dripping mist had clouded the hills and chilled the hot air.

The two men smoked silently, knocking out their ashes and refilling with the regularity of clockwork. Lewis was thinking hard, thinking of the bitterness of dashed hopes, of self-confidence clutched at and lost. He saw as if in an inspiration the trend of Marker's plans. He had been given a paltry fictitious errand, like a bone to a dog, to quiet him. Some devilry was afoot and he must be got out of the road. For a second the thought pleased him, the thought that at least one man held him worthy of attention, and went out of his way to circumvent him. But the gleam of satisfaction was gone in a moment. He could not even be sure that there was guile at the back of it. It might be all foolish honesty, and to a man cursed with a sense of weakness the thought of such a pedestrian failure was trebly intolerable.

But honesty was inconceivable. He and he alone in all the frontier country knew Marker and his ways. To Andover, sucking his pipe dismally beside him, the thing appeared clear as the daylight. Marker, the best man alive, had word of some Bada-Mawidi doings and had given a friendly hint. It was not his blame if the thing had fizzled out like damp powder. But to Lewis, Marker was a man of uncanny powers and intelligence beyond others, the iron will of the true adventurer. There must be devilry behind it all, and to the eye of suspicion there was doubt in every detail. And meantime he had fallen an easy victim. Marooned in this frontier fort, the world might be turned topsy-turvy at Bardur, and he not a word the wiser. Things were slipping from his grasp again. He had an intense desire to shut his eyes and let all drift. He had done enough. He had come up here at the risk of his neck; fate had fought against him, and he must succumb. The fatal wisdom of proverbs was all on his side.

But once again conscience assailed him. Why had he believed Marker, knowing what he knew? He had been led by the nose like a crude school-boy. It was nothing to him that he had to believe or remain idle in Bardur. Another proof of his folly! This importunate sense of weakness was the weakest of all qualities. It made him a nervous and awkward follower of strength, only to plunge deeper into the mud of incapacity.

Andover looked at him curiously. His annoyance was of a different stamp--a little disappointment, intense boredom, and the ever-present frontier anxiety. But such were homely complaints to be forgotten over a pipe and in sleep. It struck him that his companion's eyes betrayed something more, and he kicked him on the shins into attention.

"Been seedy lately? Have some quinine. Or if you can't sleep I can tell you a dodge. But you know you are looking a bit cheap, old man."

"I'm pretty fit," said Lewis, and he raised his brown face to a glass. "Why I'm tanned like a nigger and my eye's perfectly clear."

"Then you're in love," said the mysterious Andover. "Trust me for knowing. When a man keeps as quiet as you for so long, he's either in love or seedy. Up here people don't fall in love, so I thought it must be the other thing."

"Rot," said Lewis. "I'm going out of doors. I must be off pretty soon, if I'm to get to Nazri by sundown. I wish you'd come out and show me the sort of lie of the land. There are three landmarks, but I can't remember their order."

An hour later the two men returned, and Lewis sat down to an early dinner. He ate quickly, and made up sandwiches which he stuffed into his pocket. Then he rose and gripped his host's hand.

"Good-bye, Andy. This has been a pleasant meeting. Wish it could have been longer."

"Good-bye, old chap. Glad to have seen you. My love to George, if you get to Nazri. Give you three to one in half-crowns you won't get there to-night."

"Done," said Lewis. "You shall pay when I see you next." And in the most approved style of the hero of melodrama he lit a short pipe and went off into Immensity.

CHAPTER XXIX

THE WAY TO NAZRI

Our traveller did not reach Nazri that night for many reasons, of which the chief shall be told. The way to Nazri is long and the way to Nazri is exceedingly rough. Leaving the table-land you plunge down a trackless gully into the dry bed of a stream. Thence it is an hour's uneasy walking among stagnant pools and granite boulders to the foot of another nullah which runs up to the heart of the hills. From this you pick your way along the precipitous side of a mountain, and if your head is good and your feet sure, may come eventually to a place like the roof of the house, beyond which lies a thicket of thorn-bushes and the Nazri gully. At first sight the thing seems impossible, but by a bold man it can be crossed either in the untanned Kashmir shoes or with the naked feet.

Lewis had not gone a mile and had barely reached the dry watercourse, when the weather broke utterly in a storm of mist and fine rain. At other times this chill weather would have been a comfort, but here in these lonely altitudes, with a difficult path before him, its result was to confound confusion. So long as he stuck to the stream he had some guidance; it was hard, even when the air was like a damp blanket, to mistake the chaos of boulder and shingle which meant the channel. But the mist was close to him and wrapped him in like a quilt, and he looked in vain for the foot of the nullah he must climb. He tried keeping by the edge and feeling his way, but it only landed him in a ditch of stagnant slime. The thing was too vexatious, and his temper went; and with his temper his last chance of finding his road. When he had stumbled for what seemed hours he sat down on a boulder and whistled dismally. The stream belonged to another watershed. If he followed it, assuming that he did not break his neck over a dry cataract, he would be through the mountains and near Taghati quicker than he intended. Meantime the miserable George would wait at Nazri, would rouse the Khautmi garrison on a false alarm, and would find himself irretrievably separated from his friend. The thought was so full of irritation, that he resolved not to stir one step further. He would spend the night if need be in this place and wait till the mist lifted.

He found a hollow among the boulders, and improvidently ate half his store of sandwiches. Then, finding his throat dry, he got up to hunt for water. A trickle afar off in the rocks led him on, and sure enough he found water; but when he tried to retrace his steps to his former resting place he found that he had forgotten the way. This new place was conspicuously less sheltered, but he sat down on the wet gravel, lit a pipe with difficulty, and with his knees close to his chin strove to possess his soul in patience.

He was tired, for he had slept little for two days, and the closer air of the ravine made him drowsy. He had lost any sense of discomfort from the wet, and was in the numb condition of the utterly drenched. He could not spend the night like this, so he roused himself and stood staring, pipe in teeth, into the drizzle. The mist seemed clearer. He was a little stupid, so he did not hear the sound of feet on stones till they were almost on him. Then through the haze he saw a procession of figures moving athwart the channel. They were not his countrymen, for they walked with the stoop forward which no Englishman can ever quite master in his hill-climbing. Lewis turned to flee, but in his numbness of mind and body missed footing, and fell sprawling over a bank of shingle. He scrambled to his feet only to find hands at his throat, and himself a miserable prisoner.

The scene had shifted with a vengeance, and his first and sole impulse was to laugh. It is possible that if the scarf of a brawny tribesman had not been so tight across his chest he would have astonished his captors with hysterical laughter. But the jolt as he was dragged up hill, tied close to a horse's side, was unfavourable to merriment, and raw despondency filled his soul. This was the end of his fine doings. The prisoner of unknown bandits, hurried he knew not whence, a pretty pass for an adventurer. This was the seal on his ineffectiveness. Shot against a rock, held up to some sordid ransom, he was as impotent for good or ill as if he had stayed at home. For a second he longed to pull horse and captor with one wrench over the brink to the kindly gulf where all was quiet.

The bitterest ill-humour possessed this meekest of men. Normally he would have been afraid, for he was an imaginative being who feared horrors and had little relish for them. But there is a certain perfect bad temper which casteth out fear, and this held him in its grip. He cursed the mountain solitude and he cursed the Bada-Mawidi with awful directness. Then he chose silence as the easier part, and trudged like a stolid criminal till, half in a daze of weariness and sleep, he found that the cavalcade had halted.

The place was the edge of a little tableland where in a hollow among rocks lay a collection of mud-walled huts. A fire, in spite of the damp weather, blazed cheerfully in the midst of the clearing. There was commotion in the huts, every door was opened, and evil-smelling people poured forth with cries and questions. The leader of the newly arrived party bowed himself before a short, square man whom we have met before, and spoke something in his ear. Fazir Khan looked up sharply at Lewis, then laughed, and spoke something to his men in his own tongue.

Lewis comprehended barely a few words of Chil, the Bada tongue, and he knew little of the frontier speeches. But to his amazement the chief addressed him in tolerable, if halting, English. It was not for nothing that Fazir Khan had harried the Border and sojourned incognito in every town in North India.

"Allah has given thee to us, my son," he said sweetly. "It is vain to fight against God. I have heard of thee as the Englishman who would know more than is good for man to know. You were at Forza to-day."

Lewis's temper was at its worst. "I was at Forza to-day, and I watched your people running. Had they waited a little longer we should have slain them all, and then have come for you."

The chief smiled unpleasantly. "My people did not fight at Forza to-day. That was but the sport to draw on fools. Soon we shall fight in earnest, but in a different place, and thou shalt not see."

"I am your prisoner," said Lewis grimly, "and it is in your power to do with me as you please. But remember that for every hair of my head my people will take the lives of four of your cattle-lifters."

"That is an old story," said Fazir Khan wearily, "and I have heard it many times before. You speak boldly like a man, and because you are not afraid I will tell you the truth. In a very little there will be not one of your people in the land, only the Bada-Mawidi, and others whom I do not name."

"That is a still older story. I have heard it since I was in my mother's arms. Do you think to frighten me by such a tale?"

"Let us not talk of fear," said the chief with some politeness. "There are two races in your people, one which talks and allies itself with Bengalis and swine, and one which lives in hard places and follows war. The second I love, and had it been possible, I would have allied myself with it and driven the others into the sea." This petty chieftain spoke with the pride of one who ruled the destinies of the earth.

Lewis was unimpressed. "I am tired of your riddles," he said. "If you would kill me have done with it. If you would keep me prisoner, give me food and a place to sleep. But if you would be merciful, let me go and show me the way to Bardur. Life is too short for waiting."

Fazir Khan laughed loudly, and spoke something to his people.

"You shall join in our company for the night," he said. "I have eaten of the salt of your people and I do not murder without cause. Also I love a bold man."

Lewis was led into the largest of the huts and given food and warm Hunza wine. The place was hot to suffocation; large beads of moisture stood on the mud walls, and the smell of uncleanly clothing and sweating limbs was difficult to stand. But the man's complexion was hard, and he made an excellent supper. Thereafter he became utterly drowsy. He had it in his mind to question this Fazir Khan about his dark sayings, but his eyes closed as if drawn by a magnet and his head nodded. It may have been something in the wine; it may have been merely the vigil of the last night, and the toil of the past hours. At any rate his mind was soon a blank, and when a servant pointed out a heap of skins in a corner, he flung himself on them and was at once asleep. He was utterly at their mercy, but his course, had he known it, was the wisest. Even a Bada's treachery has its limits, and he will not knife a confident guest. The men talked and wrangled, ate and drank, and finally snored around him, but he slept through it all like a sleeper of Ephesus.

When he woke the hut was cleared. The village slept late but he had slept later, for the sun was piercing the unglazed windows and making pattern-work on the earth floor. He had slept soundly a sleep haunted with nightmares, and he was still dazed as he peered out into the square where men were passing. He saw a sentry at the door of his hut, which reminded him of his condition. All the long night he had been far away, fishing, it seemed to him, in a curious place which was Glenavelin, and yet was ever changing to a stranger glen. It was moonlight, still, bright and warm on all the green hill shoulders. He remembered that he caught nothing, but had been deliriously happy. People seemed passing on the bank, Arthur and Wratislaw and Julia Heston, and all his boyhood's companions. He talked to them pleasantly, and all the while he was moving up the glen which lay so soft in the moonlight. He remembered looking everywhere for Alice Wishart, but her face was wanting. Then suddenly the place seemed to change. The sleeping glen changed to a black sword-cut among rocks, his friends disappeared, and only George was left. He remembered that George cried out something and pointed to the gorge, and he knew--though how he knew it he could not tell--that the lost Alice was somewhere there before him in the darkness and he must go towards her. Then he had wakened shivering, for in that darkness there was terror as well as joy.

He went to the door, only to find himself turned back by the sheep-skin sentry, who half unsheathed for his benefit an ugly knife. He found that his revolver, his sole weapon, had been taken while he slept. Escape was impossible till his captors should return.

A day of burning sun had followed on the storm. Out of doors in the scorching glare from the rock there seemed an extraordinary bustle. It was like the preparations for a march, save that there seemed no method in the activity. One man burnished a knife, a dozen were cleaning rifles, and all wore the evil-smelling finery with which the hillman decks his person for war. Their long oiled hair was tied in a sort of rude knot, new and fuller turbans adorned the head, and on the feet were stout slippers of Bokhara make. Lewis had keen eyesight, and he strove to read the marks on the boxes of cartridges which stood in a corner. It was not the well-known Government mark which usually brands stolen ammunition. The three crosses with the crescent above--he had seen them before, but his memory failed him. It might have been at Bardur in the inn; it might have been at home in the house of some great traveller. At any rate the sight boded no good to himself or the border peace. He thought of George waiting alone at Nazri, and then obediently warning the people at Khautmi. By this time Andover would know he was missing, and men would be out on a very hopeless search. At any rate he had done some good, for if the Badas meant marching they would find the garrisons prepared.

About noon there was a bustle in the square and Fazir Khan with a dozen of his tail swaggered in. He came straight to the hut, and two men entered and brought out the prisoner. Lewis stiffened his back and prepared not reluctantly for a change in the situation. He had no special fear of this smiling, sinister chieftain. So far he had been spared, and now it seemed unlikely that in the midst of this bustle of war there would be room for the torture which alone he dreaded. So he met the chief's look squarely, and at the moment he thanked the lot which had given him two more inches of height.

"I have sent for thee, my son," said Fazir Khan, "that you may see how great my people is."

"I have seen," said Lewis, looking round. "You have a large collection of jackals, but you will not bring many back."

The notion tickled Fazir Khan and he laughed with great good-humour. "So, so," he cried. "Behold how great is the wisdom of youth. I will tell you a secret, my son. In a little the Bada-Mawidi, my people, will be in Bardur and a little later in the fat corn lands of the south, and I, Fazir Khan, will sit in King's palaces." He looked contemptuously round at his mud walls, his heart swelling with pride.

"What the devil do you mean?" Lewis asked with rising suspicion. This was not the common talk of a Border cateran.

"I mean what I mean," said the other. "In a little all the world shall see. But because I have a liking for a bold cockerel like thee, I will speak unwisely. The days of your people are numbered. This very night there are those coming from the north who will set their foot on your necks."

Lewis went sick at heart. A thousand half-forgotten suspicions called clamorously. This was the secret of the burlesque at Forza, and the new valour of the Badas. He saw Marker's game with the fatal clearness of one who is too late. He had been given a chance of a little piece of service to avert his suspicions. Marker had fathomed him well as one who must satisfy a restless conscience but had no stomach for anything beyond. Doubtless he thought that now he would be enjoying the rest after labour at Forza, flattering himself on saving a garrison, when all the while the force poured down which was to destroy an empire. An army from the north, backed and guided by every Border half-breed and outlaw--what hope of help in God's name was to be found in the sleepy forts and the unsuspecting Bardur?

And the Kashmir and the Punjab? A train laid in every town and village. Supplies in readiness, communications waiting to be held, railways ready for capture. Europe was on the edge of a volcano. He saw an outbreak there which would keep Britain employed at home, while the great power with her endless forces and bottomless purse poured her men over the frontier. But at the thought of the frontier he checked himself. There was no road by which an army could march; if there was any it could be blocked by a handful. A week's, a day's delay would save the north, and the north would save the empire.

His voice came out of his throat with a crack in it like an old man's.

"There is no road through the mountains. I have been there before and I know."

Again Fazir Khan smiled. "I use no secrecy to my friends. There is a way, though all men do not know it. From Nazri there is a valley running towards the sunrise. At the head there is a little ridge easily crossed, and from that there is a dry channel between high precipices. It is not the width of a man's stature, so even the sharp eyes of my brother might miss it. Beyond that there is a sandy tableland, and then another valley, and then plains."

The plan of the place was clear in Lewis's brain. He remembered each detail. The long nullah on which he had looked from the hill-tops had, then, an outlet, and did not end, as he had guessed, in a dead wall of rock. Fool and blind! to have missed so glorious a chance!

He stood staring dumbly around him, unconscious that he was the laughingstock of all. Then he looked at the chief.

"Am I your prisoner?" he asked hoarsely.

"Nay," said the other good-humouredly, "thou art free. We have over-much work on hand to-day to be saddled with captives."

"Then where is Nazri?" he asked.

The chief laughed a loud laugh of tolerant amusement. "Hear to the bold one," he cried. "He will not miss the great spectacle. See, I will show you the road," and he pointed out certain landmarks. "For one of my own people it is a journey of four hours; for thee it will be something more. But hurry, and haply the game will not have begun. If the northern men take thee I will buy thy life."

Four hours; the words rang in his brain like a sentence. He had no hope, but a wild craving to attempt the hopeless. George might have returned to Nazri to wait; it was the sort of docile thing that George would do. In any case not five miles from Nazri was the end of the north road and a little telegraph hut used by the Khautmi forts. The night would be full moonlight; and by night the army would come. His watch had been stolen, but he guessed by the heavens that it was some two hours after noon. Five hours would bring him to Nazri at six, in another he might be at the hut before the wires were severed. It was a crazy chance, but it was his all, and meanwhile these grinning tribesmen were watching him like some curious animal. They had talked to him freely to mock his feebleness. His dominant wish was to escape from their sight.

He turned to the descent. "I am going to Nazri," he said.

The chief held out his pistol. "Take your little weapon. We have no need of such things when great matters are on hand. Allah speed you, brother! A sure foot and a keen eye may bring you there in time for the sport." And, still laughing, he turned to enter the hut.

CHAPTER XXX

EVENING IN THE HILLS

The airless heat of afternoon lay on the rocks and dry pastures. The far snow-peaks, seen for a moment through a rift in the hills, shimmered in the glassy stillness. No cheerful sound of running water filled the hollows, for all was parched and bare with the violence of intemperate suns and storms. Soon he was out of sight and hearing of the village, travelling in a network of empty watercourses, till at length he came to the long side of mountain which he knew of old as the first landmark of the way. A thin ray of hope began to break up his despair. He knew now the exact distance he had to travel, for his gift had always been an infallible instinct for the lie of a countryside. The sun was still high in the heavens; with any luck he should be at Nazri by six o'clock.

He was still sore with wounded pride. That Marker should have divined his weakness and left open to him a task in which he might rest with a cheap satisfaction was bitter to his vanity. The candour of his mind made him grant its truth, but his new-born confidence was sadly dissipated. And he felt, too, the futility of his efforts. That one man alone in this precipitous wilderness should hope to wake the Border seemed a mere nightmare of presumption. But it was possible, he said to himself. Time only was needed. If he could wake Bardur and the north, and the forts on the passes, there would be delay enough to wake India. If George were at Nazri there would be two for the task; if not, there would be one at least willing and able.

It was characteristic of the man that the invasion was bounded for him by Nazri and Bardur. He had no ears for ultimate issues and the ruin of an empire. Another's fancy would have been busy on the future; Lewis saw only that pass at Nazri and the telegraph-hut beyond. He must get there and wake the Border; then the world might look after itself. As he ran, half-stumbling, along the stony hillside he was hard at work recounting to himself the frontier defences. The Forza and Khautmi garrisons might hold the pass for an hour if they could be summoned. It meant annihilation, but that was in the bargain. Thwaite was strong enough in Bardur, but the town might give him trouble of itself, and he was not a man of resources. After Bardur there was no need of thought. Two hours after the telegraph clicked in the Nazri hut, the north of India would have heard the news and be bestirring itself for work. In five hours all would be safe, unless Bardur could be taken and the wires cut. There might be treason in the town, but that again was not his affair. Let him but send the message before sunset, and he would still have time to get to Khautmi, and with good luck hold the defile for sixty minutes. The thought excited him wildly. His face dripped with sweat, his boots were cut with rock till the leather hung in shreds, and a bleeding arm showed through the rents in his sleeve. But he felt no physical discomfort, only the exhilaration of a rock climber with the summit in sight, or a polo player with a clear dribble before him to the goal. At last he was playing a true game of hazard, and the chance gave him the keenest joy.

All the hot afternoon he scrambled till he came to the edge of a new valley. Nazri must lie beyond, he reasoned, and he kept to the higher ground. But soon he was mazed among precipitous shelves which needed all his skill. He had to bring his long stride down to a very slow and cautious pace, and, since he was too old a climber to venture rashly, he must needs curb his impatience. He suffered the dull recoil of his earlier vigour. While he was creeping on this accursed cliff the minutes were passing, and every second lessening his chances. He was in a fever of unrest, and only a happy fortune kept him from death. But at length the place was passed, and the mountain shelved down to a plateau. A wide view lay open to the eye, and Lewis blinked and hesitated. He had thought Nazri lay below him, and lo! there was nothing but a tangle of black watercourses.

The sun had begun to decline over the farther peak, and the man's heart failed him utterly. These unkind stony hills had been his ruin. He was lost in the most formidable country on God's earth, lost! when his whole soul cried out for hurry. He could have wept with misery, and with a drawn face he sat down and forced himself to think.

Suddenly a long, narrow black cleft in the farther tableland caught his eye. He took the direction from the sun and looked again. This must be the Nazri Pass, which he had never before that day heard of. He saw where it ended in a stony valley. Once there he had but to follow the nullah and cross the little ridge to come to Nazri.

Weariness was beginning to grow on him, but the next miles were the quickest of the day. He seemed to have the foot of a chamois. Down the rocky hillside, across the chaos of boulders, and up into the dark nullah he ran like a maniac. His mouth was parched with thirst, and he stopped for a moment in the valley bottom to swallow some rain-water. At last he found himself in the Nazri valley, with the thin sword-cut showing dark in the yellow evening. Another mile and he would be at the camping-place, and in five more at the hut.

He kept high up on the ridge, for the light had almost gone and the valley was perilous. It must be hideously late, eight o'clock or more, he thought, and his despair made him hurry his very weary limbs. Suddenly in the distant hollow he saw the gleam of a fire. He stopped abruptly and then quickened with a cry of joy. It must be the faithful George still waiting in the place appointed. Now there would be two to the task. But it was too late, he bitterly reflected. In a little the moon would rise, and then at any moment the van of the invader might emerge from the defile. He might warn Bardur, but before anything could be done the enemy would be upon them. And then there would be a southward march upon a doubtful and half-awakened country, and then--he knew not.

But there was one other way. It had not occurred to him before, for it is not an expedient which comes often to men nowadays, save to such as are fools and outcasts. We are a wise and provident age, mercantile in our heroics, seeking a solid profit for every sacrifice. But this man--a child of the latter day--had not the new self-confidence, and he was at the best high-strung, unwise, and unworldly. Besides, he was broken with toil and excited with adventure. The last dying rays of the sun were resting on the far snow walls, and the great heart of the west burned in one murky riot of flame. But to the north, whence came danger, there was a sea of yellow light, islanded with faint roseate clouds like some distant happy country. The air of dusk was thin and chill but stirring as wine to the blood, and all the bare land was for the moment a fairy realm, mystic, intangible and untrodden. The frontier line ran below the camping place; here he was over the border, beyond the culture of his kind. He was alone, for in this adventure George would not share. He would earn nothing, in all likelihood he would achieve nothing; but by the grace of God he might gain some minutes' respite. He would be killed; but that, again, was no business of his. At least he could but try, for this was his one shred of hope remaining.

The thought, once conceived, could not be rejected. He was no coward or sophist to argue himself out of danger. He laid no flattering unction to his soul that he had done his best while another way remained untried. For this type of man may be half-hearted and a coward in little matters, but he never deceives himself. We have all our own virtues and their defects. I am a well-equipped and confident person, walking bluffly through the world, looking through and down upon my neighbours, the incarnation of honesty; but I can find excuses for myself when I desire them, I hug my personal esteem too close, and a thousand to one I am too great a coward at heart to tell myself the naked truth. You, on the other hand, are vacillating and ill at your ease. You shrink from the hards of life which I steer happily through. But you have no delusions with yourself, and the odds are that when the time comes you may choose the "high that proved too high" and achieve the impossibly heroic.

A tired man with an odd gleam in his eye came out of the shadows to the firelight and called George by name.

"My God, Lewis, I am glad to see you! I thought you were lost. Food?" and he displayed the resources of his larder.

Lewis hunted for the water-bottle and quenched his thirst. Then he ate ravenously of the cold wild-fowl and oatcake which George had provided. He was silent and incurious till he had satisfied his wants; then he looked up to meet George's questions.

"Where on earth have you been? Andover said you started out to come here last night. I did as you told me, you know, and when you didn't come I roused the Khautmi people. They swore a good deal but turned out, and after an infernal long climb we got to Forza. We roused up Andover after a lot of trouble, and he took us in and gave us supper. He said you had gone off hours ago, and that the Bada-Mawidi business had been more or less of a fraud. So I slept there and came back here in the morning in case you should turn up. Been shooting all day, but it was lonely work and I didn't get the right hang of the country. These beggars there are jolly little use," and he jerked his head in the direction of the native servants. "What *have* you been after?"

"I? Oh, I've been in queer places. I fell into the hands of the Badas a couple of hours after I left Forza. There was a storm up there and I got lost in the mist. They took me up to a village and kept me there all night. And then I heard news--my God, such news! They let me go because they thought I could do no harm and I ran most of the way here. Marker has scored this time, old man. You know how he has been going about all North India for the last year or two getting things much his own way. Well, to-night when the moon rises the great blow is to be struck. It seems there is a pass to the north of this; I knew the place but I didn't know of the road. There is an army coming down that place in an hour or so. It is the devil's own business, but it has got to be faced. We must warn Bardur, and trust to God that Bardur may warn the south. You know the telegraph hut at the end of the road, when you begin to climb up the ravine to the place? You must get down there at once, for every moment is precious."

George had listened with staring eyes to the tale. "I can't believe it," he managed to ejaculate. "God, man! it's invasion, an unheard-of thing!"

"It's the most desperate truth, unheard-of or no. The whole thing lies in our hands. They cannot come till after midnight, and by that time Thwaite may be ready in Bardur, and the Khautmi men may be holding the road. That would delay them for a little, and by the time they took Bardur they might find the south in arms. It wouldn't matter a straw if it were an ordinary filibustering business. But I tell you it's a great army, and everything is prepared for it. Marker has been busy for months. There will be outbreaks in every town in the north. The railways and arsenals will be captured before ever the enemy appears. There will be a native rising. That was to be bargained for. But God only knows how the native troops have been tampered with. That man was as clever as they make, and he has had a free hand. Oh the blind fools!"

George had turned, and was buttoning the top button of his shooting-coat against the chilly night wind. "What shall I say to Thwaite?" he asked.

"Oh, anything. Tell him it's life or death. Tell him the facts, and don't spare. You'll have to impress on the telegraph clerk its importance first and that will take time. Tell him to send to Gilgit and Srinagar, and then to the Indus Valley. He must send into Chitral too and warn Armstrong. Above all things the Kohistan railway must be watched, because it must be their main card. Lord! I wish I understood the game better. Heaven knows it isn't my profession. But Thwaite will understand if you scare him enough. Tell him that Bardur must be held ready for siege at any moment. You understand how to work the thing?"

George nodded. "There'll be nobody there, so I suppose I'll have to break the door open. I think I remember the trick of the business. *Then*, what do I do?"

"Get up to Khautmi as fast as you can shin it. Better take the servants and send them before you while you work the telegraph. I suppose they're trustworthy. Get them to warn Mitchinson and St. John. They must light the fires on the hills and collect all the men they can spare to hold the road. Of course it's a desperate venture. We'll probably all be knocked on the head, but we must risk it. If we can stop the beggars for one half-hour we'll give Thwaite a better chance to set his house in order. How I'd sell my soul to see a strong man in Bardur! That will be the key of the position. If the place is uncaptured to-morrow morning, and your wires have gone right, the chief danger on this side will be past. There will be little risings of wasps' nests up and down the shop, but we can account for them if this army from the north is stopped."

"I wonder how many of us will see to-morrow morning," said George dismally. He was not afraid of death, but he loved the pleasant world.

"Good-bye," said Lewis abruptly, holding out his hand.

The action made George realize for the first time the meaning of his errand.

"But, I say, Lewie, hold on. What the deuce are you going to do?"

"I am dog-tired," said the impostor. "I must wait here and rest. I should only delay you." And always, as if to belie his fatigue, his eyes were turning keenly to the north. At any moment while he stood there bandying words there might come the sound of marching, and the van of the invaders issue from the defile.

"But, hang it, you know. I can't allow this. The Khautmi men mayn't reach you in time, and I'm dashed if I am going to leave you here to be chawed up by Marker. You're coming with me."

"Don't be an ass," said Lewis kindly. This parting, one in ignorance, the other in too certain knowledge, was very bitter "They can't be here before midnight. They were to start at moonrise, and the moon is only just up. You'll be back in heaps of time, and, besides, we'll soon all be in the same box."

It was a false card to play, for George grew obstinate at once. "Then I'm going to be in the same box as you from the beginning. Do you really think I am going to desert you? Hang it, you're more important than Bardur."

"Oh, for God's sake, listen to reason," Lewis cried in despair. "You must go at once. I can't or I would. It's our only chance. It's a jolly good chance of death anyway, but it's a naked certainty unless you do this. Think of the women and children and the people at home. You may as well talk about letting the whole thing slip and getting back to Bardur with safe skins. We must work the telegraph and then try to hold the road with the Khautmi men, or be cowards for evermore. We're gentlemen, and we are responsible."

"I didn't mean it that way," said George dismally. "But I want you to come with me. I can't bear the thought of your being butchered here alone, supposing the beggars come before we get back. You're sure there is time?"

"You've three hours before you, but every moment is important. This is the frontier line, and this fire will do for one of the signals. You'll find me here. I haven't slept for days." And he yawned with feigned drowsiness.

"Then--good-bye," said George solemnly, holding out his hand a second time. "Remember, I'm devilish anxious about you. It's a pretty hot job for us all; but, gad! if we pull through you get the credit."

Then with a single backward glance he led the way down the narrow track, two mystified servants at his heels.

Lewis watched him disappear, and then turned sadly to his proper business. This was the end of a very old song, and his heart cried out at the thought. He heaped more wood on the blaze from the little pile collected, and soon a roaring, boisterous fire burned in the glen, while giant shadows danced on the sombre hills. Then he rummaged in the tent till he found the rifles, carefully cleaned and laid aside. He selected two express 400 bores, a Metford express and a smooth-bore Winchester repeater. Then he filled his pockets with cartridges, and from a small box took a handful for his revolver. All this he did in a sort of sobbing haste, turning nervous eyes always to the mouth of the cañon. He filled his flask from a case in the tent, and, being still ravenously hungry, crammed the remnants of supper into a capacious game-pocket. Then, all preparations being made, he looked for a moment down the road where his best friend had just gone out of his ken for ever. The thought was so dreary that he did not dare to delay longer, but with a bundle of ironmongery below his arms began to scramble up the glen to where the north star burned between two peaks of hill.

He did the journey in an hour, for he was in a pitiable state of anxiety. Every moment he looked to hear the tramp of an army before him, and know his errand of no avail. Over the little barrier ridge he scrambled, and then up the straight gully to the little black rift which was the gate of an empire. His unquiet mind peopled the wilderness with voices, but when, breathless and sore, he came into the jaws of the pass, all was still, silent as the grave, save for an eagle which croaked from some eyrie in the cliffs.

CHAPTER XXXI

EVENTS SOUTH OF THE BORDER

Thwaite was finishing a solitary dinner and attempting to find interest in a novel when his butler came with news that the telephone bell was ringing in the gun-room. Thwaite, being tired and cross, told him to answer it himself, expecting some frivolous message about supplies. The man returned in a little with word that he could not understand it. Then Thwaite arose, blessing him, and went to see. The telegraph office proper was on the other side of the river, on the edge of the native town, but a telephone had been established to the garrison.

Thwaite's first impulse was to suspect a gigantic hoax. A scared native clerk was trying to tell him a most appalling tale. George had not spared energy in his message, and the Oriental imagination as a medium had considerably increased it. The telegrams came in a confused order, hard to piece together, but two facts seemed to stand out from the confusion. One was that there was an unknown pass in the hills beyond Nazri through which danger was expected at any moment that night; the other was that treason was suspected throughout the whole north. Then came the name of Marker, which gave Thwaite acute uneasiness. Finally came George's two words of advice--keep strict watch on the native town and hold Bardur in readiness for a siege; and wire the same directions to Yasin, Gilgit, Chitral, Chilas, and throughout Kashmir and the Punjab. Above all, wire to the chief places on the new Indus Valley railway, for in case of success in Bardur, the railway would be the first object of the invader.

Thwaite put down the ear-trumpet, his face very white and perspiring. He looked at his watch; it was just on nine o'clock. The moon had arisen and the telegram said "moonrise." He could not doubt the genuineness of the message when he had heard at the end the names Winterham and Haystoun. Already Marker might be through the pass, and little the Khautmi people could do against him. He must be checked at Bardur, though it cost every life in the garrison. Four hours' delay would arm the north to adequate resistance.

He telephoned to the telegraph office to shut and lock the doors and admit no one till word came from him. Then he summoned his Sikh orderly, his English servant, and the native officers of the garrison. He had one detachment of Imperial Service troops officered by Punjabis, and a certain force of Kashmir Sepoys who made ineffective policemen, and as soldiers were worse than useless. And with them he had to defend the valley, and hold the native town, which might give trouble on his flank. This was the most vexatious part of the business. If Marker had organized the thing, then nothing could be unexpected, and treachery was sure to be thick around them.

The men came, saluted, and waited in silence. Thwaite sat down at a table and pulled a sheaf of telegraph forms to pieces. First he wired to Ladcock at Gilgit, beseeching reinforcements. From Bardur to the south there is only one choice of ways--by Yasin and Yagistan to the Indus Valley, or by Gilgit and

South Kashmir. Once beyond Gilgit there was small hope of checking an advance, but in case the shorter way to the Indus by the Astor Valley was tried there might be hope of a delay. So he besought Ladcock to post men on the Mazeno Pass if the time was given him. Then he sent a like message to Yasin, though on the high passes and the unsettled country there was small chance of the wires remaining uncut. A force in Yasin might take on the flank any invasion from Afghanistan and in any case command the Chitral district. Then came a series of frantic wires at random--to Rawal Pindi, to the Punjabi centres, to South Kashmir. He had small confidence in these messages. If the local risings were serious, as he believed them to be, they would be too late, and in any case they were beyond the country where strategical points were of advantage against an invader. There remained the stations on the Indus Valley railway, which must be the earliest point of attack. The terminus at Boonji was held by a certain Jackson, a wise man who inspired terror in a mixed force of irregulars, Afridis, Pathans, Punjabis, Swats, and a dozen other varieties of tribesmen. To him he sent the most lengthy and urgent messages, for he held the key of a great telegraphic system with which he might awake Abbotabad and the Punjab. Then, perspiring with heat and anxiety, he gave the bundle into the hands of his English servant, and told off an officer and twenty men to hold the telegraph office. A blue light was to be lit in the window if the native town should prove troublesome and reinforcements be needed.

Soon the force of the garrison was assembled in the yard, all but a few who had been sent on messages to the more isolated houses of the English residents. Thwaite addressed them briefly: "Men, there's the devil's own sweet row up the north, and it's moving down to us. This very night we may have to fight. And, remember, it's not the old game with the hillmen, but an army of white men, servants of the Tsar, come to fight the servants of the Empress. Therefore, it is your duty to kill them all like locusts, else they will swallow up you and your cattle and your wives and your children, and, speaking generally, the whole bally show. We may be killed, but if we keep them back even for a little God will bless us. So be steady at your posts."

The garrison was soon dispersed, the guns in readiness, pointing up the valley. It was ten o'clock by Thwaite's watch ere the last click of the loaders told that Bardur was awaiting an enemy. The town behind was in an uproar, men clamouring at the gates, and seeking passports to flee to the south. Chinese and Turcoman traders from Leh and Lhassa, Yarkand and Bokhara, with scared faces, were getting their goods together and invoking their mysterious gods. Logan, who had returned from Gilgit that very day, rode breathless into the yard, clamouring for Thwaite. He received the tale in half a dozen sentences, whistled, and turned to go, for he had his own work to do. One question he asked:

"Who sent the telegrams?"

"Haystoun and Winterham."

"Then they're alone at Nazri?"

"Except for the Khautmi men."

"Will they try to hold it?"

"I should think so. They're all sportsmen. Gad, there won't be a soul left alive."

Logan galloped off with a long face. It would be a great ending, but what a waste of heroic stuff! And as he remembered Lewis's frank good-fellowship he shut his lips, as if in pain.

The telegrams were sent, and reply messages began to pour in, which kept one man at the end of the telephone. About half-past ten a blue light burned in the window across the river. There seemed something to do in the native town of narrow streets and evil-smelling lanes, for the sound of shouting and desultory firing rose above the stir of the fort. The telegraph office abutted on the far end of the bridge, and Thwaite had taken the precaution of bidding the native officer he had sent across keep his men posted around the end of the passage. Now he himself took thirty men, for the native town was the most dangerous point he had to fear. The wires must not be cut till the last moment, and, as they passed over the bridge and then through the English quarter, there was small danger if the office was held. He found, as he expected, that the place was being maintained against considerable odds. A huge mixed crowd, drawn in the main from the navvies who had been employed on the new road, armed with knives and a few rifles, and encouraged by certain wild, dancing figures which had the look of priests, was surging around the gate. The fighting stuff was Afridi or Chitrali, but there was abundance of yelling from this rabble of fakirs and beggars who accompanied them. Order there was none, and it was clear to Thwaite that this rising had been arranged for but not organized. His men had small difficulty in forcing a way to the office, where they served to complete the cordon of defence and the garrison of the bridge-end. Two men had been killed and some half-dozen of the rioters. He pushed into the building, and found a terrified Kashmir clerk sternly watched by his servant and the Sikh orderly. The man, with tears streaming down his face, was attempting to read the messages which the wires brought.

Thwaite picked up and read the latest, which was a scrawl in quavering characters over three telegraph forms. It was from Ladcock at Gilgit, saying that he was having a row of his own with the navvies there, and that he could send no reinforcements at present. If he quieted the trouble in time he would try and hold the Mazeno Pass, and meanwhile he had done his best to wake the Punjab. As the wires would be probably cut within the next hour there would be no more communications, but he besought Thwaite to keep the invader in the passes, as the whole south country was a magazine waiting for a spark to explode. The message ran in short violent words, and Thwaite had a vision of Ladcock, short, ruddy, and utterly out of temper, stirred up from his easy life to hold a frontier.

There was no word from Yasin, as indeed he had expected, for the tribes on the highlands about Hunza and Punial were the most disaffected on the Border, and doubtless the first to be tampered with. Probably his own message had never gone, and he could only pray that the men there might by the grace of

God have eyes in their heads to read the signs of the times. There was a brief word from Jackson at Boonji. There attacks had been made on the terminus and the engine-sheds since sunset, which his men had luckily had time to repulse. A large amount of rolling-stock was lying there, as five freight trains had brought up material for the new bridge the day before. Of this the enemy had probably had word. Anyhow, he hoped to quiet all local disturbances, and he would undertake to see that every station on the line was warned. He would receive reinforcements from Abbotabad by the afternoon of the next day; if Bardur and Gilgit, or Yasin as it might be, could delay the attack till then everything might be safe--unless, indeed, the whole nexus of hill-tribes rose as one man. In which case there would be the devil to pay, and he had no advice to give.

Thwaite read and laughed grimly. It was not a question of a day's delay, but of an hour's, and the hill-tribes, if he judged Marker's cleverness rightly, would act just as Jackson feared. The business had begun among the navvies at Bardur and Gilgit and Boonji. In a little they would have news of real tribal war-- Hunzas, Pathans, Chitralis, Punialis, and Chils, tribes whom England had fought a dozen times before and knew the mettle of; now would be the time for their innings. Well supplied with money and arms--this would have been part of Marker's business--they would be the forerunners of the great army. First savage war, then scientific annihilation by civilized hands--a sweet prospect for a peaceful man in the prime of life!

He returned to the fort to find all quiet and in order. It commanded the north road, but though the eye might weary itself with looking on the moonlit sandy valley and the opaque blue hills, there was no sight or sound of men. The stars were burning hard and cold in the vault of sky, and looking down somewhere on the march of an army. It was now close on midnight; in five hours dawn would break in the east and the night of attack would be gone. But death waited between this midnight hour and the morning. What were Haystoun and the men from Khautmi doing? Fighting or beyond all fighting? Well, he would soon know. He was not afraid, but this cursed waiting took the heart out of a man! And he looked at his watch and found it half-past twelve.

At Yasin there was the most severe fighting. It lasted for three days, and in effect amounted to a little tribal war. A man called Mackintosh commanded, and he had the advantage of having regulars with him, Gurkhas for the most part, who were old campaigners. The place had seemed unquiet for some days, and certain precautions had been taken, so that when the rioting broke out at sunset it was easy to get the town under subjection and prepare for external attack. The Chiling Pass into Chitral had given trouble of old, but Mackintosh was scarcely prepared for the systematic assaults of Punialis and Tangiris from the east and south. Having always been famous as an alarmist he put the right interpretation on the business, and settled down to what he half hoped, half feared, might be a great frontier war. The place was strong only on the north side, and the defence was as much a question of engineering as of war. His Sepoys toiled gallantly at the incomplete defences, while the rest fought hand to hand--bayonet against knife, Metford against Enfield--to cover their labour. He lost many men, but on the evening of the next day he had the satisfaction of seeing the fortifications complete, and he awaited a siege with equanimity, as he was well victualled.

On the second night the enemy again attacked, but the moon was bright, and they were no match for his sharpshooters. About two in the morning they fell back, and for the next day it looked as if they proposed to invest the garrison. But by the third evening they began to melt away, taking with them such small plunder as they had won. Mackintosh, who was a man of enterprise, told off a detachment for pursuit, and cursed bitterly the fate which had broken his ankle with a rifle-bullet.

In the south along the railway the warnings came in good time. At Rawal Pindi there was some small difficulty with native officials, a large body of whom seemed to have unaccountably disappeared. This delayed for some time the sending of a freight-train to Abbotabad, but by and by substitutes were found, and the works left under guard. The telegram to Peshawur found things in readiness there, for memories of old trouble still linger, and people sleep lightly on that frontier. Word came of native riots in the south, at Lahore and Amritsar, and the line of towns which mark the way to Delhi. In some places extraordinary accidents were reported. Certain officers had gone off on holiday and had not returned; odd and unintelligible commands had come to perplex the minds of others; whole camps were reported sick where sickness was least expected. A little rising of certain obscure rivers had broken up an important highway by destroying all the bridges save the one which carried the railway. The whole north was on the brink of a sudden disorganization, but the brink had still to be passed. It lay with its masters to avert calamity; and its masters, going about with haggard faces, prayed for daylight and a few hours to prepare.

George had sent his men to Khautmi before he entered the telegraph hut, and he followed himself in twenty minutes. Somewhere upon the hill-road he met St. John with a dozen men, who abused him roundly and besought details.

"Are you sure?" he cried. "For God's sake, say you're mistaken. For, if you're not, upon my soul it's the last hour for all of us."

George was in little mood for jest. He told Lewis's tale in a few words.

"A pass beyond Nazri," the man cried. "Why, I was there shooting buck last week. Up the nullah and over the ridge, and then a cleft at the top of the next valley? Does he say there's a pass there? Maybe, but I'll be hanged if an army could get through. If we get there we can hold it."

"We haven't time. They may be here at any moment. Send men to Forza and get them to light the fires. Oh, for God's sake, be quick! I've left Haystoun down there. The obstinate beggar was too tired to move."

Over all the twenty odd miles between Forza and Khautmi there is a chain of fires which can be used for signals in the Border wars. On this night Khautmi was to take the west side of the Nazri gully and Forza the east, and the two quickest runners in the place were sent off to Andover with the news. He was to come towards them, leaving men at the different signal-posts in case of scattered assaults, and if he came in time the two forces would join in holding the Nazri pass. But should the invader come before, then it fell on the Khautmi men to stand alone. It was a smooth green hollow in the stony hills, some hundred yards wide, and at the most they might hope to make a fight of thirty minutes. St. John and George, with their men, ran down the stony road till the sweat dripped from their brows, though the night was chilly. Mitchinson was to follow with the rest and light the fires; meantime, they must get to Nazri, in case the march should forestall them. St. John was cursing his ill-luck. Two hours earlier and they might have held the distant cleft in the hills, and, if they were doomed to perish, have perished to some purpose. But the holding of the easy Nazri pass was sheer idle mania, and yet it was the only chance of gaining some paltry minutes. As for George, he had forgotten his vexatious. His one anxiety was for Lewis; that he should be in time to have his friend at his side. And when at last they came down on the pass and saw the camp-fire blazing fiercely and no trace of the enemy, he experienced a sense of vast relief. Lewis was making himself comfortable, cool beggar that he was, and now was probably sleeping. He should be left alone; so he persuaded St. John that the best point to take their stand on was on a shoulder of hill beyond the fire. It gave him honest pleasure to think that at last he had stolen a march on his friend. He should at least have his sleep in peace before the inevitable end.

He looked at his watch; it was almost half-past eleven.

"Haystoun said they'd be here at midnight," he whispered to his companion. "We haven't long. When do you suppose Andover will come?"

"Not for an hour and a half at the earliest. Afraid this is going to be our own private show. Where's Haystoun?"

George nodded back to the fire in the hollow, and the tent beside it. "There, I expect, sleeping. He's dog-tired, and he always was a very cool hand in a row. He'll be wakened soon enough, poor chap."

"You're sure he can't tell us anything?"

"Nothing. He told me all. Better let him be." Mitchinson came up with the rearguard. Living all but alone in the wilds had made him a silent man compared to whom the taciturn St. John was garrulous. He nodded to George and sat down.

"How many are we?" George asked.

"Forty-three, counting the three of us. Not enough for a good stand. Wonder how it'll turn out. Never had to do such a thing before."

St. John, whose soul longed for Maxims, posted his men as best he could. There was no time to throw up earthworks, but a rough cairn of stone which stood in the middle of the hollow gave at least a central rallying-ground. Then they waited, watching the fleecy night vapours blow across the peaks and straining their ears for the first sound of men.

George grew impatient. "It can't be more than five miles to the pass. Shouldn't some of us try to get there? It would make all the difference."

St. John declined sharply. "We've taken our place and we must stick to it. We can't afford to straggle. Hullo! it's just on twelve. Thwaite has had three hours to prepare, and he's bound to have wakened the south. I fancy the business won't quite come off this time."

Suddenly in the chilly silence there rose something like the faint and distant sound of rifles. It was no more than the sound of stone dropping on a rock ledge, for, still and clear and cold though the night was, the narrowness of the valley and the height of the cliffs dulled all distant sounds. But each man had the ear of the old hunter, and waited with head bent forward.

Again the drip-drip; then a scattering noise as when one lets peas fall on the floor.

"God! That's carbines. Who the devil are they fighting with?" Mitchinson's eye had lost its lethargy. His scraggy neck was craned forward, and his grim mouth had relaxed into a grimmer smile.

"It's them, sure enough," said St. John, and spoke something to his servant.

"I'm going forward," said George. "It may be somebody else making a stand, and we're bound to help."

"You're bound not to be an ass," said St. John. "Who in the Lord's name could it be? It may be the Badas polishing off some hereditary foes, and it may be Marker getting rid of some wandering hillmen. Man, we're miles beyond the pale. Who's to make a stand but ourselves?"

Again came the patter of little sounds, and then a long calm.

"They're through now," said St. John. "The next thing to listen for is the sound of their feet. When that comes I pass the word along. We're all safe for heaven, so keep your minds easy."

But the sound of feet was long in coming. Only the soft night airs, and at rare intervals an eagle's cry, or the bleat of a doe from the valley bottom. The first half-hour of waiting was a cruel strain. In such moments a man's sins rise up large before him. When his future life is narrowed down to an hour's compass, he sees with cruel distinctness the follies of his past. A thousand things he had done or left undone loomed on George's mental horizon. His slackness, his self-indulgence, his unkindness--he went over the whole innocent tale of his sins. To the happy man who lives in the open and meets the world with a square front this forced final hour of introspection has peculiar terrors. Meantime Lewis was sleeping peacefully in the tent by the still cheerful fire. Thank God, he was spared this hideous waiting!

About two Andover turned up with fifteen men, hot and desperate. He listened to St. John's story in silence.

"Thank God, I'm in time. Who found out this? Haystoun? Good man, Lewis! I wonder who has been firing out there. They can't have been stopped? It's getting devilish late for them anyhow, and I believe there's a little hope. It would be too risky to leave this pass, but I vote we send a scout."

A man was chosen and dispatched. Two hours later he returned to the mystified watchers at Nazri. He had been on the hill-shoulder and looked into the cleft. There was no sign of men there, but he had heard the sound of men, though where he could not tell. Far down the cleft there was a gleam of fire, but no man near it.

"That's a Bada dodge," said Andover promptly. "Now I wonder if Marker trusted too much to these gentry, and they have done us the excellent service of misleading him. They hate us like hell, and they'd sell their souls any day for a dozen cartridges; so it can't have been done on purpose. Seems to me there has been a slip in his plans somewhere."

But the sound of voices! The man was questioned closely, and he was strong on its truth. He was a hillman from the west of the Khyber, and he swore that he knew the sound of human speech in the hills many miles off, though he could not distinguish the words.

"In thirty minutes it will be morning," said George. "Lord, such a night, and Lewis to have missed it all!" His spirits were rising, and he lit a pipe. The north was safe whatever happened, and, as the inertness of midnight passed off, he felt satisfaction in any prospect, however hazardous. He sat down beneath a boulder and smoked, while Andover talked with the others. They were the frontier soldiers, and this was their profession; he was the amateur to whom technicalities were unmeaning.

Suddenly he sprang up and touched St. John on the shoulder. A great chill seemed to have passed over the world, and on the hill-tops there was a faint light. Both men looked to the east, and there, beyond the Forza hills, was the red foreglow spreading over the grey. It was dawn, and with the dawn came safety. The fires had burned low, and the vagrant morning winds were beginning to scatter the white ashes. Now was the hour for bravado, since the time for silence had gone. St. John gave the word, and it was passed like a roll-call to left and right, the farthest man shouting it along the ribs of mountain to the next watch-fire. The air had grown clear and thin, and far off the dim repetition was heard, which told of sentries at their place, and the line of posts which rimmed the frontier.

Mitchinson moistened his dry lips and filled his lungs with the cold, fresh air. "That," he said slowly, "is the morning report of the last outpost of the Empire, and by the grace of God it's 'All's well.'"

CHAPTER XXXII

THE BLESSING OF GAD

"Gad--a troop shall overcome him, but he shall overcome at the last."

Lewis peered into the gorge and saw only a thin darkness. The high walls made pits of shade at the foot, but above there was a misty column of light which showed the spectres of rock and bush in the nullah beyond. It was all but dark, and the stars were coming out like the lights on a sea-wall, hard and cold and gleaming. Just in the throat of the pass a huge boulder had fallen and left a passage not two yards wide. Beyond there was a sharp descent of a dozen feet to the gravelled bottom which fell away in easier stages to the other watershed. Here was a place made by nature for his plans. With immense pains he rolled the biggest stones he could move to the passage, so that they were poised above the slope. He tried the great boulder, too, with his shoulders, and it seemed to quiver. In the last resort this mass of rock might be sent crashing down the incline, and by the blessing of God it should account for its man.

He brought his rifles forward to the stones, loaded them and felt the cartridges easy in his pocket. They were for the thirty-yards range; his pistol would be kept for closer quarters. He tried one after the other, cuddling the stocks to his cheek. They were all dear-loved weapons, used in deer-stalking at home and on many a wilder beat. He knew the tricks of each, and he had little pet devices laughed at by his friends. This one had clattered down fifty feet of rock in Ross-shire as the scars on the stock bore witness, and another had his initials burned in the wood, the relic of a winter's night in a Finnish camp. A thousand old pleasant memories came back to him, the sights and scents and sounds of forgotten places, the zest of toil and escapade, the joy of food and warmth and rest. Well! he had lived, had tasted to the full the joys of the old earth, the kindly mother of her children. He had faced death thoughtlessly many times, and now the Ancient Enemy was on his heels and he was waiting to give him greeting. A phrase ran in his head, some trophy from his aimless wanderings among books, which spoke of death coming easily to one "who has walked steadfastly in the direction of his dreams." It was a comforting thought to a creature of moods and fancies. He had failed, doubtless, but he had ever kept some select fanciful aim unforgotten. In all his weakness he had never betrayed this ultimate Desire of the Heart.

Some few feet up the cliff was a little thicket of withered thorns. The air was chilly and the cleft was growing very black. Why should not he make a fire behind the great boulder? He gathered some armfuls and heaped them in a space of dry sand. They were a little wet, so they burned slowly with a great smoke, which the rising night wind blew behind him. He was still hungry, so he ate the food he had brought in his pockets; and then he lit his pipe. How oddly the tobacco tasted in this moment of high excitement! It was as if the essence of all the pipes he had ever smoked was concentrated into this last one. The smoke blew back, and as he sniffed its old homely fragrance he seemed to feel the smell

of peat and heather, of drenched homespun in the snowy bogs, and the glory of
a bright wood fire and the moorland cottage. In a second his thoughts were
many thousand miles away. The night wind cooled his brow, and he looked into
the dark gap and saw his own past.

The first picture was a cold place on a low western island. Snow was drifting
sparsely, and a dull grey Atlantic swell was grumbling on the reefs. He was
crouching among the withered rushes, where seaweed and shells had been
blown, and snow lay in dirty patches. He felt the thick collar of his shooting-coat
tight about his neck, while the December evening grew darker and colder. A
gillie, who had no English, was lying at his right hand, and far out at sea a string
of squattering geese were slowly drifting shorewards with the wind. He saw the
scene clear in every line, and he remembered the moment as if it had been
yesterday, It had been one of his periods of great exultation. He had just left
Oxford, and had fled northward after some weeks in Paris to wash out the taste
of civilization from his mouth among the island north-westers. He had had a
great day among the woodcock, and now was finishing with a stalk after wild
geese. He was furiously hungry, chilled and soaked to the bone, but riotously
happy. His future seemed to stretch before him, a brighter continuation of a
bright past, a time for high achievement, bold work, and yet no surcease of
pleasure. He had been master of himself in that hour, his body firm and strong,
his soul clear, his mind a tempered weapon awaiting his hands.

And then the scene changed to a June evening in his own countryside. He
was deep in the very heart of the hills beside a little loch, whose clear waves
lapped on beaches of milky sand, it was just on twilight, and an infinite sighing
of soft winds was around him, a far-away ineffable brightness of sunset, and the
good scents of dusk among thyme and heather. He had fished all the afternoon,
and his catch lay on the bent beside him. He was to sleep the night in his plaid,
and already a fire of heather-roots behind him was prepared for supper. He had
been for a swim, and his hair was still wet on his forehead. Just across a conical
hill rose into the golden air, the highest hill in all the countryside, but here but a
little thing, for the loch was as high as many a hill-top. Just on its face was a
scaur, and there a raven--a speck--was wheeling slowly. Among the little islands
broods of mallard were swimming, and trout in a bay were splashing with wide
circles. The whole place had seemed caught up into an ecstasy, a riot of gold and
crimson and far-off haunting shades and scents and voices. And yet it was no
wild spectacle; it was the delicate comfort of it all which had charmed him. Life
seemed one glorious holiday, the world a garden of the gods. There was his
home across the hills, with its cool chambers, its books and pictures, its gardens
and memories. There were his friends up and down the earth. There was the
earth itself waiting for his conquest. And, meantime, there was this airy land
around him, his own by the earliest form of occupation.

The fire died down to embers and a sudden scattering of ashes woke him
out of his dreaming. The old Scots land was many thousand miles away. His past
was wiped out behind him. He was alone in a very strange place, cut off by a
great gulf from youth and home and pleasure. For an instant the extreme

loneliness of an exile's death smote him, but the next second he comforted himself. The heritage of his land and his people was his in this ultimate moment a hundredfold more than ever. The sounding tale of his people's wars--one against a host, a foray in the mist, a last stand among the mountain snows--sang in his heart like a tune. The fierce, northern exultation, which glories in hardships and the forlorn, came upon him with such keenness and delight that, as he looked into the night and the black unknown, he felt the joy of a greater kinship. He was kin to men lordlier than himself, the true-hearted who had ridden the King's path and trampled a little world under foot. To the old fighters in the Border wars, the religionists of the South, the Highland gentlemen of the Cause, he cried greeting over the abyss of time. He had lost no inch of his inheritance. Where, indeed, was the true Scotland? Not in the little barren acres he had left, the few thousands of city-folk, or the contentions of unlovely creeds and vain philosophies. The elect of his race had ever been the wanderers. No more than Hellas had his land a paltry local unity. Wherever the English flag was planted anew, wherever men did their duty faithfully and without hope of little reward--there was the fatherland of the true patriot.

The time was passing, and still the world was quiet. The hour must be close on midnight, and still there was no sign of men. For the first time he dared to hope for success. Before, an hour's delay was all that he had sought. To give the north time for a little preparation, to make defence possible, had been his aim; now with the delay he seemed to see a chance for victory. Bardur would be alarmed hours ago; men would be on the watch all over Kashmir and the Punjab; the railways would be guarded. The invader would find at the least no easy conquest. When they had trodden his life out in the defile they would find stronger men to bar their path, and he would not have died in vain. It was a slender satisfaction for vanity, for what share would he have in the defence? Unknown, unwept, he would perish utterly, and to others would be the glory. He did not care, nay, he rejoiced in the brave obscurity. He had never sought so vulgar a thing as fame. He was going out of life like a snuffed candle. George, if George survived, would know nothing of his death. He was miles beyond the frontier, and if George, after months of war, should make his way to this fatal cleft, what trace would he find of him? And all his friends, Wratislaw, Arthur Mordaunt, the folk of Glenavelin--no word would ever come to them to tell them of his end.

But Alice--and in one wave there returned to him the story which he had striven to put out of his heart. She had known him in his weakness, but she would never think of him in his strength. The whimsical fate pleased him. The last meeting on that grey autumn afternoon at the Broken Bridge had heartened him for his travellings. It had been a compact between them; and now he was redeeming the promise of the tryst. And she would never know it, would only know that somewhere and somehow he had ceased to struggle with an inborn weakness. Well-a-day! It was no world of rounded corners and complete achievements. It was enough if a hint, a striving, a beginning were found in the scheme of man's frailty. He had no clear-cut conception of a future-that was the happy lot of the strong-hearted--but he had a generous intolerance of little success. He did not ask rewards, but he prayed for the hope of a good beginning or a gallant failure. The odd romance which lies in the wanderer's brain welcomed the paradox. Alice and her bright hair floated dim on the horizon of his vision, something exquisite and dear, a memory, a voice, a note of tenderness in this last exhilaration. A sentimental passion was beyond him; he was too critical of folly to worship any lost lady; and he had no love for vain reminiscences. But the girl had become the embodied type of the past. A year ago he had not seen her, now she was home and childhood and friends to him. For a moment there was the old heart-hunger, but the pain had gone. The ineffectual longing which had galled him had perished at the advent of his new strength.

For in this ultimate moment he at last seemed to have come to his own. The vulgar little fears, which, like foxes, gnaw at the roots of the heart, had gone, even the greater perils of faint hope and a halting energy. The half-hearted had become the stout-hearted. The resistless vigour of the strong and the simple was his. He stood in the dark gully peering into the night, his muscles stiff from heel to neck. The weariness of the day had gone: only the wound in his ear, got the day before, had begun to bleed afresh. He wiped the blood away with his handkerchief, and laughed at the thought of this little care. In a few minutes he would be facing death, and now he was staunching a pin-prick.

He wondered idly how soon death would come. It would be speedy, at least, and final. And then the glory of the utter loss. His bones whitening among the stones, the suns of summer beating on them and the winter snowdrifts decently covering them with a white sepulchre. No man could seek a lordlier burial. It was the death he had always craved. From murder, fire, and sudden death, why should we call on the Lord to deliver us? A broken neck in a hunting-field, a slip on rocky mountains, a wounded animal at bay--such was the environment of death for which he had ever prayed. But this--this was beyond his dreams.

And with it all a great humility fell upon him. His battles were all unfought. His life had been careless and gay; and the noble commonplaces of faith and duty had been things of small meaning. He had lived within the confines of a little aristocracy of birth and wealth and talent, and the great melancholy world scourged by the winds of God had seemed to him but a phrase of rhetoric. His creeds and his arguments seemed meaningless now in this solemn hour; the truth had been his no more than his crude opponent's! Had he his days to live over again he would look on the world with different eyes. No man any more should call him a dreamer. It pleased him to think that, half-hearted and sceptical as he had been, a humorist, a laughing philosopher, he was now dying for one of the catchwords of the crowd. He had returned to the homely paths of the commonplace, and young, unformed, untried, he was caught up by kind fate to the place of the wise and the heroic.

Suddenly on his thoughts there broke in a dull tread of men, a sound of slipping stones and feet upon dry gravel. He broke into the cold sweat of tense nerves, and waited, half hidden, with his rifle ready. Then came the light of dull lanterns which showed a thin, endless column beneath the rock walls. They advanced with wonderful quietness, the sound of feet broken only by a soft word of command. He calculated the distance--now it was three hundred yards, now two, now a bare eighty. At fifty his rifle flew to his shoulder and he fired. His nerves were bad, for one bullet clicked on the rock, while the second took the dust a yard before the enemy's feet. Instantly there was a halt and the sound of speech.

The failure had steadied him. The second pair of shots killed their men. He heard the quick cry of pain and shivered. He was new to this work and the cry hurt him. But he picked up his express and fired again, and again there was a cry and a fall. Then he heard a word of command and the sound of men creeping in the side of the nullah. Eye and ear were marvelously acute at the moment, for he picked out the scouts and killed them. Then he loaded his rifles and waited.

He saw a man in the half-light not five yards below him. He fired and the man dropped, but he had used his rifle and the great spattering of earth showed his whereabouts. Now was the time for keen eye and steady arm. The enemy had halted thirty yards off and beneath the slope there was a patch of darkness. He kept one eye on this, for it might contain a man. He fixed his attention on a ray of moonlight which fell across the floor of the gully. When a man crept past this he shot, and he rarely failed.

Then a command was given and the column came forward at the double. He fired two shots, but the advance continued. They passed the ray of light and he saw the whites of their eyes and the gleam of teeth and steel. They paused a second to fire a volley, and a storm of shot rattled about him. He had stepped back into his shelter, and was unscathed, but when he looked out he saw the enemy at the foot of the slope. His weapons were all loaded except the express, and in mad haste he sent shot after shot into the ranks. The fire halted them, and for a second they were on the edge of a panic. This unknown destruction coming out of the darkness was terrifying to the stoutest hearts. All the while there was wrath behind them. This stopping of the advance column was throwing the whole force into confusion. Angry messages came up from the centre, and distracted officers cursed their native guides.

Meanwhile Lewis was something wholly unlike himself, a maddened creature with every sense on the alert, drinking in the glory of the fight. He husbanded the chances of his life with generous parsimony. Every chance meant some minutes' delay and every delay a new link of safety for the north. His cartridges were getting near an end, but there still remained the stones and his pistol and the power of his arm hand to hand.

Suddenly came a second volley which all but killed him, bullets glancing on all sides of him and scraping the rocks with a horrid message of death. Then on the heels of it came a charge up the slope. The turn had come for the last expedient. He rushed to the stone and with the strength of madness rooted it from its foundations. It wavered for a second, and then with a cloud of earth and gravel it plunged downwards. A second and it had ploughed its way with a sickening grinding sound into the ranks of the men below. There was one wild scream of terror, and then a retreat, a flight, almost a panic.

Down in the hollow was a babel of sound, men yelping with fright, officers calming and cursing them, and the shouting of the forces behind. For Lewis the last moment was approaching. The neck of the pass was now bare and wide and half of the slope was gone. He had lost his weapons in the fall, all but his express, and the loosening of the stone had crushed his foot so that he could scarcely stand. Then order seemed, to be restored, for another volley rang out, which passed over his head as he crouched on the ground. The enemy were advancing slowly, resolutely. He knew that now there was something different in their tread.

He was calm and quiet. The mad exhilaration was ebbing and he was calculating chances as dispassionately as a scientist in his study. Two shots, the six chambers of his pistol, and then he would be ground to powder. The moon rode over the top of the cleft and a sudden wave of light fell on the slope, the writhing dead, and below, the advancing column. It gave him a chance for fair shooting, and he did not miss. But the men were maddened with anger and taunts, and they would have charged a battery. They came up on the slope with a fierce rush, cursing in gutturals. He slipped behind the old friendly jag of rock and waited till they were abreast. Then began a strange pistol practice. Crouching in the darkness he selected his men and shot them, making no mistake. The front ranks of the column turned to the right and lunged with their bayonets into the gloom. But the man knew his purpose. He climbed farther back till he was above their heads, looking down on ranks of white inhuman faces mad with slaughter and the courage which is next door to fear. They were still advancing, but with an uncertain air. He saw his chance and took it. Crying out he knew not what, he leapt among them with clutched rifle, striking madly to right and left. There was a roar of fright, and for a moment a space was cleared around him. He fought like a maniac, stumbling with his crushed foot and leaving two men stunned at his feet. But it was only for a moment. A bayonet entered his side and his rifle snapped at the stock. He grappled with the nearest man and pulled him to the ground, for he could stand no longer. Then there came a wild surge around, a dozen bayonets pierced him, and in the article of death he was conscious of a great press which ground him into the earth. The next moment the column was marching over his body.

Dawn came with light and sweet airs to the dark cleft in the hills. Just at that moment, when the red east was breaking into spires and clouds of colour, and the little morning winds were beginning to flutter among the crags, two men were standing in the throat of the pass. The ground about them was ploughed up as if by a battery, the rock seamed and broken, and red stains of blood were on the dry gravel. From the north, in the direction of the plain, came the confused sound of an army in camp. But to the south there was a glimpse through an aperture of hill of a far side of mountain, and on it a gleam as of fire.

Marka, clad in the uniform of a captain of Cossacks, looked fiercely at his companion and then at the beacon.

"Look," he said, "look and listen!" And sure enough in the morning stillness came the sound as of a watchword cried from post to post.

"That," said he, "is the morning signal of an awakened empire and the final proof of our failure."

"It was no fault of mine," said Fazir Khan sourly. "I did as I was commanded, and lo! when I come I find an army in confusion and the frontier guarded." The chief spoke with composure, but he had in his heart an uneasy consciousness that he had had some share in this undoing.

Marka looked down at a body which lay wrinkled across the path. It was trodden all but shapeless, the poor face was unrecognizable, the legs were scrawled like a child's letters. Only one hand with a broken gold signet-ring remained to tell of the poor inmate of the clay.

The Cossack looked down on the dead with a scowling face. "Curse him-- curse him eternally. Who would have guessed that this fool, this phrasing fool, would have spoiled our plans? Curse his conscience and his honour, and God pity him for a fool! I must return to my troops, for this is no place to linger in." The man saw his work of years spoiled in a night, and all by the agency of a single adventurer. He saw his career blighted, his reputation gone. It is not to be wondered at if he was bitter.

He turned to go, and in leaving pushed the dead man over with his foot. He saw the hand and the broken ring.

"This thing was once a gentleman," he said, and he went down the pass.

But Fazir Khan remained by the body. He remembered his guest of two days before, and he cursed himself for underrating this wandering Englishman. He saw himself in evil case. His chances of spoil and glory had departed. He foresaw expeditions of reprisal, and the Bada-Mawidi hunted like partridges upon the mountains. He had staked his all on a desperate chance, and this one man had been his ruin. For a moment the barbarian came out, and in a sudden ferocity he kicked the dead.

But as he looked again he was moved to a juster appreciation.

"This thing was a man," he said.

Then stooping he dipped his finger in blood and touched his forehead. "This man," he said, "was of the race of kings."

The Echo Library
www.echo-library.com

Please visit our website to download a complete catalogue of our books. We specialise in out-of-copyright reprints in all subjects. We publish a range of Large Print Editions of classic titles.

Books for re-printing

Suggestions for re-printing can be sent to titles@echo-library.com. Titles must be out-of-copyright or you must own the copyright. They can be in digital or published form.

If we do not wish to add the title to our catalogue then we can reprint for you. Costs depend on the format of the manuscript or book and its size.

Feedback

Because we have no direct contact with our customers we would welcome constructive comments to feedback@echo-library.com

Complaints

If there is a serious error in the text or layout please advise us by sending details to complaints@echo-library.com and we will supply a corrected copy, usually within 15 working days (it may take longer outside the UK and USA).

If there is a printing fault or the book is damaged please refer to your supplier.

Printed in the United Kingdom
by Lightning Source UK Ltd.
119464UK00003B/291